SAFE

SAFE

— A NOVEL —

S. K. BARNETT

DUTTON

DUTTON

An imprint of Penguin Random House LLC
penguinrandomhouse.com

Copyright © 2020 by James Siegel
Penguin supports copyright. Copyright fuels creativity, encourages diverse voices, promotes free speech, and creates a vibrant culture. Thank you for buying an authorized edition of this book and for complying with copyright laws by not reproducing, scanning, or distributing any part of it in any form without permission. You are supporting writers and allowing Penguin to continue to publish books for every reader.

DUTTON and the D colophon are registered trademarks of Penguin Random House LLC.

LIBRARY OF CONGRESS CATALOGING-IN-PUBLICATION DATA
Names: Barnett, S. K., 1954– author.
Title: Safe : a novel / S. K. Barnett.
Description: New York : Dutton, an imprint of Penguin Random House LLC, [2020] |
Identifiers: LCCN 2019031321 (print) | LCCN 2019031322 (ebook) |
ISBN 9781524746520 (hardcover) | ISBN 9781524746544 (ebook)
Subjects: GSAFD: Suspense fiction.
Classification: LCC PS3569.I3747 S24 2020 (print) | LCC PS3569.I3747 (ebook) |
DDC 813/.54—dc23
LC record available at https://lccn.loc.gov/2019031321
LC ebook record available at https://lccn.loc.gov/2019031322
Export ISBN: 9780593182796

Printed in the United States of America
1 3 5 7 9 10 8 6 4 2

Book design by Nancy Resnick

This is a work of fiction. Names, characters, places, and incidents either are the product of the author's imagination or are used fictitiously, and any resemblance to actual persons, living or dead, businesses, companies, events, or locales is entirely coincidental.

To Laura—with whom I once rode a Ferris wheel to the stars from which I have never ever come down

SAFE

PROLOGUE

The first poster was put up within a day of the disappearance. In the end there'd be over 1,500 of them, plastering what seemed like every available inch of the village. All of them mass-produced by the owner of a local printing company who barely knew the scared-out-of-their-minds parents but figured it was the least he could do.

It was nail-gunned to a telephone pole in front of Fredo's Famous Pizzeria, an example of doubly false advertising, since its pizza wasn't famous or even well-known, and the pizzeria wasn't owned by anyone named Fredo. The owner was a Serbian named Milche, who thought an Italian name made more fiscal sense. Being an aficionado of The Godfather, he'd picked Fredo over Michael, which seemed to him too Anglicized. Like many pizza parlors throughout Long Island, it had evolved into a hangout for the too-young-to-drink crowd, and when Milche would shoo the local adolescents out of the store at closing time, the reigning fourteen-year-old wiseass would turn and utter this famous if mis-quoted line: "You broke my heart, Fredo, you broke my heart."

What was really breaking hearts was the subject of the poster placed on the telephone pole outside Fredo's on July 10, 2007. **MISSING** it said in black letters printed in Helvetica bold, and underneath, a picture of six-year-old Jennifer Kristal. It was her first-grade school photo, a little girl all dolled up and smiling for the camera.

It was a dichotomy that was particularly hard to comprehend for any parent strolling by—what was innocence doing plastered to a telephone pole? Telephone poles were for garage sale notices, local politicians' campaign posters, and handyman ads with phone number slips hanging down like stripper tassels. They weren't for a six-year-old girl with a traffic-stopping smile who'd walked down the block to her best friend's house one day—yes, she was just six, but it was only two houses away and it was summer, and it wasn't like they lived in the projects or something. This was upper-class suburbia, for God's sake, and her mom, Laurie, had walked her to their screen door and even stood and watched a bit while Jenny skipped down the front steps—whereupon Jenny disappeared. Never showed up at her best friend Toni's front door, never came home.

Poof.

That was hard for people to get their head around. A child just disappearing like that—like one of those sequined assistants in a magic act. It made existence seem too ephemeral, made them question their assumptions about everyday life. If little girls could just disappear into thin air, then what else was possible?

People didn't know quite what to say to Laurie and Jake either—it was Jake who'd put up that first poster. People would generally avoid them if they had enough time to see them coming.

Neighbors would duck into a store or pantomime that they must've left something in their car so that they had an excuse to turn around and go look for it. It was as if grief was catching. But, really, what do you say to parents whose kid had been stolen from them, whose only daughter had been taken God knows where—four states away by now, or in some dank basement, or the kind of place you didn't even want to think about.

At first, there were some impressive and enthusiastic community efforts at pitching in. Not just from the owner of the local printing company, but from Laurie and Jake's inner circle—the Kellys, whose daughter, Toni, was the best friend Jennifer had been on her way to see that afternoon, and the Shapiros, Kleins, and Mooneys, who were all fixtures at Laurie and Jake's Fourth of July barbecues. The blowouts always featured a kick-ass fireworks show, courtesy of Jake's stepbrother Brent, who drove up a truckload of cherry bombs and bottle rockets from North Carolina and, rumor had it, sold them on consignment to the neighborhood teens.

In fact, people who'd never even met the Kristals joined in the search, people from the neighborhood whose daughter or son was in the same first-grade class as Jennifer, or on the same soccer team. People who didn't know Jennifer at all but had kids of similar age and experienced "there but for the grace of God" moments. And there were those who helped because they were simply drawn to that sort of thing.

There were Jennifer Park Searches, where volunteers groggily gathered at six A.M. in Hunter Park. They'd form a line straight across, not unlike the first wave of a football onside-kick formation, combing the tangled shrubs straight down to the lake. There was a Jennifer Hotline manned round the clock in those first few weeks, fueled by prodigious amounts of coffee provided gratis by the local Dunkin' Donuts. A rotating support group set up shop in the Kristals' house on Maple Street, bringing baked ziti, casseroles, bagels, and other assorted nourishment so that Laurie, Jake, and their son, Ben, could have something to eat. Not that Laurie or Jake consumed many calories that first week, but Ben, who was all of eight, walked around with a perpetual smear of doughnut glaze across his upper lip.

There was even a mass rally held at the local school auditorium, where the teary parents addressed the overflow crowd, beseeching anyone who'd seen anything, anything at all—a strange car, an odd-looking person—or overheard even a mildly suspicious comment to please, please report it to the Jennifer Hotline. The detective in charge of the investigation, Looper, a veteran of some twenty years, weighed in, providing the somewhat morose admonition that the first few days were crucial to there being a happy conclusion here—saying this even as the first few days were, in fact, coming to a close.

After Looper came to a dead end, there would be others placed in nominal authority: a private investigator hired by the Kristals named Lundowski who charged five hundred dollars a day to "beat the bushes"; Madame Laurette, a psychic, who claimed to have helped the police solve a number of baffling missing persons cases; and later on—much later—a cold case detective named Joe Pennebaker who would scrupulously go over every single piece of evidence again. Which sounds more impressive than it was, since there really wasn't any evidence—not any physical evidence, anyway.

There were, of course, the usual false alarms—a registered sex offender who lived within running distance of the Kristals, a volunteered confession from an elderly man named Tom Doak, who kept a cache of pornography in his basement featuring young girls *of indeterminate age. But the sex offender was found to have an airtight alibi, and Doak a long history of providing false confessions to the police—including copping to the assassinations of Medgar Evers, John Lennon, and, yes, even President Kennedy, though Doak would have been beginning second grade at the time.*

After a while, that first poster, like the community's interest in Jenny's disappearance, slowly began to fade. As hard as that was to grasp for her grief-stricken parents, it happens that way. Life intrudes; there are family matters good, bad, and banal to contend with—graduations and divorces, anniversaries and funerals. A kind of communal attention deficit disorder seems to be on the uptick in this country anyway—the result of the internet, probably, where the next cigarette-smoking baby or celebrity train wreck is just seconds away. People lose interest at warp speed.

And there were other tragedies to wallow in for those who liked that sort of thing. For committed Republicans throughout the neighborhood—and Long Island was one of their last remaining downstate bastions—one of those tragedies was war hero John McCain losing the presidential election to a Chicago liberal who'd been a US senator for about ten seconds. A McCain/Palin poster was placed directly beneath Jenny's, which despite almost a year and a half of inclement weather still retained her radiant smile, though her eyes had pretty much faded to two dull coins. Someone had crossed out MCCAIN/PALIN with blue spray paint and substituted HOPE AND CHANGE, BABY.

Hope was all but dead at the house on Maple Street, where Jake and Laurie remained. They'd refused to abandon the scene of the crime, because it was, after all, the scene of everything else involving Jennifer—her first birthdays, her first words, her first steps. And also because it happens to be what the parents of missing children do—stay put, because how else will their child ever find their way home?

By 2012, only half the poster remained, buried beneath ones for Mitt Romney and Chuck Schumer. Only the upper half, so you could still make out Jennifer Kristal's eyes, which, like the Mona Lisa's, seemed to be staring at you no matter which side of the street you were coming from. There were people who passed by and didn't know whom the poster was for—people newly arrived in the neighborhood, and even some of the older residents, who'd simply forgotten that there'd ever been a missing child.

Her parents didn't have that luxury. Five years from the date of Jenny's disappearance, Jake made a new plea on a local Long Island TV station—like the messages NASA places on interstellar satellites rocketed into the void, doubtful anyone will read them, but willing to give it a shot: "Jenny, if you're out there, I want you to know we will never stop looking for you. And if her kidnapper sees this, I want them to know that we just want her back. Please. That's all we want. We won't go to the police. We just want our daughter back."

The local reporter followed with some depressing stats concerning the odds of Jennifer—or any missing child—still being alive after all that time. About on par with winning the New York Lottery (1 in 3,838,380, according to the New York State Bureau of Statistics). Yet, in an effort to provide some small sliver of hope, a few cases were cited—Elizabeth Smart, the girl found in Utah, for example, and a few other cases where a missing child was miraculously tracked down or simply walked into a police station one day and announced their identity. The same picture that had been nail-gunned to the telephone pole was prominently displayed on-screen, next to a police artist's rendering of what Jennifer might *look like now. A teenager who didn't look very much like Jenny anymore, devoid of her neon smile and laughing eyes, as if the artist had tried to imbue it with whatever myriad horrors might have been perpetrated on her during all that time.*

It was seven years later, when the original poster was only marginally visible, faded to almost complete white—the barest ghost image lurking there—when rain and snow and mud and time had mostly obliterated me, that I finally came home.

ONE

Forest Avenue, the neighborhood hub, three lanes on each side, with the Forest Avenue Diner—early-bird specials starting at five P.M., dessert and coffee included—standing watch on the northwest corner, or was it the north*east* corner? Note to self: Check which way's which. No matter, I remembered it.

I'd eaten in that diner, a Sunday tradition for the Kristal family, starting when I was small enough to fit into one of those red plastic baby chairs.

I wondered if they ate there now—Mom and Dad and Ben—maintaining the tradition against all odds, or if they'd long ago given it up, picked some other diner to eat their Sunday breakfasts in, or just stopped going out at all.

Just as I passed it, the door flew open. I could smell a mixture of pancakes, syrup, and fried eggs wafting through the door. Okay, I was hungry. But then I was always hungry—had been hungry as long as I could remember.

I had what felt like two dollars scrunched in my jeans pocket.

Not enough for a muffin or even one egg. Coffee maybe . . . but what good would that do?

I floated on—floating is what it felt like, as if I were hovering over this little neighborhood, like you do in a dream, when you're both in it and above it, everything half-remembered and half-not, things looking just the same and startlingly different. Just like me.

It was late fall, warm enough to think about ditching my zippered jacket. The brown leaves littering the sidewalk were so brittle they crunched into dust when I stepped on them.

I was making a game of it, in fact, not so much walking down the block as announcing my presence with each leaf-obliterating step. *Hello, I'm back.* Advancing in a kind of zigzag pattern—some of the shopkeepers had swept the leaves into piles, forcing me to lunge here and there to keep it going, wondering if I looked high on something, like someone staggering home after an all-nighter.

That's when I saw it—when I locked eyes with my former six-year-old self. Such *barely there* eyes—you really had to squint into the white void to see them. It was on a telephone pole outside a pizzeria. A dog was checking out the base of the pole, deciding whether or not it was going to grace it with its piss, the owner—a middle-aged woman—languidly scrolling through her phone and pretty much acting as if she wasn't holding a leash with a dog attached to it.

I wanted to walk up to that pole and take a good look, but dogs scared me. So I waited until the lady finally stopped staring at her cell and moved on, yanking the dog away in mid-pee.

It was kind of like looking in a mirror, I thought, when I stepped up to the poster, except it was more like a magic mirror where you can look back in time—this parallel crazy world lurking just on the other side of it. I was coming *back* from that crazy world. And I was going to step back into my six-year-old room where all my toys were lined up just as I'd left them. *Remember:* The Bratz. Elmo. The two Barbies. A herd of plastic horses—one of them a Palomino I'd named Goldy.

Remember . . .

"Yoh."

It took a second nasal *yoh* to understand that someone was actually speaking to me.

A guy. Nothing new about that. Put me on a sidewalk somewhere and odds are some dude will come chat me up. He might've been older than me but was somehow dressed younger, a red bandanna poking out of the back pocket of his low-slung jeans—which were precariously balanced on his hipbones and showing an inch or more of ugly brown boxers.

"You got a smoke?" he asked.

"No."

He still hung around; maybe he was showing off for his friends, since there seemed to be an audience of boys—they looked like boys, too, younger than him—lurking by the pizzeria entrance.

"You're not from around here," he said, half as a question.

"Who *said*?"

"Never seen you, thas all . . ." He was trying to grow in a goatee—emphasis on *trying,* because it looked like the scraggly tufts you see on cancer patients.

"Okay, you got me," I said.

"So you're not . . . ?"

"Not *what*?"

"From around here."

"Sure I am. Just not *lately*."

"Oh . . ." He looked confused by that. Stared at the pole for a second, where I saw his eyes connect with mine. My old eyes. Before they saw a bunch of things they shouldn't have.

He shifted his feet, seemingly out of things to say now.

I turned away and resumed looking at the pole, a nonverbal *Screw off.* After a few more seconds, he took the hint—okay, more of a directive—and slunk away, mission still accomplished, I guess, since I heard muted hoots and high fives from the peanut gallery.

When I glanced back at him, after finishing my face time with my own face—what was left of it—I saw him still staring at me, but this time without the put-on smirk. Something else. For a moment, I thought I knew what it was. A look of recognition, only the kind where you're not sure what it is you're recognizing.

No. Not possible.

I walked on, faster than I'd intended, even if it was still kind of aimlessly, although I had a vague aim in mind. It didn't feel as if I were floating anymore. I was good and grounded. I felt a sudden gut-gripping panic as people flowed past me on either side—it was a *Saturday,* right? Lots of people out and about, enjoying the surprisingly balmy weather.

I was being swallowed up by them—this surging crowd that seemed in a hurry to get somewhere and to take me with them, and I'd been there, done that, thank you very much, uh-uh. I was losing control of the situation. I was not the boss of me.

Stop.

Deep breaths. In, out. Deep breaths . . .

I found myself leaning against a gray car in the middle of the sidewalk. Finding yourself doing something you didn't know you were doing was a weird feeling, as if I'd been sleepwalking and someone had just turned on the lights.

I saw a woman staring at me—someone with a stroller and a kid in it with a blue pacifier stuck in its mouth. Blue is for boy. She was hovering there, seeing what was up with me, I guess.

"Are you . . . uh, okay?" She was suddenly next to me—had left the stroller a few feet away to attend to this girl in a tan zippered jacket and dirty jeans. I wanted to say to her, *Don't, don't leave that stroller. You don't know what can happen. You think you're this close to it, sure, but you're this close to the unimaginable. The unforgivable. Go back.*

That's what I wanted to say.

But what I said was this:

"I need a policeman. Please. I'm Jenny Kristal and I need a policeman."

TWO

The detective questioning me was a woman, which must be standard operating procedure. They'd passed me from a cop who kept eyeing me in his rearview mirror, the entire ride to the station, to the desk person, who was about fifty pounds overweight—on a good day—to this woman detective who said her name was Mary.

She was pretty courteous, asking me if I was hungry—*Yeah, starved*; if I needed to use the bathroom—*Yeah, I've been holding it in for hours*; if I needed a doctor—*No, I'm fine*.

Then she asked me my name again—for the record.

"Jenny Kristal." This was the third person I'd told my name to in the last half hour—*fourth*, if you include the woman wheeling the baby stroller, who'd called 911 for me, but only after telling me my name sounded kind of familiar.

She'd told the same thing to the cop who showed up five minutes later, after he'd placed me in the back seat of his cruiser for safekeeping.

There was a little girl that vanished when I was in high school, the woman whispered. *It was kind of a big deal around here. I think her name was Jenny Kristal . . . It can't be her, can it . . . ?*

The cop said he didn't know. But when he got into the front seat, he asked me.

He'd already asked me if I was on some kind of narcotics—the woman thought I might be high on something since she'd found me hugging a parked car. *She just kind of collapsed,* she'd told the cop, whose name was Farley.

I told him I wasn't on drugs and he could test me if he didn't believe me, that I just needed to talk to someone at the station.

Well, what's wrong with you? She said you keeled over—you on percs or something?

I haven't eaten in a while. Please, can you take me to the station?

I'm going to call an ambulance, Miss . . .

I don't need an ambulance. I need a Big Mac.

So you're refusing an ambulance . . . ?

Can you just take me to the station . . . ?

I need you to say that you're refusing an ambulance. That's the protocol. You're allowed to refuse it if you want to, but you have to say so. Are you over eighteen?

Yes.

And you're refusing an ambulance.

Yes.

That's when he put me in the back seat.

But before starting the car, he turned around and stared at me through the mesh partition—pretty much at tits level—and asked me if I had ever been a kidnap victim.

Your Good Samaritan said someone with your name—she thinks it's the same name—was kidnapped from here about twelve years ago. Is that you . . . ?

My Good Samaritan thought she was reporting a drug addict who needed to be yanked off the streets. I wanted to talk to someone at the station instead of Officer Farley, because when he'd asked me if I was over eighteen, he'd asked it like he wanted to be sure he wasn't committing statutory.

I stopped talking.

I counted corners instead, trying to ignore the various people—an old lady using a walker, a black UPS guy balancing six packages in his arms, two kids on bikes—peeking into the back seat to see who was being carted off to jail today. *One, two, three, four, five . . .* Counting gave me something to do other than talk to Farley or think about what they were going to look like now and what they were going to say and what it would feel like to hold them again. One corner pretty much like another, leaf strewn and empty, though I spotted chalked hopscotch lines on the corner of Elm, trying to remember what it was like to *play* hopscotch—throwing a pebble into a chalked square and then hopping over to grab it without falling down, that was the tricky part.

Eleven was a corner with a deep weblike crack stretching from one end to the other, and just like that, it caught me and wouldn't let me go.

What's the matter? Farley asked from the front seat.

Had I shouted something? Had I banged on the window and pleaded to be let out?

Maple Street . . . Is this where you used to live . . . ?

Detective Mary had her hair pulled back in a severe bun—in fact, her whole face was pretty severe. I guess that's how you look when your job is dealing with lowlifes every day.

"Okay, Jenny," Detective Mary said, "Officer Farley said you told him you used to live on Maple Street. That's where a girl named Jenny Kristal lived before she disappeared. Are you saying you're *her*?"

Note to self: Detective Mary hadn't said *when* Jennifer Kristal disappeared—the actual date it happened. She was going to make me say it.

The crack on the corner of Maple Street was suddenly front and center. Was it really wide enough to have swallowed me whole?

"Yeah," I said. "I'm . . . Jenny Kristal. I was walking to my friend Toni Kelly's house and I was *taken*." Detective Mary had sent someone out to get me that Big Mac I'd been jonesing for, and I suddenly remembered something. "The night before . . . before I was kidnapped, we'd all gone to McDonald's. It was the last night I saw my dad, because he was gone the next morning, you know, for work . . ."

Detective Mary lost some of her severity then. She was recording everything, had asked me if I minded—*Nope*—I think because she wanted to maintain eye contact with me instead of having to scribble everything down, and I saw it there in her eyes, a kind of softening.

"When was that exactly, Jenny? When you were taken?"

Okay, she was still verifying.

"It was summer. July tenth, 2007."

"Hmmm . . . ," Detective Mary said, as if I'd said something really interesting. "Just wondering—you were how old then . . . ?"

"Six," I said again.

"Uh-huh. You were six years old and you remember the *exact date*? Just curious about that, since most children that young don't really take account of time the way we do."

"I remember the date because it's my birthday."

She looked up as if she'd just caught me in a huge lie, a sudden tightness to her mouth.

"You were taken on your birthday?"

"It *became* my birthday."

"I don't understand."

"My *new* birthday. He said it was the beginning of my new life, so it would be my new birthday." I felt something wet at the corner of each eye.

"He. Who's *he*, Jenny?"

"Father."

"Father? The one who took you? What was his actual name?"

"That was his name. Father. That's what I had to call him."

"Before we get into that, which I know must be very hard for you, Jenny, you mind if we talk about that day again—about the time before it all happened?"

"Why?" I knew why—of course I did—but I wanted to make her say it this time.

"That's the way we do things, I'm afraid. Procedure. Proceed chronologically. From A to B. Is that okay?"

"Sure, no problem."

"Great. So can you take me back a little? What was that summer like? What do you remember about your mom and dad, for instance? And the rest of your family . . . do you have any siblings?"

"Ben," I said, "my brother," even though she knew damn well whether I had any siblings, and she knew his name was Ben. She probably knew he had a scar on the inside of his left knee, too, where I'd pushed him onto a metal tomato stake in the backyard when he was six. And that his favorite food was jelly beans—at least it was back then—and at Halloween I would trade my jelly beans for his Almond Joys. And that Ben's middle name was Horace because our grandfather's name was Horace. And that Ben liked to build sand castles at the beach, and his favorite cartoon character on TV was Thomas the Train—and he would use his toy train, which he'd named Thomas too, to move the sand from one pile to another.

She probably knew all of that already, but she was going to ask anyway.

"Right, *Ben,*" she said. "Younger?"

"Two years *older.* He was eight when . . . when it happened."

"Right. And your mom and dad?"

"What about them?"

"I don't know. Tell me about them. If you don't mind."

I wondered what would happen if I said, *Yeah, actually I do mind. I was kidnapped, so is it okay if I don't undergo the third degree here? Is that all right with you? Do you mind if I mind . . . ?*

I kept talking.

"My mom, sometimes it was hard for me to remember, you know. I had this new mother—but I had to hold on to my real one . . ."

"This Father—he had a *wife?*"

"Uh-huh. *Mother.* Mother and Father and Jobeth. My new name. They let me pick it and they even let me keep the first letter of my real name. Really kind of them, don't you think? Such nice people. Such *selflessness.*" *Stop crying,* I told myself. *Stop.*

"I know this is hard for you, Jenny. We're going to get to all that . . . promise. Can we stick to your family first?"

"You asked me. About Mother."

"I did, I know. Got a little ahead of myself there." She smiled, at least what passes for a smile from someone who looked like that lady in *American Gothic.* Okay, I was being mean—she wasn't *that* bad. She was just getting on my nerves, Detective Mary was. "How about we stay with your mother for now," she said.

"Okay," I said. "I tried hard to remember her. Tried every night, to hold on to her, you know? They wanted me to forget. Told me my mom and dad didn't want me. That *they* were my mom and dad from now on. That my mom and dad had *asked* them to take me. I knew they were lying. I knew it. But you're like six, you know? And part of you doesn't know. But part of you does—and that part was the part I held on to. The part I listened to every night, after . . ."

If you move, it's going to hurt more . . .

". . . when I was back in bed. When I was by myself. I forced myself to remember things—everything I could, about Mom and Dad and Ben and Grandpa and Grandma, and everyone. Going to Disney World when I was five—how we waited for like two hours to ride the Dumbo, and it only lasted like six seconds, but I asked my dad if we could do it again and we waited on line for another two hours. And how Ben got lost on Tom Sawyer Island—he got lost in the cave there—and we all had to look for him, and when we found him, he was crying and we bought him this humongous ice cream cone—he got a bigger one than I did just because he'd been the one lost—and I thought that was so *unfair*—and after I was kidnapped, when I was lying in bed remembering this, I'd think if they found me, if my mom and dad ever found *me* now— then I should get a whole ice cream *store,* a whole Baskin-Robbins of my own."

I told you to stop moving, didn't I?

"You okay, Jenny? We can take a break if you want."

"I'm fine."

"And your dad?"

"I told you. He was a . . . *dad.* I loved him. He took me to Disney World. He would let me ride him around my room as if he was a horse. 'Cause when I was little I loved horses. He called me Jenny Penny because he used to do this trick with a penny where he hid it in between two fingers and then he'd pull it out of my ear—and I could never figure out how, and I would always ask him to do it again, do the penny trick, so he started calling me Jenny Penny."

Detective Mary asked me if I needed a tissue.

I shook my head.

"After a while," I said, "they became like my *storybook* mom and dad. Like the kind you make up, because I started to forget what they looked like. And what they sounded like, their voices, you know? And Father and Mother were real because they were *there*. And you're six and seven and eight and nine, and this is your family now. And, okay, it was a real bizarro family—you know those Superman comics about the planet Bizarro. Father had whole stacks of these old comics. Anyway, there's this planet Bizarro where there's another Superman and Lois Lane and Jimmy Olsen but they're all, well . . . *bizarre*; they're like the opposite of the ones here on Earth. And it used to, like, terrify me . . . those Bizarro Superman comics—because that's what I was *living*, see? That's what this family was . . . because back on Earth, your father doesn't well, you know . . . he doesn't . . ."

I took the tissue from Detective Mary. This was what happened— I talked about being six, and seven, and eight, and nine, and I turned into six and seven and eight and nine. I reverted.

"Where did they take you?" Detective Mary said. "After they kidnapped you . . . where did you go?"

"Down the rabbit hole," I said.

THREE

This is what I found out later.

Detective Mary called the house on Maple Street. No one answered because both my parents were working and Ben was at school—high school, even though he should've easily been in college by now, meaning he must've screwed up big-time. Some detective there did some detective work and found out Mom worked at Mooney Realty and called there. When she answered the phone Detective Mary said, *I don't want to get your hopes too high, but there's someone here claiming to be your daughter.*

Mom fainted—that's what she told me later. *The next thing I saw was the ceiling.*

After she was picked up off the floor by Tom Mooney—the Mooneys used to show up at our Fourth of July blowouts and somehow he'd become her boss, just like somehow she'd become a Realtor—Mom called Dad, who still worked at the same production company in the city but was now its executive producer, whatever that meant. *He takes people to lunch,* Mom explained.

Mom told Dad what the detective had told her—word for word, because she didn't want to get anything wrong. *I don't want to get your hopes too high, but there's someone here claiming to be your daughter.* Mom's hopes were apparently already floating somewhere past Jupiter, but Dad reminded her that the year after I'd disappeared, they'd been told that two separate girls might be me.

One of them was black, he said.

He was coming to the station anyhow.

Before Detective Mary slipped outside to call my parents, she asked me if taking my picture would be okay—still being courteous. I asked her what the point was, even though I kind of knew what the point was. "Is this my mug shot or something?"

"No, Jenny. No one's arresting you." Fake smile. "Just standard procedure."

Smile for the camera, I said, or thought I said. Or both.

Mary snapped two—I smiled in one but not in the other. Then she said she'd be back in a few minutes.

"In the meantime, I'll send Officer Farley in to keep you company, okay?"

"I'm fine with me, myself, and I."

"Afraid it's procedure again."

I was tempted to ask if it was procedure for police officers to drool all over you, but I was starting to hyperventilate.

"My *parents?*" I asked her. "Have you talked to them yet?"

But Mary was already out the door, and Officer Farley was in.

"Hey there, stranger," he said, still his friendly lecherous self.

"I really don't need babysitting, you know. I'm legal."

"Noted," he said. "You want anything to drink?"

"Jack Daniel's. Straight up."

"How about some coffee?"

"No, thanks."

He sat down in Detective Mary's chair, looked around the room a little as if he'd never been there—maybe he hadn't, since this must be where detectives did their questioning and he wasn't one. He drummed his fingers on the desk—he had bitten-down fingernails—and sighed. Then cleared his throat. Then sighed.

I wanted to be alone. I wanted to focus. In a little while they'd be walking into the room.

What if I become a fish and swim away from you? Baby Bunny asked. *Then I will become a fisherman and fish for you,* Mommy Bunny answered. *What if I become a bird and fly away from you?* Baby Bunny asked. *Then I will be a tree that you come home to,* Mommy Bunny answered.

Mom used to read *The Runaway Bunny* to me every night. It's how I went to sleep. No matter what Baby Bunny did, no matter how far he ran or swam or flew or jumped, Mommy Bunny would go after him. Baby Bunny would never get away from her.

"Are you feeling all right?" Officer Farley asked me.

"I'm cold."

"Yeah? Feels like a furnace to me."

"Glad you're nice and toasty."

"I can go check the thermostat, but . . ." He hesitated.

"But what?"

He looked confused, the way he had in the car when he was supposed to help me but looked like he wanted to help *himself* to me instead.

"You can't leave me alone in here, is that it? Am I on suicide watch or something?"

"*Suicide?* Of course not."

"Could've fooled me. I'm freezing."

"You sure you don't want that coffee?"

"I'm sure."

What I wanted was about to come through the door. *You want me to make it better?* Mom asked when I roller-skated into that crack on the corner of Maple and opened up a bloody gash on my knee. *Yes. Please.*

"You're shaking," he said.

"No shit. Are they here?"

"Your . . . parents?"

"Yeah."

"I don't know. Maybe."

"I'm scared . . ." It just came out. I hadn't meant it to, but that happened with me sometimes, like when Detective Mary took my picture and I said, *Smile for the camera,* even though I was just thinking it. *You're talking to yourself again,* Father would say to me. *Shut up.*

"Yeah," Farley said, "it must be . . . well, it must be really weird for you. I understand you being scared, I mean, it makes sense."

I didn't answer him. Partly because I'd been only ninety-nine percent sure that I'd actually said this thing out loud, but him responding to it had made it one hundred percent positive. And also because I *was* scared, I was scared shitless, and being scared shut me up.

I won't say anything again . . . I promise . . . please . . . don't . . .

"You know . . . ," Farley said, "when I used to get nervous out on patrol—I did two tours in Iraq, and trust me, if you were *sane* you were scared. I saw some bad shit go down over there. I used to focus on the end game, understand? I'd imagine being back at base—actually picture it and everything, like what I was eating, and who I was jawing with—because that made it, well . . . real. It's called *visualization.*"

Farley was trying, but he was talking over someone else.

You bet your ass you won't say anything . . .

"So what I'm saying is . . . think about being home with them. And I know even that must be kind of scary for you, but after a while, it won't be, right? Everyone will get to know each other again and it'll be just like . . . well, like it never happened, maybe not exactly, of course not, but close maybe. So *visualize* it. You'd be surprised it really works."

Okay, Officer. I hear you. I'm trying.

"See. You look better already," he said.

I was visualizing sitting in my old living room, with the big TV where I used to watch *Arthur* and *Dora,* and on top of the TV were Monopoly and the Game of Life, which we would play as a family, and I always chose the pink car because I was a girl, of course, and now we were all sitting there together, Mom, Dad, and grown-up Ben, and we were eating a pizza and Mom was saying, *Eat over the plate, Jenny,* and Dad was telling one of his corny jokes and we were a big, happy family.

Only other things were starting to crowd into my head, like when that security guard had opened the doors at the Sioux City Mall on the day after Thanksgiving to let me get to my job at Bed Bath & Beyond and all the customers waiting outside surged in after me. Good luck keeping anyone out, even though it was fifteen minutes before opening time. The security guard kept shouting, *Please, it is not opening yet, please . . . ,* but he might've been talking to himself for the amount of good that did.

The security guard in my head was like that Sioux City Mall guard—Mr. Hammard his name was, though we called him Mr. Hammered because you could sometimes smell alcohol on his breath when he opened the door for you in the morning. He wasn't threatening or anything, which was maybe the problem, because as a security guard he basically wasn't worth shit. Neither was the security guard in my head—because no matter how many times he said, *Stay out*, tried to keep certain persona non grata out of my head, they'd sneak in anyway.

They were doing that now, sneaking into the living room where we Kristals were pigging out on pizza and making up for lost time. There were Father and Mother suddenly standing there telling me it was time for me to go to my room and I was getting that sick, sour feeling in my stomach.

"Hey . . . ," Farley said, "*hey . . .*"

Now Officer Farley was in the living room with us, only the living room had turned into the room at the police station and it was just the two of us.

"I want my mommy," I said. "Now."

FOUR

'd pictured them the way they looked then.

Mom still looking like Snow White—the one at the Magic Kingdom who'd posed for photos with my brother, Ben, and me. She would hug me the way Mommy Bunny hugged Baby Bunny when he promised never to run away from home again.

Dad would look very big because I'd been very small. He probably wouldn't let me ride him around the room anymore, but he might lift me in his arms and carry me all the way home to Maple Street.

When they walked into the room, Mom looked like Snow White's aunt on her cousin's side. Her long brown hair was short, layered, and streaked with iridescent blond highlights. Her pale white skin had been zapped by one of the several hundred tanning salons I'd passed on Forest Avenue. She'd made a few too many trips to Dunkin' Donuts.

Not Dad.

He'd shrunk.

They were standing just inside the door and I was clear on the other side of the room, and I was trying to calculate the actual physical distance between us.

Twelve years.

I think they were doing the same thing I was—photoshopping the picture they'd carried around in their heads, the same one still plastered to that telephone pole.

Maybe Mary had played the tape for them—about Ben getting lost in Disney World and riding Dumbo and Jenny Penny and maybe she'd played them some of the uglier stuff too.

Where did Father take you?

To bed.

I meant where did you live, Jenny?

All over. Ohio. Iowa. Michigan. Arizona. We kept moving. We squatted a lot. You know, houses nobody lives in. Last place was an abandoned trailer outside Sioux City. It had a hole in the roof.

Maybe the detective showed them the photos she'd snapped of me and said, *Is* this *your daughter? Before you book the family reunion, how about we make sure.* Or maybe she'd done it just to prepare them for what time can do to a six-year-old. And they'd stared and stared at those pics the way they were doing now.

"Mom . . . ?"

Don't cry, I was thinking, *don't cry,* only I went and said it out loud. Like I was saying it to them instead of me, *Don't cry, Mom and Dad, don't . . .* which was okay, because suddenly that's what they were doing, Mom at least. Crying.

Me too.

Both of us crying, and the tears somehow meeting, because—

and here's the weird part—I'd been on one side of the room and now I was completely on the other side. Somehow I'd traveled twelve years just like that. Mommy had her arms around me like I was back on those roller skates, and she was making it better, just like she'd promised she would several eons ago.

FIVE

After they'd led me into the house and asked me if I remembered it and I said yes and no, after they'd shown me my old room where my toys were *not* lined up like I'd left them, but where there was a TV, Xbox, and fold-out couch—*We'll get you a beautiful bed tomorrow, Jenny*—after we huddled around the kitchen table, because that's what it felt like, huddling around a fire to keep warm but the fire was *me,* after we talked a little about this and that but not really about *it,* after they asked me what I wanted for dinner—Dad said let's order in, but Mom said I was getting a home-cooked meal, *chicken and mashed potatoes, that was your favorite*—Ben came home.

Dad had to go get him. First, he'd tracked him down by phone—*Is Ben there?* he'd asked at least three different people—because Ben wasn't answering his cell. When he finally got a yes and then actually got Ben on the phone, he said, *Hold tight, I'm coming to get you.*

Ben must've asked why he'd be coming to get him when he had his own car and was perfectly capable of getting home on his own.

Leave it parked there, Dad said. *I'll explain.*

What do you say in a situation like this? *Hey, Ben, your sister's back?* Wait for him to walk back into the house, then yell *Surprise?*

Some news can only be delivered in person.

Dad gave me a brief, awkward hug before walking out the door. Then it was just me and Mom, and that was awkward too, suddenly not like the police station where we couldn't stop holding each other, but like sitting in a house with a distant relative you'd once met as a kid. Mom brought out a photo album.

"I haven't looked at this since . . . since, well . . . we lost you. Would you like to see it?"

"Sure," I said.

Jennifer Kristal, it said on the cover. A photo album of me.

Jenny's First Day was written at the top of page one. Me in the hospital—lying, eyes closed, on Mom's chest, Mom looking like Snow White again, or frankly more like Sleeping Beauty waking up from general anesthesia. Then me in Dad's arms. Then me being held by some older person.

"Do you remember him?" Mom asked. We were sitting on the living room couch, nestled up against each other, back to being snug as two bugs in a rug.

"Grandpa?" I said.

Mom nodded. "He adored you, you know. When you . . . disappeared, it took everything out of him. Grandma had already passed on, so you were kind of it for him. His Jenny."

"I remember he used to bring me Tootsie Rolls, but I had to guess which hand they were in first."

"You remember that?" Mom smiled. "He did the same thing to me when I was a girl."

"He must've had them in both hands because I never missed. Never. I always got a Tootsie Roll."

"How about him?" Mom said, pointing out someone else holding me that day in the hospital, very delicately, as if he thought he might drop me.

"Not sure. Looks kind of familiar, but . . ." I shrugged.

"Your uncle Brent. Dad's stepbrother. You don't remember him at all?"

"Oh sure," I said. "Uncle Brent. I remember. You got mad at him once because he let Ben light a firecracker on the Fourth of July, and Ben's hand got burned, and you got real upset at him."

Mom turned and gave me a super-surprised look, like maybe I deserved *two* Tootsie Rolls for remembering something from that long ago. Go, me.

"That's right," she said slowly. "I did get real upset at him. Ben still has the scar."

She went back to the album. To my first birthday. Me blowing out a single candle on the cake—though it looked like Dad was the one really blowing it out, since I was just sitting there with a stupid expression on my face. Me with chocolate birthday cake smeared all over my face. Me sitting on Mom's lap surrounded by lots of ripped-open presents. *Jenny Turns One* this page was titled.

Then me on a pony ride, the kind where someone holds on to you the whole time around the ring. I was wearing a pink cowboy hat and looked scared shitless.

"You used to love horses," Mom said, "remember?"

It went on like this, Mom providing the commentary as we progressed through the terrible twos, the terrific threes, the fabulous fours, on our way to the sexually abused sixes.

"You cried when you touched snow for the first time," she said.

I could understand why, because there was a picture of me sitting on this snowy hill at about age four, pretty much swallowed up by an oversize down jacket. I looked like a Thanksgiving Day balloon. *Our little Snow Bunny*, it said.

"Really?" I said. "I don't remember, Mom."

I liked how the word sounded coming out of my mouth. *Mom. Mom. Mom. Mom. Mom. Mom.* It was my new favorite word. Me and Mom leafing through old times, and soon Dad would come home with my big brother. Maybe we'd take the Game of Life out of mothballs, and I'd spin the wheel and go speeding down the road in my pink convertible, and who knows where it would take me? It had finally taken me back here, hadn't it? And what were the odds of that happening? It would be just like I visualized it when that policeman told me to, after I admitted I was scared. I was still scared. I'd had the trembles sitting around the kitchen table earlier, but sitting this close to Mom gave me the warm fuzzies.

When we passed my first-grade pic—the one I'd seen stapled to that telephone pole, Mom quickly turned the page as if she couldn't bear to look at it. Then the album stopped. It was like the screen going dark in a movie theatre when a projector jams. Smack in the middle of this great story, and suddenly you're staring at blankness. I wanted my money back—the story had been interrupted, and this was my story.

The very last picture in the album was taken at a beach—it must've been right before it happened. We'd made a sand castle complete with moat—Mom and me—and someone had written *Kristals' Castle* on it, each letter dug into the sand, and we were standing in front of it like proud sentries. Like no one was getting into this castle, no one—it was, what's that word . . . *impregnable*. Only it wasn't impregnable—someone had breached the castle walls and stolen the princess from right under their noses.

Mom slowly traced her finger down the opposite blank page. It reminded me of a blind person I'd once seen reading braille on a bus. *Jenny's gone,* this page read.

"That's it," she said. "That's all. We never got to take another picture . . ."

I took her hand and squeezed tight.

"We can take more pictures now, Mom, and put them in the album. Why not?"

Then the door opened and Ben walked in.

We recognized each other. Not like *Wow, you're my sister* and *You're my older brother.*

No.

Like *Shit, you're the guy who was hitting on me outside that pizzeria,* and *Fuck, you're the girl I tried to bum a smoke from.* Both of us staring at each other and probably wondering if we should say so out loud. At least, I was.

He said zip and stayed frozen right inside the front door, even when Dad gave him an encouraging nudge from behind.

"I know this is really strange for you, Ben, it's strange for all of us, but how about you say hello to your sister."

He didn't say hello. He gave an almost imperceptible nod and remained right where he was, as if he wasn't sure if he'd walked into the right house—it was entirely different from the one he'd left this morning . . . and it *was.* Sure it was.

"Hey, Ben," I said. "Long time no see."

I was trying to be funny, or trying to be something, but no one laughed. Dad managed a weak smile, walked into the living room, and sat down next to us on the couch.

"Ummm, Ben?" Mom said. "How about we all sit down and talk a little?"

Apparently, Ben didn't feel like talking.

"Ben . . . ?" Mom said again.

It took her a few more entreaties, delivered with increasing levels of frustration, before Ben actually joined us, if you could call it that, since he took the seat farthest away from everyone—way across the room on an orange love seat. Not that there seemed to be much love coming from it.

I'd noticed what must've been an old science project of Ben's sitting in what used to be my bedroom—a papier-mâché diorama of the solar system—and if me, Mom, and Dad were the sun, Mercury, and Venus, Ben was an outer planet. Pluto maybe, the one they'd downsized to a speck of cosmic dust.

Sides were being drawn.

"So, would you like to say anything to your sister, Ben?" Mom said.

That would be a no.

"Okay. You must have a thousand questions, Ben, we all do," Mom said. "Jenny's had a really hard time out there, and I think we should just get to know each other again. Can we do that? No one's expecting you to feel like a brother to her—not yet—I understand that. This will take time. A lot of time. But maybe if we just talk, if we just get the ball rolling . . ."

Ben wasn't in a ball-rolling mood. He rolled his eyes instead, just enough to get a tired sigh out of Dad. The kind of sigh that said, *We've been here before, haven't we, and I'm tired of it.* Okay, so maybe things hadn't been too rosy around the Kristal home lately.

"Jenny, I think this is just a real shock to Ben. I'm sure he's trying to process it. To understand. We all thought you were . . . you know . . .

"Dead," I said.

That seemed to be a buzzkill. Using a word like that. Anyway, it shut everybody up.

"I'm really tired," I said. "Can I go to sleep?"

"Of course," Dad said. "You must be . . . Jesus, we should have realized . . ."

Mom said she'd make up the sofa bed for me.

"Is that okay?"

"Sounds comfy," I said. Then we all stood up as if we were leaving a restaurant. Everyone except Ben, who stayed where he was, eyeing me the way security guards eyeball shoplifters—good security guards, not ones like Mr. Hammered.

I waited inside my old room while Mom brought in sheets and pillows, Dad grunting as he pulled out the mattress from the inside of the couch, both of them trying very hard to show me how happy they were that I was back home.

"Can I give you a nightgown?" Mom asked. "I think we're about the same size."

"A T-shirt's fine," I said. "That's what I'm used to wearing."

"Really, you sure? Okay, I've got plenty of those."

She brought in a blue T-shirt that said COSTA RICA on it, and Dad asked me if I wanted him to turn up the thermostat.

"No, it's fine, Dad."

It was the first time I'd called him that, *Dad*, and I saw him physically flinch, then blush. "Okay . . . well, good night," he said, standing awkwardly by the door, looking like a first date who doesn't know if he should kiss or quit.

"See you in the morning," he said.

Mom gave me a hug—a real one—but after she left and closed the door behind her, she tiptoed back in with something in her hand. I'd already turned off the lights and slipped into bed, so I couldn't see what it was at first. Then I did.

"I don't know why I kept it," she said. "Dad made me throw everything out. After the third year. Because it was too painful, I guess. He was right. It was. But I kept one thing, just *one* . . . for in case. Good night, Jenny . . ."

Goldy.

I nestled it under my neck, where the soft mane tickled my throat. I thought it smelled of childhood. The good kind.

Just before I drifted off, I heard someone walking up the stairs, then stopping just outside my door.

"Ha," Ben said.

SIX
Laurie

She woke up at least five times during the night—she counted, the way other people count sheep. She'd been dreaming about Jenny—the six-year-old Jenny, who used to haunt her dreams on a regular basis, forever screaming for help that never came.

Laurie had been given industrial-strength sleeping pills back then, courtesy of her psychiatrist, Dr. Leslie, but she'd never taken them, even though she'd sometimes pretend to in order to stop Jake from hounding her about it. She understood—it was *him* being jolted awake by his dissembling wife's sobbing on a near nightly basis.

Can you describe your emotional state? Dr. Leslie had asked her.

No, can you?

The thing is, she hadn't wanted to stop seeing Jenny. She couldn't see her daughter wide-awake, so seeing her in nightmares had to do. Being terrified awake or sleeping—was there really a difference?

She was deep into her short-lived God phase by then—having run back to the church the way you run back to your mother's arms when you're desperate for the comfort of home. If psychiatry couldn't save her, maybe the church could—where you were allowed to call dream figures souls, and your emotionally wrenching nightmares visions.

Over the years, the frequency of those visions began to lessen, and Jenny became an unreliable guest. Laurie would go months without seeing her, years even, only to have her unexpectedly pop in like that family member who'd long ago moved away but couldn't pass through without saying hi.

Tonight was different. As if someone had blown the dust off that family album and made it magically spring to life. Jenny wasn't screaming anymore. She was shrieking with six-year-old glee as she galloped through the house on her favorite Palomino—life-size and snorting plumes of hot vapor—then suddenly performing pirouettes across the basement floor in Laurie's cavernous high heels. They may have been the best dreams Laurie ever had.

After she woke up for the fifth time, she slipped out of bed. She had to see if an actual eighteen-year-old was sleeping down the hall.

Was that actually possible?

When she got to the door, she hesitated for a moment, wondering if all she'd see was a closed fold-out couch, unused Xbox, and dusty diorama—a daughter's bedroom remodeled into virtual unrecognizability in an effort to obliterate memory. They'd been like Stalinists, Jake and her, airbrushing a once-important personage out of the picture as if she'd never existed.

The most excruciating part had been removing Jenny's things, because they were the closest things to Jenny. Each toy or doll or dress they threw into the cavernous packing box felt like throwing clumps of dirt onto her coffin—her final burial. Laurie had to take a break in the middle of it just in order to breathe. And there was all that unexpected stuff they stumbled across—a birthday card Jenny had drawn for her brother—*Hapy birhdy Bne*—three silver dollars and an Indian-head nickel she'd been given by her grand-father, a stable she'd constructed from Popsicle sticks and Elmer's glue. Each item cracking open another door into memories they were dutifully trying to suppress, and each door opening inward, pressing painfully into what was left of her heart.

Once the room was empty, it was easier. Then they could pretend it was just a room: four walls, a floor, and a ceiling. They bought the desk where Ben would do his homework and Laurie would pay her bills, they mounted that big flat-screen TV to the wall and hooked it up to Ben's Xbox. A home office, a game room—call it whatever you wanted, as long as you didn't call it Jenny's bedroom.

Of course, Laurie kept one toy from banishment to Goodwill, a golden horse belonging to a golden child, stashing it under a precarious tower of shoeboxes in her clothing closet—the one Jake never ventured into without a search warrant.

She'd pretty much forgotten about that toy—until she'd seen it today in one of the photos in the album. Four-year-old Jenny dancing Goldy across the floor of her bedroom, oblivious to the camera being held by a mother equally oblivious of what was to come. That unimaginable moment, when life would be separated into before and after.

Laurie pushed the door open.

For a moment, blackness. She had to wait a few seconds for her eyes to acclimate to the dark before she could see that the fold-out couch was actually folded out, and, yes, there was a person lying on top of it.

Laurie could hear her breathing, ragged and restless like a broken-down air conditioner. She wondered what she was dreaming about. Something horrible, probably, remembering what the female detective had told them.

Why did she wait so long to run away? Laurie had asked her.

They were her parents since she was six years old. They were monsters, sure—but they were her monsters.

And Laurie had thought there was something awful about relegating *monster* to a relative term. Even if it was true. There were all sorts of monsters let loose in this world, the detective was saying, and some of them belonged to you.

This is Jenny, she told herself.

Their friends the Shapiros had adopted twin daughters from Colombia, and as they were walking into the room where two complete strangers were going to be ushered into their arms, Amy Shapiro had whispered a kind of mantra to herself: *These are my daughters,* she'd told herself, *Meghan and Molly Shapiro, these are my daughters.*

That's what Laurie was doing now.

This is my daughter, Jenny.

She didn't look like Jenny—Jenny was six years old with dimpled knees. She didn't act like Jenny—Jenny liked to gallivant around the house singing songs from *Mulan.* She didn't talk like Jenny either, whose missing front tooth made her *t*'s whistle.

It didn't matter.

This is my daughter, Jenny.

Who suddenly shifted and moaned, throwing an arm up as if to ward off a bad dream, her hand clenched into a tight fist. Her hair was a tangled mess and so was the blanket, as if she'd been wrestling with it before finally pinning it into a kind of submission.

Laurie let herself sink into the lumpy mattress the way you

slowly lower yourself into a hot bath, then tentatively brushed away several strands of gold that were stuck to Jenny's forehead. She stroked her hair and whispered, "Shhhhh."

"Shhhhhh . . ."

Jenny's eyes blinked open.

Jake had once set a trap for a possum that'd been mauling their backyard gardenias, but it'd been Laurie who'd first discovered it hissing and writhing in its makeshift prison. It was the possum's eyes that still haunted her—twin beacons of panic.

That's what Jenny's eyes looked like now.

"Once there was a little bunny who wanted to run away," Laurie whispered, continuing to stroke her hair.

"So he said to his mother, 'I am running away . . .'"

Jenny blinked.

"'If you run away,' said his mother, 'I will run after you . . .'"

She blinked again, and Laurie could see a single tear slowly rolling down her cheek. The panic was leaving her, going back to that subterranean place where it caused sleeping hands to ball into angry fists.

"'For you,' said his mother, . . ."

Jenny curled herself into Laurie's lap and shut her eyes.

"'. . . are my little bunny . . .'"

SEVEN

Where am I?

It wasn't the first time I'd asked myself that question. It should've been old hat by now.

Where the fuck am I . . . ?

I'd woken up in too many places not knowing where I was, and some of those places had turned out to be pretty awful.

I didn't recognize anything.

A window of rippling silver.

A potted cactus with a dead flower half attached to it.

A desk with a blank computer sitting on it.

A miniature universe.

Focus.

The window was rippling because a heating vent was blowing the silvery shades up and down, up and down.

The universe was not a universe but a dusty diorama, slowly crystallizing into an actual and recognizable object.

It belonged to Ben. Ben's diorama. Ben had stopped outside my door last night and gone, *Ha . . .*

But there'd been someone *in* this room last night.

I could swear it.

I'd been flitting in and out of half-remembered nightmares— that was old hat too—and when I managed to escape from a particularly terrifying one—I was chained to a tree at the bottom of a lake lit on fire—not exactly waking up, but not exactly sleeping either, someone was stroking my hair. And whispering to me.

Someone like Mom.

I stayed right there. In bed, which was really a couch, a couch bed, letting the sun creep through the shimmering blinds and up over my legs, like someone slowly pulling a warm woolen blanket up over me. I could hear waking-up sounds. They comforted me, those sounds: shuffling slippered feet, soft voices meant not to wake anyone, muted clanging from down in the kitchen.

What day was it?

Sunday.

I'd always had a kind of love-hate thing going with Sundays, since it was the first day of the rest of the week, and usually the rest of the week was going to suck. It was also the day they made newbies work at the Sioux City Mall, so you had to watch everybody else enjoying themselves on their day off, while you busted your ass fetching them BB&B catalogues and plastic hanger racks.

But before I joined the retail ranks, there'd be some Sundays where I actually did Sunday things. Like lying outside in the grass and picking out crazy shapes in the clouds or drawing my latest comic book—I'd started by tracing the Superman ones in Father's stash. The hero of my comics was a thirteen-year-old girl with superpowers who was able to make herself invisible. Super Invisible Girl.

Ha! Just try and find me!

No need for invisible powers now.

I'm home, I thought.

Or said.

Or thought and said.

"I'm home." This time purposely saying it out loud, so I could hear what it sounded like. Home at last. Home for good.

I sat up and looked for my jeans, which I could swear I'd flipped over the chair last night but were somehow missing. I looked on the floor, under the bed, in the closet, but they weren't there either. I tried the bed, but when I lifted the blanket, I saw Goldy's dead eyes staring back at me.

So now what?

I went over to the door and cracked it open. I was in a blue T-shirt and panties. Cheap lime-green H&M, with my tattoo peeking out over the left hip, the only tattoo I'd ever gotten because having a needle punch holes in your skin actually hurts like hell. Zonked on Xanax, I had thought it was a great idea at the time, which says something about great ideas, because afterward I'd wanted no part of it, even though it was part of me. *VIDI.* That's Latin for *I saw.* The whole point of tattoos, as far as I could tell, was picking a language no one speaks, so people have to ask you what it means.

I saw, I'd tell them. *That's what it means.*

Saw what?

Things.

What things?

Things you don't want to know.

Which usually ended the conversation, because most people *don't* want to know, even when they said they did.

Someone was coming up the stairs.

"Hey there," Mom said, spying me through the crack in the door. "Good morning. Are you okay . . . ?"

"I can't find my jeans."

"Oh, sorry. Hope you don't mind. They were kind of . . ."

"What?"

"In need of a wash. I was doing a load anyway, is that all right?"

"They're my only clothes, and I didn't know where they were."

"I didn't want to wake you."

"Okay. Just didn't know where they were, that's all."

"Sorry about that."

"What do I, like, walk around in . . . ?"

"I have some sweats. Is that all right for now?"

"I guess."

"Hold on." She passed by the door on the way to her room, where I heard her rummaging around a drawer. She came back and pushed a pair of red sweatpants through the door, like someone sliding a meal tray into the cell of a possibly dangerous prisoner.

"Last night . . . ," I asked, still holding the sweats in my hand, still talking to her through that crack in the door, "did you . . . ?"

"What . . . ?"

"I don't know . . . come into my room? I kind of remember you being here . . ."

"You were having a nightmare, I think."

"Why . . . was I saying anything?"

"Not saying anything. Just, I don't know . . . agitated."

"Oh." It was like waking up draped over a car with that woman leaning over me. Someone seeing me do something when I didn't know I'd been doing it.

"I held you till you calmed down. I didn't mean to invade your privacy," Mom said.

"Just not used to it," I said.

"To being . . . comforted?"

"To privacy."

"I understand. Look, Jenny, I know I'm going to be making mistakes here. A ton of them probably. It's going to take a while for all of us to get reacquainted, right? We're making up for a lot of lost time . . ."

Lost time, as if someone had simply misplaced it, draped it over a chair one night and woken up in the morning to find it missing.

"Oh . . . the FBI called." Mom saying it the way she might've said, *Uncle Brent called,* or *Oh, some guy selling life insurance called,* as if it were a normal occurrence around here, getting personal telephone calls from the FBI.

"Why?" I said.

"Why? I think . . . I'm not sure about this, but I think the police, they need to alert the FBI when there's a kidnapping across state lines . . . something like that. Anyway, they want to talk to you. The FBI. About the people who kidnapped you. This . . . Father and Mother. They need your help to find them."

"I don't know where they are. I can't help them."

"They're hoping there's things you do know. Things that might turn out to be important. They just want to talk to you, Jenny . . ."

"I don't have the slightest idea where they are. None. They could be anywhere by now."

Detective Mary had called the Sioux City police and directed them to the trailer. The deserted trailer, it turned out. Not surprising, Detective Mary had explained to Mom over the phone yesterday, since I'd left it more than two years ago, and they hadn't really expected to find my kidnappers just sitting there waiting to invite the police in. Mom told me they'd be investigating the trailer for clues. Which is what they wanted to do to me now.

That crack in the door—I felt like shutting it. Like crawling back into bed and staying there for a long time.

"Look, Jenny," Mom said softly, "I know this has to bring up horrible memories for you. I'm sure it's the last thing in the world you want to do right now—talk about *that*. I get it. Would it help if I just put them off for a while?"

"Yes."

"Then that's what I'll do."

"Thanks."

"They'll have to understand. I mean, we just got you back. You need a little time to . . . come to yourself. To just be Jenny again."

"I *am* Jenny."

"I know you are. I meant you need some time to . . . acclimate to things."

"Sure."

"Want some breakfast?" Mom asked, changing the subject.

"I'm starved," I said, and I was, and for more than just breakfast.

When I got to the kitchen, Dad was staring out the window at the backyard, but he quickly turned and said good morning. He looked happy to see me but a little fuzzy on who I was, like my branch manager at Bed Bath & Beyond, who was always glad to see me show up but kept confusing me with another girl, named Josie.

"What about some eggs?" Dad asked me.

"You got any Nutella?"

"Nutella? What's that?"

Mom had come in from the living room with a cup of coffee in her hand. "Yes," she said. "What's a Nutella?"

I blushed. "It's like half-chocolate and half-nutty. I don't know. You put it on bread."

"Sorry," Dad said. "All out."

"I can go get some from the market," Mom said. "Take me a minute."

"That's all right," I said, "eggs are cool. Ummm . . . where's Ben?"

"Ben?" Dad said, as if I'd just said *Nutella* again. "Ben doesn't deign us with his presence until dinnertime. Ben sleeps."

"Well, it's Sunday."

"Yeah, well, he sleeps on Saturdays too."

"Ben's in that phase," Mom said. "Sorry about last night, by the way . . . how he acted."

"I wouldn't worry about it," Dad said. "You're in good company. He acts that way with everybody."

"I was kind of just dropped on him. It's cool."

"Glad you think so. How do you like them, sweetheart?" Dad asked. "Your eggs?"

"Sunny-side up," I said.

After all, it kind of fit my mood.

I was really hungry," I said, after slurping down the yolks in two seconds—I always saved them for last.

"You want more? Just take me a minute," Mom said.

"I'm good."

"The detective," Mom said, "she told us you were out on your own. For like . . . over two *years*?"

I nodded.

"How did you manage?" she said softly. "I mean . . . what did you *eat*?"

"Nutella," I said.

On the way back from the police station, Mom had promised

they wouldn't ask me any questions about what I'd been through unless I felt like talking about it. My days on the streets—that time between the worst thing that ever happened to me and the best— she must've felt that was a gray area.

"Where did you . . . sleep?" Mom asked tentatively, like she didn't really want to hear the answer.

"Anywhere I could find. Not like I was used to staying in four-star hotels. I got by." I decided to leave out the part about how I got by. She definitely wouldn't want to hear about that.

We reverted to small talk.

Dad asking if I'd slept okay—*Yeah, absolutely,* even as I was wondering if Mom had told him about my nightmare. Mom telling me there was an extra toothbrush in the bathroom cabinet, and me saying thanks, Dad saying he hoped the warm weather would continue, and me agreeing that'd be nice, all right, the conversation doing some serious dwindling, and then pretty much coming to a stop. We were sitting around the kitchen table like nothing had changed, even though everything had.

"How about we get you a real bed today?" Mom said, breaking the silence, which seemed on its way to eternity.

"The couch is fine." It was fine, more than fine compared to some things I'd slept on over the years. For one thing, there were no creepy crawlers in it. Sleep tight, don't let the bedbugs bite. For another thing, no one was going to try to come share it with me in the middle of the night.

"Don't be silly," Mom said, "you need a real bed now. And some clothes. Why don't we take a trip to the Roosevelt Field Mall?"

Mom gave me a button-down shirt of hers, and my freshly cleaned jeans, which smelled of bleach. On the way to the mall, she let me blast the radio as loudly as I wanted.

We went to T.J.Maxx first. Every time I tried something on, I came out of the dressing room so Mom could see it on me.

Great, she'd say, or, *I think you need a smaller size,* or, *You sure you like that color?*

When she told me how pretty I looked in a yellow scoop-neck blouse, I said, "Thanks, Mom. For taking me shopping."

"You don't have to thank me, Jenny."

The final tally: three pairs of skinny jeans, five tops, two sweaters, three pairs of shoes, a winter coat, ten pairs of Hanky Panky panties, and a brown leather belt.

In Bed Bath & Beyond I sat on three different beds because Mom said, "You need to try them out." On the Sealy Posturepedic Plus with actual firmness controls, I pretended to conk out, closing my eyes and fake snoring. "Wake up, Sleeping Beauty," Mom said. I opened my eyes and laughed, until I saw Mom staring at me with one of those "I've just seen a ghost" looks.

"What's wrong?" I said.

"Nothing . . . ," she said.

"Seriously? Did I do something wrong? I'm sorry . . ."

"You didn't do anything wrong, Jenny. *Nothing.* It's just . . . the detective yesterday—she asked us if you had any identifiable physical characteristics. Like beauty marks, things like that. You know, when we first got there, before we actually saw you . . ."

"Okay . . . ?"

"I told her how your eyes . . . they used to crinkle when you laughed."

"Huh . . . ?"

"They just did. When you smiled."

A saleswoman was staring at the bed as if she wanted me off it. The PA system was asking, *Will the mother of Leshaun Washington please report to the front register.* I didn't feel like Sleeping Beauty anymore.

"They're . . . beautiful, Jenny. Like little dimples."

"If you say so."

Say so . . . please . . . say so . . .

I ended up picking the bed without firmness controls, which I believe is for older people with bad backs; then we picked out three sets of sheets with floral patterns and a pink comforter.

When we went to pay for it, I stared at the girl across the counter, who looked about my age, and wondered if she was as bored as I used to be. Probably.

The bed came later that day, and two delivery guys in stained wifebeaters carried it up the stairs after they'd taken the couch bed down to the basement. "Now Ben has two places to sleep all day," Dad said.

Speaking of which, he wasn't there. Ben.

"He's sleeping at Zack's," Dad said.

"Really?" Mom said. "On Jenny's second day home?"

He shrugged, one of those "What are you going to do?" shrugs, which maybe had become second nature when it came to Ben.

"Jesus, Jake . . . ," Mom said.

Later, I heard them furiously whispering about it, thinking they were out of earshot, which they might've been, if I hadn't been snooping outside their bedroom door.

I only heard pieces of their back-and-forth, but it was enough.

". . . hard on him . . ."

". . . suddenly she shows . . ."

". . . he's angry . . ."

". . . dammit . . ."

After dinner—Mom made spaghetti and meatballs, my second-favorite dish—Mom said she was going to call the rest of the family and tell them the good news, that she might even ask them to come over the next day to see me, the ones who lived close by, anyway, like Dad's stepbrother, Brent. Only if that was okay with me, though?

"Sure," I said.

When I woke up after another shitty night I was stuck to my new bed as if I'd sweated through it—I thought they were already there, and that the family must've been bigger than I remembered, since it seemed like they'd all come at once to say good morning. It sounded like an honest-to-God commotion just outside my window.

I opened the blinds to tell them to please knock it off.

EIGHT

Remember when Uncle Brent would tickle us till we said *uncle*?" Ben asked. "Remember that?"

Ben talks.

"Sure," I said.

"And then he'd say, 'What?' And keep tickling us, and we'd say *uncle* again, and he'd say, 'What?' It was his big, stupid joke, right?"

"Right. I remember."

Uncle Brent was right there in front of us during this little discussion, looking older than the photo where he was holding a just-born me in the hospital, but then everyone else in the photo album had aged right along with him.

He was the first member of the family to show up, looking me over like a window-shopper trying to decide if he's going to splurge.

"So," he said after a few moments that seemed tons longer than that, "you going to give your uncle Brent a hug?"

Sure. One of those perfunctory ones where you both keep your distance. He smelled of cigarettes.

"I saw you had quite a show out there today," he said. "Everything good?"

"Terrific. I always like to start my day out with a riot."

No one laughed.

When I'd opened the blinds of my bedroom window, I'd thought maybe I was still dreaming—it was possible, right? Just having one of my off-the-wall nightmares—and in a minute Mom would come in and wake me.

When I blink, they will all go poof.

They were taking up the entire sidewalk and half the street. It would've been the whole street if their vans weren't taking up the rest of it—big ones with satellite dishes on the roofs and numbers painted on their sides: 2, 4, 7, 9.

It took me a while to understand that they were all there for *me*. "Jenny," I heard some of them shouting, "Jenny," as if they knew me or something, and I almost shouted back at them: *What the fuck do you want?* I shut the blinds and retreated to my bed, but I felt like retreating even farther, to the back of my closet maybe.

I was sitting there holding tight to Goldy when Mom rushed in.

"So sorry about this, Jenny," she said. "I have no clue how they found out."

I did.

The phone had rung in the middle of the night, and since I was already wide-awake, I'd picked it up.

"Hello," a voice said. "Is this Mrs. Kristal?"

"No."

Pause.

"Is this . . . *Jenny* Kristal?"

"Who's this?"

"Max Westfield. *Newsday*."

"*Who?*"

"Max Westfield. I'm a reporter."

He'd gotten word from a source at the precinct, he said. That I'd been found. If it was me he was talking to, that is? And if it was, he'd love to be the first to say welcome back. And the first to hear my story, too, if that was okay. Being that this was a real bona fide miracle.

I kept quiet.

"Look, Jenny . . . I am talking to Jenny, right? You have no idea how many people have been praying for you over the years—for your safe return. And how a story like this will impact them. Not just them . . . everyone. Parents of other kidnapped children—give them some hope that maybe their kids will come home . . ."

"I'm pretty tired . . . ," I said.

"Of course, Jenny. You have every right to be. With what you've been through. I can call you Jenny, right?"

"It's one in the morning. That's why I'm tired."

"Right, sorry. I only need a minute of your time. If I could just ask you a few questions? I understand you were kidnapped by a couple of, well . . . sexual deviants, and they more or less . . ."

Click.

I didn't tell Mom. Even as she was apologizing for the entire world finding out about me and telling me they were going to make the reporters go away.

How the hell is she going to do that? I thought, but Mom said Dad had called the police.

"You're soaked, Jenny," she said, putting a hand to my forehead. "Do you have a fever?" I didn't bother telling her this is how I woke up most mornings, as if I'd been through the wash-and-spin cycle.

"Why don't you get dressed," she said, laying out a new pair of jeans and that scoop-neck top she'd bought me at the Roosevelt

Field Mall. "Stay here," she said, "we'll deal with this," before shutting my door and marching back downstairs.

After I slipped on my clothes, I peeked through the blinds again. Sure enough, there was a police car right in the middle of the crowd, one of the cops looking like he was trying to shoo all the reporters away. Only the reporters didn't seem to really give a shit, because no one was actually moving anywhere.

Then my dad was out on the porch.

I heard him tell them to please respect our privacy, but they were shouting questions at him, questions about me, and it was so freakin' weird to hear myself being talked about when I wasn't actually part of the conversation—not that it was actually a conversation; it was more of a cluster fuck, since Dad was having trouble getting a single word in.

That word being *getthefuckouttahere.*

Dad was telling them that there wasn't going to be any interview, there wasn't going to be any anything, but they weren't listening and they weren't leaving either, so Dad did, slamming the front door so hard, it made the house shake.

Mom had told me to stay put, but I felt trapped up there, so I went downstairs, slinking down each step as if the reporters could somehow see me. I ended up spooking Mom and Dad, who jerked around as if they thought one of the TV people had somehow snuck into the house.

"I told you to stay upstairs," Mom said.

"Goldy didn't want to." I was still holding her in my hand. Mom motioned for me to come join them on the couch.

"I don't know if the police can make them leave . . . I mean legally," Dad explained to me. "But maybe they'll get the message we don't want them here and we're not going to talk to them."

Which was the same message Mom and Dad gave the people

who began calling the house, then didn't stop. Apparently some people still used landlines—at least when they didn't have your cell number. Every time Mom or Dad put the phone down, it just rang again, *ringggg, ringggg, ringggg,* a network, a newspaper, a talk show. All of them asking about me. Finally, they took the phone off the hook.

"Good thing Ben's not here," Mom said.

"Shit," Dad said, "I've got to tell him to stay at Zack's. That's all we need—Ben bouncing up the front walk."

Too late. Ben had seen the commotion on the news and was already worming his way through the crowd. We could actually see him on the living room TV—kind of surreal watching your house on the news as you're sitting in it. And your brother flailing his way through a sea of mics like a swimmer about to go under.

After he slammed the front door behind him, he blinked at me. Like, *What's wrong with this picture? A cat, a dog, a bird, a sister— circle which one doesn't belong.*

He took his customary place on the love seat and asked Mom to please change the channel—he'd *seen* this show already. One *Ink Master* and half a *Bar Rescue* later, Dad said, "I think they're gone."

"You sure?" Mom said.

Dad peeked through the drapes. "Yep. They've left. Thank God."

Eventually two policewomen showed up at our front door and explained that the reporters might be coming back—they didn't actually have the authority to make them disperse, just to make sure they kept off our property, but if they wanted to sit out there on the sidewalk all day, there wasn't much they could do about it.

"Thanks anyway," Dad said. "Appreciate your help."

Given the all clear, Uncle Brent showed up an hour later, and then the rest of the family began trickling in. There was Mom's aunt Gerta, who looked around sixty-five and suffered from emphysema, and her daughter Trude, who brought her two kids over—all of them my cousins, I guess. And there were some of Dad's relatives—his cousins Arnie and Cecille, and his uncle Samuel. Dad's mom—my grandmother—was living in Florida; his father had died years ago, but they called her on the phone and made me talk to her.

"My darling Jenny," she said. "Oh, my darling . . . This is *Nanny*. Do you remember me?"

"A little," I said.

Which is what I told all of them—*I remember you a little*—because every single person asked me. Uncle Brent and Aunt Gerta and Trude and Arnie and Cecille and Samuel.

The last time I saw you, you were two . . . or *three . . .* or *one . . .* or *six . . .* or *just born,* they said. *You were laughing . . .* or *crying . . .* or *sleeping . . .* or *chattering away . . .* or *playing with your horses.*

And I said, *Really?*

Aunt Gerta couldn't stop crying. She kept a wrinkled tissue inside her sleeve, and she kept pulling it out to dab at her red-rimmed eyes, which reminded me of a magician pulling one of those long scarves out of their belly buttons. Samuel—who had to be eighty, easy—just kept shaking his head from side to side as if he couldn't believe I was really standing there in front of him, and Trude just beamed at me.

Samuel settled next to me on the couch and asked me what it was like living all those years with my kidnappers, and things suddenly went quiet.

"Uncle Sammy," Dad said gently. "Jenny doesn't need to talk about that right now."

"Huh?" Samuel looked confused.

"When she's ready to talk about all that, I'm sure she will. But not yet."

All of them were looking at me now, while munching on the chips and pretzels and hummus Mom had bought from Trader Joe's. Like I was the star attraction, and they were the audience waiting for me to do something interesting.

"Yeah. I'd just rather not think about that right now, if that's okay," I said.

That seemed to sour the air a little, Samuel asking about my kidnappers and me not answering. It reminded everybody that this wasn't some ordinary family reunion, but the kind where everyone needed a police escort just to make it into the house.

"So," Trude said, with her smile still stuck on high beam, "what are your plans now?"

"Yeah," Ben said. "What are your plans now, *sis*?"

"Just take it easy, I guess."

"Sure," Trude said. "That makes sense."

"How about after you take it easy?" Ben said.

Mom shot him a nervous glance. Ben ignored it.

"I don't know. I haven't really thought about it." They were still staring at me, these pretty much perfect strangers—asking me questions like I'd just come back from college or something, because they needed to tiptoe around where I'd really come back from.

"There's no rush," Mom said. "Jenny can figure that all out later."

"Of course she can," Trude said.

"Want to play *Gobble Gobble* now?" Melissa, the nine-year-old, asked me, showing me her phone.

"Sure," I said.

She demonstrated the finer points of the game, using her middle finger to stuff pieces of candy into this fat frog's mouth. There were thirty-nine different levels and she seemed determined to take me through all of them.

"That's one full frog," I said.

"It's not a frog," Melissa giggled. "It's a monster."

"Yeah," Sebastian, the five-year-old, said. "It's a monster."

"That's one full monster, then."

"You're funny . . . ," Sebastian said.

"Yeah, I'm hysterical." I'd always felt irritated around kids—probably because I'd never been allowed to be one. Chalk it up to jealousy.

"Don't annoy your cousin," Trude admonished them.

Good idea, I thought.

"Someone should take a picture," Aunt Gerta said, and finally Arnie obliged, using his cell phone to snap a family portrait. This one would be titled: *Melissa and Sebastian Annoy Their Cousin Jenny.*

Ben was staring at me from across the room.

"Want a turn?" Melissa asked me.

"I'd rather eat the candy myself," I said. "Screw the frog."

"Mommy . . . Jenny said a *curse* word."

Trude looked like she was about to say something to me, but then the little voice in her head must've said, *We have to make allowances for poor Jenny,* and she scolded Melissa instead.

"I said don't annoy your cousin."

"But she said a curse word."

"Yeah," Sebastian said, giggling, "she said *screw!*"

"Sebastian! Do we use language like that? Do we?"

Sebastian tried to explain that he was merely telling her what language his cousin Jenny had used, but since cousin Jenny was apparently off-limits to any parental correction, Trude remained purposelessly oblivious.

"*Never* use language like that again, Sebastian."

Smash. Sebastian flung his sister's iPhone to the floor.

"What are you doing, mister!" Trude wagged her finger at him.

I would've been happy to explain. *He's telling you to screw off in five-year-old.*

Melissa started to cry because her iPhone had a big crack in it now—*See what he did, Mommy . . . see*—and then Sebastian joined in, creating a kind of stereo bawling.

"I'm sorry for my children's behavior," she said, directing most of that toward them.

"No problem," I said.

Everything had been knocked off-kilter. Trude wasn't smiling anymore; Aunt Gerta wasn't dabbing at her eyes; Arnie wasn't taking pictures. Dad's uncle Samuel still looked confused, as if he was wondering where all the forced cheeriness had gone.

Ben was still staring at me.

Trude said it was time to get her *incorrigible* kids home, and that started a mass exodus, everyone probably tired of maintaining their smiles for that long.

I received a rapid-fire series of good-bye hugs and kisses.

Before Ben stomped upstairs, he brushed past me and whispered something in my ear.

"That game where Uncle Brent tickled us till we said *uncle*? Guess what? I *made it up*. Never happened. Weird that you remember it, huh?"

NINE

The two FBI agents sitting in the living room with us were named Hesse and Kline. But I was picturing them as one of those wannabe YouTube comedy duos, because that made it easier when they kept asking me questions I didn't feel like answering—even with Mom telling them to stop because it was upsetting me.

"Sorry," Hesse said—the woman half of the comedy team—"we appreciate this is hard for both of you, but the more we know about what happened to you, the better chance we have of finding them. Don't you want them locked up, Jenny?"

What I wanted was for them to stop asking *When did the sexual abuse start?* And *Can you describe exactly what he did to you?* And *Did this Father use protection when he raped you?*

Jenny wanted to go upstairs and take a nap or go back to the Roosevelt Field Mall with Mom to buy some new tops.

"I don't want to think about them anymore," I said.

"Of course," Hesse said, "that's totally understandable. But they've committed a very serious crime. *Several* serious crimes. And they need to be taken off the streets before they do that to someone else. You can understand that, can't you, Jenny?"

Mom had tried to push the interview back, but the FBI pushed harder. Every day they waited could make it tougher for them to find my kidnappers, they'd told her.

"Why do you want to know about the . . . you know . . . that stuff?"

Hesse looked over at Kline as if she was asking him the same question. But she was just passing the baton, which was their standard operating procedure. Every time me or Mom made a stink about having to answer a question—mostly about the sex stuff—Hesse would hand the questioning over to Kline. Who'd change the subject—like asking me about where we'd lived in Iowa.

I told FBI agent Kline about the deserted trailer at the edge of a dump. About the two ripped beds and the roach-infested cabinets and the sink that didn't work. About the hole in the ceiling where the freezing rain poured in.

"She told Detective Schilling all about Iowa," Mom said. "At the police station. Don't they share all that with you?"

"The mobile home's been checked out," Kline said. "It was empty."

"Well, you didn't think they'd . . . like . . . stay there?" I said.

"Not if they thought you'd be going to the police," Kline said. "Would they have thought that?"

I shrugged. "How would I know?"

"When you left, what exactly were the circumstances?"

"The *circumstances*?"

"Did you have a fight that day? Did you confront them . . . about the sexual abuse, about them having kidnapped you . . . about anything in particular?"

"It wasn't like that."

"Okay, Jenny," Kline said gently. "What was it like?"

"I just wanted to get out of there. So, one day I did."

"How?"

"I walked out and didn't come back."

They'd already asked if I'd been restrained in any way.

"Sometimes."

This is the way we tie your arms, tie your arms, tie your arms, this is the way we tie your arms, early in the morning . . .

Had they let me attend school at any point?

"No." (Hesse explaining to Mom that homeschooling made perfect sense, since the less interaction kidnappers have with people in authority, the better, and me explaining to Hesse that it wasn't homeschooling—I'd learned English by reading all those DC comics Father collected, math by counting the empties he picked up in the streets.)

"But eventually, they gave you more freedom," Kline said.

"If you want to call it that." I'd already told them about the shitty job they let me get at the mall, mostly so I could kick in for family expenses.

"So there wasn't any argument the day you left? No confrontation with either of them?"

"No."

"What made you decide to do it that particular day? You were how old then?"

"Sixteen, almost."

"So why leave that day? Why not the day before, or the day after . . . or the month before?"

"I don't know. I just felt like it. It wasn't like some big planned decision or anything."

"Where did you go?"

"I told you. I hitched a ride. I got off the first place that seemed far enough away."

"Which was?"

"I told you that too. What does that have to do with finding them?"

"I know this must seem repetitive."

"Because it *is* repetitive. You ask me the same stuff a million times."

"Sometimes it takes a couple of times before people remember things, Jenny. Things they didn't remember before. Sorry, I know this isn't fun."

I sighed and looked over at Mom, who looked like she was sorry too, but not enough to go to bat for me again.

"Do you remember who picked you up that day?" Kline asked. "The car, for instance?"

"It was like two years ago."

"Man? Woman?"

"Boy."

"What did he look like?"

"Like a boy."

"That's it?"

"Yeah, that's it. It was just a ride. I didn't care what he looked like."

"Okay. And where did he leave you off?"

"I told you. Illinois. Peoria."

"Did they come looking for you, Jenny?"

"Who?"

"Father and Mother?"

"How do I know?"

"You never contacted them after you left?"

"No. Why would I?"

"I don't know . . . because they were your parents all those years. Because you wanted to tell them off, maybe. You must've been angry at them—angry enough to leave that day."

"I wanted to forget they ever existed; that's what I wanted to do. Besides, how would I have contacted them? It's not like they had a phone or computer or anything."

"Right. Maybe you could've sent them a letter?"

"Maybe I couldn't have, because maybe they didn't have a mailbox or, like, even an address. It was a junked trailer."

"Speaking of that trailer, Jenny"—Hesse piping in again, the baton having been invisibly exchanged without my noticing—"what were the sleeping arrangements like?"

"Sleeping arrangements?" *How stupid did that sound?* I wanted to say. What would she ask next—what were the seating arrangements at dinner?

"Did you all sleep in the same area?"

"My bed was in the back," I said. "Not a bed exactly. Just a mattress"—thinking that they would probably be combing it for hair and stuff. Of course they would.

"And Mother and Father . . . they slept in the front?"

"Uh-huh."

"And when Father, sorry, when he sexually assaulted you, he would leave Mother and go to your bed in the back?"

"Uh-huh."

"And what would Mother do?"

"Snore."

"So she would be sleeping when he assaulted you?"

"Mostly."

"But not all the time? Sometimes she wasn't sleeping? She was up? She could hear what was going on?"

"She knew what was going on."

"I'm talking about when the assaults were actually taking place?"

"I don't know."

"You don't know if she was ever up and could actually hear it?"

"I was kind of occupied." My voice had an edge to it now, and I pictured it as an actual solid thing, made of steel, razor sharp, and able to slice Hesse and Kline to ribbons.

"We've been over this already," Mom said. "Do we really need to keep harping on it?"

"Just a few more questions," Hesse said. "I'm sorry."

No, she wasn't.

"Was Mother," she asked, "I don't know . . . ever sympathetic?"

"What's that mean?"

"I mean did she ever try and help you? Tell Father to stop. You know, try and protect you?"

"No."

"Why do you think that was?"

I felt it coming on, the stupid quivers. I was back on the planet Bizarro, where there was an opposite Jenny who didn't eat nails for breakfast like the one here on Earth.

"'Cause she was a massive bitch, I guess."

There was a brief silence, as if they needed to let my anger have its own space for a while.

"What do you remember about the day they took you?" Kline asked, switching tacks again.

"Huh?"

"The day they kidnapped you? What do you remember?"

Hold on, I thought. *Hold on . . .*

"I was walking down the block to my friend Toni's house. And I was taken . . ."

"Yes, we know that. But how? Did they drive by in a car and pull you in? Was it just Father? Or both of them?"

"I don't remember. It's . . . it's kind of a blur."

"Can you take a minute and think about it?"

I spent the minute thinking about what Ben had whispered to me instead. *I made it up . . . Weird that you remember it, huh?*

"So?" Kline said. "Was it just him . . . Father? In a car? Or the both of them?"

"Just him."

"In a car?"

"Yes."

"What kind of car? Do you remember?"

"I was six."

"Sure. But maybe they kept that car for a while?"

"No. I mean . . . I don't think so."

"And he grabbed you while you were walking down the side-walk?"

"Yes. Right."

"How?"

"How . . . ?"

"Did he come up behind you and just grab you? Or did he stop you first? Maybe say something to you."

"He . . . stopped me."

"And said something to you?"

"Yeah."

"What? Do you remember what he said?"

"He said my mom had asked him to pick me up."

"But you knew that was a lie, right? You were walking down the block to your friend Toni's house. Your mom"—looking over at her now—"she'd just let you out the door. So you knew that wasn't true—that this stranger wasn't supposed to pick you up."

"Uh-huh. Right."

"So what happened then? You didn't go with him like he wanted. That's when he grabbed you?"

"Yes."

"Did you scream?"

"Scream? I don't . . . yes."

I suddenly remembered what it's like to scream but not hear anything coming out of your mouth, because you can't open it.

If you keep moving it's going to hurt worse . . .

"So what did he do? Did he gag you with something?"

"His hand."

"He gagged you with his hand. And he pulled you into the car?"

"Yes."

"Then what?"

"I don't . . ."

"Were you still screaming when he had you in the car?"

"Yes."

"So what did he do?"

"I told you. He had his hand across my mouth."

"Even while he was driving?"

"I guess. I don't remember."

"Okay. Where did he take you?"

"I don't know . . . to Mother, I guess. I was scared. I was scream-ing."

"You don't remember where Mother was? Where he drove you to?"

"No."

"A house? An apartment?"

"I . . . it was an apartment, I think."

"Do you remember if it was a long drive? From where he took you?"

"I don't remember. It felt long."

"How long did you stay there? At the apartment?"

"I don't know. A while."

"A month? A year?"

"I don't really remember. Longer than a month."

"Were there any neighbors around the apartment?"

"I don't remember any."

"You sure? No one? So far, of all the places you can remember living with them, you don't remember a single person ever interacting with them? A neighbor, the postman, a pizza delivery guy . . . ?"

"No."

"Not one person ever knocked on the front door?"

"Sure. I mean, I guess so."

"Okay. Who?"

"I don't know. . . . no one specific comes to mind."

"You sure? You want to think about it?"

"I told you. I don't remember anyone in particular."

"I wish you wouldn't badger her like that," Mom said, standing up for me again. "If you haven't noticed, she's been through hell. She told you she doesn't remember anyone showing up wherever they happened to be living. We're talking about abandoned houses here. Junked trailers. So who exactly was going to pay them a visit?"

"You'd be surprised, Mrs. Kristal. As much as people keep to themselves, they still have to go out into the world. They run into people; people run into them. Maybe some of them came by the houses. Or the trailer. If there are other people who actually knew them, who saw them, even spoke to them, it'd obviously be a major help to us. Your daughter's description to the police was kind of vague."

"I told them exactly what they looked like," I said.

"I'm not sure that's accurate, Jenny." Kline looked down at his notes. "You described Father as being about five ten. Brown eyes.

Graying hair. A beard about medium length. No other distinguishing features. Mother as being about five five. Brown hair. Brown eyes. Medium build." He looked up. "Doesn't give us all that much to go on."

"I said he had *scraggly* gray hair."

"Right. Scraggly . . . sorry, that's in the notes. Did you sit down with a sketch artist at the precinct?"

"Detective Schilling asked us about it," Mom said. "Frankly, we just wanted to get Jenny home at that point."

"Of course. I completely understand. You mind if we send one over tomorrow, Jenny?"

I shrugged. "Sure."

"I know we've been over this already, but you never heard them exchange actual names? Real names? It was always just Father and Mother?"

Stop . . . I'll be good . . .

Stop, WHO . . . ?

Please . . . I promise . . .

Please, who . . . ?

FATHER . . .

"Yeah."

"And you never asked them? About their real names? The way kids, you know, like to ask their parents about everything?"

"They *weren't* my parents."

Kline reiterated that there'd be just a few more questions, but he lied, because the questions kept coming.

"What about doctors—they never took you to one?" Father didn't believe in them, I said. "Never took you shopping?" Nope— they stole clothes out of the Goodwill bins. "Never took you to a grocery store?" I don't remember. And so on. They asked about all the places we lived, most of which I couldn't recall, and then they asked about them again, and I still couldn't remember most of them.

Finally, Mom said, "Enough."

I'd begun unconsciously shrinking into the couch, as if I was trying to physically get away from them, from Hesse and Kline and all their stupid questions, and I guess I was. I was tired of being a good sport.

Hesse and Kline reluctantly agreed to end the interview.

Kline shook my hand and Hesse patted me on the shoulder and told me that it was very common for victims to remember other things after talking to them, and if that happened, to please get in contact with them right away.

"If you could remember other people who met Father and Mother, who knew them, no matter how briefly, we need to hear about it," she said.

"Haven't you asked people in Sioux City? People around the neighborhood?" Mom asked.

"There isn't a neighborhood," Kline said. "The trailer's at the edge of a dump. There's some houses about a quarter mile away—pretty run-down. A few of the people have remembered seeing Jenny. No one remembers seeing anyone matching her description of them. Father and Mother. Don't worry"—Kline looked over at me—"we'll keep digging."

TEN

Ben

Ben was trying to explain it to his best bud, Zack.

But how exactly?

Even his dad had trouble spitting it out on that ride home Saturday, Ben stewing in the front seat, wondering why he'd been hunted down—two of his friends texting him that his dad had put out a virtual APB on him—and Ben still percolating on some nice Skywalker weed, which usually made him chill but not when his dad was making him leave his car parked outside Dom's house and dragging him home like he was eight years old.

"So what's the problem?" Ben had asked him in a perfectly polite tone, that politeness somehow eluding his dad, who asked him why he always had to be so snotty.

"Perception isn't reality," Ben answered, which was a line he'd seen in a car ad in his senior communications course and then immediately appropriated. He'd already used it on the boys' dean, who'd asked him if he was high, and then on his history teacher, who'd asked him why he hadn't studied for the test on which he'd just received a big fat F. Both of them not exactly amused by it, so it wasn't totally surprising that his dad wasn't either.

"Guess I'm making it up," his dad said. "That it?"

"Intent is two-thirds of the law," Ben said, although he suspected he'd jumbled that up, that it was *possession* that was two-thirds of the law or something like that. What he was really trying to say was that he hadn't intended to be snotty so therefore was innocent as charged.

"Huh?" his dad said. "Intent is two-thirds of what? Look, forget it, I need to tell you what's happened."

Except he couldn't seem to manage that. Ben could see his jaw trying to formulate the words, as if he'd just gotten two shots of novocaine at the dentist, and Ben, still high, found it pretty funny.

"We got a call today . . . ," his dad said. Then: "Your mother got a call today . . ." Then: "You won't believe this . . ." Then: "Okay, I'm not sure how to tell you this . . ."

By this time, Ben was trying so hard not to laugh out loud that he'd completely lost focus on what his dad was saying, or trying to say. So that when his dad finally said it, Ben didn't react, because he hadn't actually processed it.

"Did you hear what I said, Ben?" his dad said, in this soft, reverential voice that Ben found perfectly hysterical.

"Sure."

"You heard what I said just now? You heard me?"

"Aye, aye, Captain."

His dad pulled over to the curb and stopped the car, which finally brought Ben's hysteria to a screeching halt.

"Are you stoned, Ben?" his dad asked. Ben was about to repeat his perception-reality line, the one he'd already offered to that very same question in the dean's office, or maybe he would just remind his dad that he was legally an adult so he could do whatever he felt like—even though that would mean suffering through one of those "you're still under my roof" speeches—but his dad's overly earnest face made him stop.

"Dope . . . I mean . . . nope." He'd done that on purpose, a response he'd honed in the past, figuring that if he was cool enough to joke about it, then he obviously wasn't. Stoned, that is.

"I just told you about Jenny. And you're cracking up."

"Huh? Who?"

"*Jenny.* Your . . . sister."

"My sister?"

It went like this for a while, his dad saying things and Ben repeating them, like they had to do in Spanish class, and with just about as much comprehension. His dad saying, "Jenny, your sister"—and Ben wondering WTF he was talking about, although starting to feel his pot head going up in smoke, so to speak. Because there was some dark, urgent undertone here, or was it *undertow,* this scary force insistently trying to suck him under.

"Jenny . . . what? I don't . . ."

"Your sister," Dad said. "She's come back. Didn't you hear what I said?"

And now, at last, he had. But it was like the kind of thing you hear when you smoke too much weed laced with speed, and the words aren't real, just coming from your own buzzing brain. This couldn't be real either, could it?

"My sister's what? She's . . . back? Back where . . . ?"

"Here. Jenny's home, Ben. I know this must be absolutely incomprehensible to you, it's incomprehensible to us too, but sometimes amazing things happen; they just do . . ."

"Whoa . . . ," Ben said. "Wait a minute . . . You're telling me that . . . my sister, she's home. Home . . . like our *house*?"

"Jenny escaped from her kidnappers. She got away from them. And now she's home."

The undertow had him now, and he couldn't breathe. He was going to drown right here in the front seat of his dad's car, and then the family would be three people again, except a different three people: Ben gone, and his sister, Jenny, here instead.

"You okay, Ben?" His dad reaching out, as if he were going to hug him, and Ben not remembering the last time his dad had done that—maybe when he'd scored two goals in soccer when he was twelve—so he found himself instinctively shrinking back, because it was just too weird, everything, his sister, Jenny, back . . . back home, and him dying here in the car when he got the news, and his dad trying to hug him.

"It's okay, Ben," his dad said, "I know this is a shock to you," and Ben thinking no, a shock was when the boys' dean caught you in mid-toke and you had to swallow smoke, or when you saw a picture of your supposed girlfriend, Darla, swapping spit with your supposed friend AJ on Snapchat, those were shocks, but this was more like being hit by lightning—he'd once seen this news shot of a smoking body being carted off to the morgue.

"When . . . like, *today* . . . ?" Ben asked, which seemed pretty stupid even as he said it, because of course it was today, since yesterday his sister was dead and buried—well, not buried, because they'd never found her. And maybe she wasn't buried metaphorically either—kudos to his English teacher for last week's assignment on metaphors versus similes—because Ben had kept her alive all these years, created a kind of shrine to her, or what he remembered of her, which he visited religiously along with a number of other devotees. If you didn't believe him, check out the number of Facebook visitors, which currently stood at 983, excluding his parents, who had no idea it even existed.

The thing was, when he looked in the mirror, he felt like he saw a kind of thalidomide baby staring back. Zack had turned him on to that particular horror when they were twelve or so—this website on medical malformations, which featured kids without legs and arms, the result of this sleeping pill called thalidomide that all these pregnant women had taken back in the Stone Age. And when Ben saw these kids—wanting to look and needing to look away at the same time—he thought, *That's me.* Maybe no one else could see it, but he could. When they took his sister, Jenny, that day, whoever they were, they'd ripped out a part of him as well—he couldn't say exactly which part, only that he never felt entirely whole again. He'd apparently lost all memory of what happened that day Jenny disappeared because he'd completely freaked out— *childhood traumatic grief* being the official diagnosis—and he was stuck in a kids' funny farm for more than a year. Sure, they'd *called* it a school, but every student was dumbed down on meds of one kind or another, and if it was a school, why did he end up two grades back when he finally reentered the general population, huh? Already twenty, and still stuck in high school.

He couldn't put it together in any logical way. It was like playing pickup sticks, trying to pull out one memory or another, but the whole thing crashing down before he could finish. Sometimes on particularly good weed—a blunt of mellow Sour Diesel, let's say—he felt like he was getting this close, like he was right there, only he never got any further. What was perplexing, particularly perplexing, was he'd never felt that he and his kid sister were that close, as much as any eight-year-old could understand that sort of thing. They were practically Irish twins, yet it seemed to him that they hadn't been tight at all. In fact, he seemed to remember them fighting half the fucking time. But when she disappeared, so did a crucial piece of him—his ability to function like a normal kid, for one thing, at least, for a while—and when he tried to remember things about her, about that day, it was like someone had turned out the lights. Wanting to know and *frightened* of knowing all at the same time.

Which is why he'd started that memorial page on Facebook, which was as much a shrine to that lost part of himself as to her, and where, bit by bit, he'd been letting in a few cracks of light. And where other people, some of whom had lost family members of their own, had started to congregate to more or less cry on one another's shoulders.

His dad had eventually pulled away from the curb—after Ben somehow pulled it together enough to look happy about this great news, which somehow he wasn't happy about, another thing he was forced to mull over on the ride home, namely, why exactly that was.

Maybe because it was entirely too amazing to be true, or maybe because his whole being had been shaped by the absence of something—his sister, Jenny—so suddenly having her back was like erasing *himself*. Like, who was he now exactly?

They remained dead quiet on the rest of the ride home, his dad giving him time to digest it, he guessed, even though he could hardly breathe, much less think. Just about the time Jenny disappeared, he'd gone flying down the stairs like he always did when his mom called them to dinner, only he'd missed a step and went literally flying down the stairs, landing on his left arm, which went *crack*. It didn't hurt at first—just this all-encompassing numbness that was somehow worse, because you knew, you just knew what was coming. Ben felt like that now, struck numb, with a world of pain lurking right around the corner.

When they got to the house, Ben didn't actually want to walk in, but it wasn't like there was exactly an alternative.

For a second, he thought this was all some stupid prank. The hot chick from Fredo's was sitting next to his mom on the couch.

"Hey, Ben, long time no see," she said, after they finished their staring contest.

No, it wasn't, he thought. It was just a few *hours* since he'd last seen her.

He was going to say that, then thought maybe he shouldn't, then thought why not, then didn't know what to think, as his mom began begging him to come and join the family reunion.

These lyrics from the Clash started playing in his head . . . maybe it was the pot—*should I stay or should I go*—and as a result, he did neither, just stood there as his mom kept asking him to come in and his dad gave him a push from behind. "Say hello to your sister," they both begged him, but she wasn't his sister, she was the girl from Fredo's, and besides, everyone knew his sister was dead. You could look it up on Facebook.

When he finally entered the living room, because there was only so long he could stand there doing nothing and he couldn't just turn around and walk out, he picked the spot geographically farthest from everyone.

His mom asked him if he wanted to say something to his sister, and he felt like saying, *Sure, where is she?* And then the girl from Fredo's said she was tired and wanted to go to sleep, so they all got up—excluding himself—and they disappeared upstairs.

Ben stayed right where he was, on the pumpkin-colored love seat, which made him think of that stupid fairy tale, the one where the girl turned into a pumpkin at midnight—or was it her coach that did? He couldn't remember—but maybe something like that would happen here, the girl from Fredo's turning into a pumpkin and ending this fairy tale, because that's what it was. Of course it was.

Eventually his mom came back downstairs and asked if he was all right and murmured something about taking time to let it all sink in, and Ben just nodded, because he suddenly felt very tired too, as exhausted as the girl from Fredo's. They'd put her in the den, and when Ben walked by the closed door on the way to his room, he had a sudden memory of running into this room when he was eight years old, or had he been running *away* from it? Whatever. The girl inside it was going to disappear at midnight.

Ha.

The next day, she was gone—the couch bed back to being just a couch again, and no sign of her anywhere, and Ben was beginning to attribute the whole thing to that pretty intense Skywalker OG he'd toked with Zack.

But when he went down to the kitchen to grab some OJ, his dad was drinking coffee by the sink and said, "Jenny and Mom went to the mall."

There went that theory. Ben was going to ask his dad to stop calling the girl from Fredo's Jenny, but he was still suffering from shock, or maybe aftershock—that thing after the original earthquake when everyone sticks their heads out of the rubble thinking it's all over, and they all get a big surprise—so he said nothing, and even forgot why he'd come down to the kitchen in the first place. His dad tried to start a conversation with him, but Ben bolted out of the kitchen as if he'd just heard a text popping up on his cell, which he'd left somewhere in the hall, only he *sent* one instead—to Zack, telling him Ben needed to come over pronto.

When he got to Zack's house and Zack asked him, "What's up?" he said nothing, and he kept saying nothing until the next day, when his house was plastered all over the TV news.

ELEVEN

Mom was at her real estate office and Dad was in the city being an *executive producer. Maybe I'll take you to work one day and show you around,* he told me, and I said, *Cool.* Mom had asked me if it was okay if she went back to work, and I said, *Why not?*

I want to be sure you can handle being alone, Jenny.

I felt like asking her what was so bad about being alone, given that there were plenty of times when being alone was exactly what I was down on my knees praying for, when I wasn't down on my knees doing something else.

No problem, I said to Mom. *It's fine.*

I was tired. Not "physically can't keep my head up" tired, though I wasn't exactly getting what you'd call a good night's sleep. The freak-show nightmares took care of that. Just tired of us all dancing around each other—what we could talk about and what we couldn't, how I should or shouldn't act. Trying to navigate between the past and present, like constantly switching a car radio from contemporary to oldies.

Last night Dad called me Jenny Penny, as he pulled a penny out of my ear.

I almost said, *How'd you do that, Dad?* Still wanting to believe in magic.

Penny for your thoughts, he'd said, sticking it into my hand.

Sure. My thoughts were about being six years old again and still feeling like you could be carried through life on your dad's back. My thoughts were I just might take him up on that offer to visit his production company, just so he could parade me around the office and say, *This is my daughter, Jenny. She's home. She's back.*

We're never going to let her out of our sight again.

My thoughts right now were about falling into a long, sweet nap where I'd dream about old times, the kind where you wake up feeling like you're on fake Xans.

I might've if it wasn't for the phone.

It kept ringing.

We were still adhering to a strict "don't answer the phone" policy around here. Mostly because there were only so many ways you can say no. Like, *No, thanks,* and, *I told you we weren't interested,* and, *If you call here again I'm going to call the police*—which seemed to be Dad's new hobby, calling the police. That reporter from *Newsday* who'd buzzed me in the middle of the night—what was his name? Max, right—had managed to weasel Dad's cell phone number from somebody, and Dad had not so politely told him to fuck off. Just like he told the booking agent from Fox News, the reporter from *Time* magazine, the producer from *Ellen,* and Dr. Phil himself—kind of cool the Philster would personally call to try to get me on his show. Dad told him thanks but no thanks, refraining from using the F word only because Mom was a true fan.

The phone was ringing now.

I tried to ignore it, but sometimes trying to ignore something only makes you that much more aware of it, and the ringing started to sound like a car alarm in the middle of the night.

I picked it up, enjoying the silence for a moment before actually putting it to my ear.

"Hello, is Mrs. Kristal there?" A man's voice.

"She's out," I said.

"Oh." Quiet. "Is this . . . never mind. Wait—can you tell her Joe Pennebaker says sorry, he won't be calling again. That's all. Just please let her know."

"Sure," I said, wondering why someone would call just to say that they wouldn't be calling. "No problem."

After I hung up, I started wishing everyone else out there felt the same way. The phone had started in again.

When it reached earsplitting, I bailed.

Opening the front door took some real effort, not because it was particularly heavy, but because the last time I'd gone through it, it'd been from the other direction. We'd been under siege, and I was finally opening the stockade gates.

But there was only a police car moseying down the street, and the officer who'd picked me up that first day—I think it was him—waved at me.

"Hey. Everything okay?" he shouted.

"No," I said.

"Why, what's wrong?"

"I'm being questioned by the police."

He squinted.

"Just kidding," I said.

"Copy that," he answered. "Your dad asked us to keep an eye out, that's all."

"Great."

"Well, have a good day, miss." Zoom. The police car accelerated down the street.

About a half minute too soon.

I spotted her halfway down the block.

A reporter, I thought.

She was hanging back, nearly blocked by a row of moth-eaten rhododendron bushes at the end of the block. Peeking. Which is exactly what a reporter would be doing, right? Trying to snap a photo of the girl who'd made it back. Mom had shown me the head-line on the website of the local paper: LOST AND FOUND. On the left was the picture from the telephone pole, and on the right was one of the photos Detective Mary had snapped at the precinct—the one where I'd mugged for the camera. Mom didn't understand how the paper could've gotten hold of that one and said she was going to call the precinct to complain. I couldn't stop thinking that the girl on the right looked like she wouldn't have much in common with the girl on the left.

I stopped dead, the sound of the police car pulling away still echoing in my ears, that face staring at me from behind the bushes.

Was a camera crew about to jump me?

When she walked out where I could see all of her, she was alone. It didn't make her any less threatening. There was something about her face I didn't like.

Her expression, for one thing, which seemed to be alternating between shyness and anger.

The other thing about her face was that I thought I recognized it.

"I just want to speak with you . . . ," she said.

I ran. Fast. Panic can do that to you, suddenly turn you into Usain Bolt. I zoomed back down the block to my front door.

Which wouldn't open.

It. Would. Not. Open.

It must've locked automatically. No one had given me any keys.

"Please . . ." I heard her voice behind me. "You need to stop this."

If I don't look, she's not here.

I ran around to the back of the house. To the sliding glass door—did anyone ever actually bother locking it?

It slid open.

As soon as I dived through, I locked it shut from inside. I ran into the living room and pulled the drapes tighter than they already were—tight enough to pretty much block out every single molecule of light.

I retreated to the couch where Mom and Dad and I had huddled together the morning the reporters surrounded the house shouting my name. Now someone else was out there doing it.

Deep breaths . . . deep breaths . . .

Knock.

Knock.

Knock. Knock. Knock. Knock. Knock. Knock. Knock. Knock. Knock. Knock. Knock. Knock. Knock. Knock. Knock . . .

In between banging on the front door, she was shouting something. I couldn't actually hear the words because I'd put both hands up over my ears.

If I wait and do nothing, she'll go away.

She can't keep knocking on a door that won't open.

She can't keep screaming at someone who won't answer.

The knocking stopped.

It stopped.

I lowered my hands and held my breath. I'd been hugging my knees with my head between my legs—what they tell you to do when a plane's about to crash.

I waited for the banging to start up again. Then waited some more.

After a while, I slowly unfolded myself from the couch, crept over to the blinds, and peeked. All clear. I should've felt okay then. I should've felt home free.

Only the phone starting ringing. Again.

There was a one-tenth of one percent possibility it wasn't her. I started to believe in that possibility, to embrace it like faith. It was another talk show. Another newspaper. It was Mr. Pennebaker admitting he'd lied, that he was going to call back just one more time.

"Finally," she said when I picked it up.

I didn't say anything back. My lungs were pressing up against my ribs.

"*Remember*," she said, "I know who you really are."

TWELVE

Who I really am.

There was a little girl who I don't remember anymore whose mom belted her into her stroller one morning, even though the little girl was five and three-quarters years old and had stopped needing to be strolled anywhere.

Maybe this had something to do with her mom's decaying yellow teeth and several black gaps where her teeth were actually missing, and those big red splotches on her face—*Sunburn,* her mom explained, even though it didn't look anything like sunburn to the little girl—or maybe it had to do with the fact that her mom had the helpless heebie-jeebies that morning, which seemed to go away only when she sucked on that glass pipe of hers, which the little girl said looked like crystal, making her mother laugh out loud.

It had been a few days since the little girl had seen her mom smoking on that pipe, and her mom had spent those days rocking back and forth in their bedroom and scratching herself like crazy—

I got a bad itch. And then she'd stopped saying anything at all to the girl, racing out of the apartment a few times but always trudging back looking worse than before.

She'd made a lot of phone calls saying *Please . . . please . . .* but the little girl never heard her say thank you. And then her mom made another phone call that morning, whispering something into the phone that the little girl couldn't quite hear, just the last part, where her mom said, *Fine . . . yeah . . . we'll be there.*

After that, her mom dressed her in a T-shirt and overalls, which had crusted food on them—the little girl couldn't remember the last time her mom had actually washed anything—then stuffed some of the little girl's other clothes in a big plastic bag, and the little girl asked her mom if they were going swimming, since that was the only other time she could remember her mom bringing clothes with them, that day they'd gone to the big municipal pool that stank of chlorine.

Her mom didn't answer her, just told her to get into the stroller, and when the little girl said no, she wanted to walk, her mom screamed at her, then picked her up and stuffed her in the blue stroller herself, strapping her in tight. *It hurts,* the little girl said, because the straps were digging into her—it felt like that time her mom had squeezed her into the baby swing at the park when she was already too old for it, and she'd complained she couldn't breathe, but her mom hadn't listened and had even disappeared, leaving the little girl dangling there for hours.

Her mom told her to *Shush . . . stop your complaining,* so she did, because there was really no way to get her mom to listen when she was like this, all jumpy and frazzled and out of sorts.

They seemed to stroll for a really long time, and the little girl wondered where they were going, since she could swear the park was in the other direction, and the pool, too, and now that she thought about it, it had to be too cold for swimming anyway, since it wasn't even summer yet.

"Where we going, Mommy?"

Her mom was huffing and puffing like the big, bad wolf in that nursery story, and she stopped for a minute to get her breath.

"We're meeting Mommy's friend," she said.

"Who?"

But her mom didn't bother answering—just started pushing the stroller again. They passed block after block with boarded-up stores and metal cages over the ones that were still open, and the little girl pretended that they were at the zoo and the people inside were animals. She was really good at pretending; her mom said she was going to grow up to be an actress, because she would imitate the people she saw on TV like *Hannah Montana*—back when they had a TV—and her mom would clap and tell her that she was good enough to be on TV herself. She would play pretend with kids she met at the playground, too, not just making believe that the plastic bridge they were running over was the one that the Billy Goats Gruff scampered across, but pretending other things—like when one of the kids asked her if that woman was her mom, pointing to the woman with red splotches all over her face who'd fallen asleep on the bench with a lit cigarette still in her mouth. *No,* the little girl had answered, *she's the nanny.*

So when they kept strolling to who knows where, the little girl kept pretending that the people inside the caged stores were lions and tigers and bears, although it was the people outside the stores, the ones lolling on stoops and against cars, who seemed more dangerous.

Some of them looked like her mom, with the same red splotches, sunken cheeks, and missing teeth. They had the same look on their faces too, like they were sleeping even though they were awake, the way her mom looked after she'd sucked on that pipe that looked like crystal.

One of the men leaning against a rusted-out car stumbled toward them and asked her mom if she had any *scratch,* which maybe had to do with her mom itching so terribly before, but her mom didn't answer him, just kept pushing the stroller forward. The man called her a *bitch,* which the little girl knew was a bad word, because her mom used it about Grandma, who she didn't like anymore—*Goddamn bitch,* she'd mutter when she got off the phone with Grandma, *you'd think I was asking her for a million dollars*—the little girl wondering if Grandma was one of the people her mom had said please to over the phone before, but not thank you. She wondered what friend they were going to visit, because some of her mom's friends were men who'd come over to the apartment and suck on that pipe with her, men who looked like the one who'd just called her mom a bitch.

They stopped in the parking lot of a motel, passing the office window, which had the same kind of metal bars over it and a glowing red sign. What kind of animal was in there? the little girl wondered. There was no one else in the parking lot, so the little girl thought maybe they'd stopped so her mom could catch her breath again.

But then a car door opened, and a man came out. He began shuffling over to them. He had a big belly and scraggly thin hair and he was smiling at her. He'd left someone in the car—a woman peering out the window at them.

"I want to get up, Mommy," the little girl said.

"In a minute," she said. "Mommy has to talk to her friend."

The little girl tried to unlatch the straps herself, but Mommy slapped at her hands.

"I said in a minute."

"I gotta go to the bathroom," the little girl said.

"Not *now.*" Her mom looked even more jittery than she had this morning, shaking like their neighbor's white cat, Lulu, when she got caught in the rain.

"Hey there, sweetheart," the man said to the little girl—he was suddenly standing right next to them. "We'll get you to the bathroom real soon, okay?"

The little girl didn't answer him, because she didn't know who he was, and the last thing she wanted was a stranger taking her to the bathroom.

"What's your name?" the man asked. "*Jobeth,* right?"

The little girl nodded, because that's what you're supposed to do when someone asks you your name.

"Isn't that pretty," the man said. "Pretty name for a pretty girl."

She looked down at her lap, where the pink strap was cutting into her stomach.

"Say thank you," her mom said.

"Thank you," the little girl mumbled. She didn't like the way the man was talking to her, or the way he was smiling, which didn't feel like a smile.

"Well . . . you're very welcome."

"Do you have it?" her mom asked the man.

"Impatient, aren't you?" He chuckled and said, "Why don't we step into my office."

The little girl wondered if the man owned the motel, because that was the only office there, but after her mom told her to just sit tight, the man led her mom back to his car. The woman in the front seat was still peering out at them, and when she saw the little girl looking at her, she smiled back.

The man opened the back door and her mom got in, and the little girl felt a sudden panic, thinking that her mom and the man were just going to drive away and leave her there. But the car stayed where it was, and she could see her mom and the man talking in the back seat. Her mom looked like she was asking him for something—maybe that thing she'd asked about before—and the man was shaking his head at her, and then her mom was putting both hands together by her mouth like she was praying, which the little girl hadn't seen her mom do since the last time they'd been to church, which was just about forever ago, and then the man nodded toward the little girl, and her mom put her face in her hands like she was crying, and maybe she was because her shoulders were heaving up and down, up and down, but then after a while, her mom lifted her head out of her hands and nodded. The little girl saw the man pass something to her mom, and then the man patted her on the shoulder.

Her mom was getting out of the car now, and the little girl thought, *Good, we can go home now,* even though her mom's face was all red, even redder than usual, and she wasn't looking at the little girl, but past her, at a place where the girl wasn't.

"Can we go?" the little girl asked, waiting for her mom to start pushing the stroller back home.

"Mommy's friend . . . ," she said, choking up. "Mommy's friend . . . he's going to *watch* you, okay?"

"I don't want someone to watch me," the little girl said. "I want to go home."

"You need to do what Mommy *says* . . ."

"No!" Suddenly that panic was back, because the car was going to drive away, and her mom was telling her *what?* That she was going to be in it? She didn't understand . . . why was she asking those strangers to babysit her? Why couldn't they just go home?

The man got out of the car and walked toward her again, with that same smile that didn't seem like a smile, and her mom started to back away, and suddenly the little girl was grabbing at the strap buckles, trying to undo them.

"Hey there, Jobeth," the man said.

She managed to get the straps open and was slipping out of them, even as the man was saying, "Whoa . . . whoa, there."

She clambered out of the stroller and ran right to her mom, who was almost past the office window. But instead of picking her up, instead of taking her little girl into her arms for a warm, tight hug, her mom just stood there with her arms folded across her chest, as the little girl wrapped herself around one of her mom's legs.

"I want to go home!"

She was crying now, the kind of crying that just pours out of you, like when you get sick and can't stop throwing up. The man had stopped by the empty stroller and he wasn't smiling anymore.

"Now, we had a deal here," he said to her mom. "You're not some kind of welsher, are you?" When her mom didn't answer, he said, "You know what we do to welshers where I come from, don't you?"

Her mom still didn't say a word. Her leg—the one the little girl was holding on to for dear life—was shaking up and down like her mom was freezing or something.

"All right," the man said. "I believe you have something that belongs to me, then. Give it back."

"No need," her mom said, "really . . . it's okay," and the little girl thought, *Yes, it's okay,* because she was back with her mom and any minute now they were going to start heading home, where she would play with her Hannah Montana doll, but first use the bathroom, because she really had to go something awful.

Only her mom began prying the little girl's arms off her leg, one arm at a time, even though the little girl was still crying like there was no tomorrow—which was what her mom always said to her, *Stop crying like there's no tomorrow,* which meant there was a tomorrow, and it would be better than today.

"Now, what did I tell you before, huh?" she said, still choking up. "Mommy's friend is going to watch you, okay?"

"No!" Shouting this between sobs, trying to cling to her mom's leg, but her mom fending her off as if she were a stray dog.

And then suddenly, she felt someone's arms around her, lifting her right off her feet.

"Now, Jobeth, you stop crying and we'll get you a nice ice cream cone," the man said.

But she didn't stop crying, she couldn't, and the man, who smelled of some kind of perfume, said, "You going to listen to me or *not?*" not sounding friendly anymore like before when he'd said she had a pretty name, but sounding like her mom when the little girl did something bad.

"Only good girls get ice cream cones," he said. "You going to be a good girl or not?"

"Mommy!" the little girl shrieked, but her mom had turned and was already walking away. *"Mommy!"*

But the man was taking her back to his car, holding her as tight as the straps had, and when the little girl squirmed around enough to look for her mom, she was already disappearing around the corner of the motel, and the little girl couldn't hold it in anymore, she just couldn't, and the man yelled, "Dammit, what did you do?"

And that was the last time the little girl, who I don't really remember anymore, ever saw her mother.

THIRTEEN

Karen Greer.
    Alexa Kornbluth.
    Terri Charnow.
Sarah Ludlow.
Jenny Kristal.
Sometimes I'd slip up.

I counted at least two times already. Once when I called Dad's mom Eloise, which was the name of a different grandmother belonging to an entirely different girl, and once when I talked about going to first grade at Hollyhock Elementary School, when Jenny Kristal had gone to Lakeside. Both times, I corrected myself . . . *Whoops, I meant Lakeside,* I said, and Mom hadn't seemed to notice.

Of course, it was three times if you included what I'd said to Ben. *Sure I remember Brent tickling us till we said uncle.* And Ben mentioning how weird it was that I remembered something that never happened.

Usually, they'd cut you some slack. You'd been kidnapped and abused, and everything was so long ago. Of course you were going to get some things wrong, jumble a few names, forget a few faces, screw up a few dates. It was to be expected, wasn't it? It was a miracle you could remember anything, considering the hell you'd been put through. Isn't that the word Mom used with the FBI? *If you haven't noticed, she's been through hell.* Go, Mom.

And since most everyone else had noticed what I'd been through, most of them wouldn't catch the other things, like me calling Grandma the wrong name, or mentioning a first-grade class that happened to be in Ohio, or even me laughing over the corny antics of Uncle Brent—though Ben had certainly caught it, since he'd made a point of nailing me on it.

I was just trying to be nice. That's what I'd tell Ben if he brought it up again. *I really didn't remember Brent tickling us like that and making us say* uncle *over and over, but since you did and you seemed to get such a goddamn kick out of it, I played along. And on that subject, why'd you make it up in the first place? Could it be you don't trust me, Ben?*

There were always Bens.

Sometimes it was the dad. Or the mom. Or the sister. Or the uncles. Or the grandmother or grandfather—though they were usually too old to notice anything. But sometimes it was Ben.

The key was to absolutely believe it. Not just pretend to believe it.

Really believe it.

Kind of like that visualization thing that policeman suggested, except he was talking about imagining something in the future, while I needed to imagine things in the past.

Being six years old, for example, and having my mom let me out the front door to go play with my best friend, Toni Kelly, and then being taken. And all the stuff from my life before that. Riding my dad around the bedroom floor like a horse. Watching a kick-ass fireworks show in the backyard every summer on the Fourth of July. Going to Disney World, where my big brother, Ben, got himself lost in Tom Sawyer's cave, boohoo. Ben had graciously filled in most of the blanks for me on that weird Facebook page of his, the one he'd dedicated to his dead sister, crammed with all sorts of scattered memories, including that useful tidbit about the family gorging on Happy Meals right before Jenny went missing. I just remembered something, I'd told Detective Mary—and I had. Sometimes it was only a few words—I remember my sister Jenny fighting with me because she caught me shooting BBs at Goldy—but usually it was long, rambling, stream-of-consciousness stuff, like when he wrote about being lost in that cave, ending that particular entry by wondering, Is this what it was like for my sister, being lost in a deep, dark hole, but never being found?

Yeah, Ben, kind of.

And I hadn't just read things. Remember, the internet's an interactive medium. I struck up a conversation with the grieving brother, because, after all, I'd lost a sister, too, I told him, so we were virtually kindred spirits. And he'd written back, warily at first, just yeses and nos. It was only after I went ahead and shared some very intimate and painful memories—I've never told anyone this before—that he started reciprocating, and after a while, he was like a faucet you couldn't turn off. Not that I wanted to.

What was she like? I asked him. What do you remember most about her?

That's just it, he'd told me. He must've blocked a lot of that stuff out, because for a long time he couldn't remember very much at all. That's why he'd started the page in the first place—to fill in the holes. And it was working, he said. Things were coming back. He remembered being in the backyard with Jenny and her pushing him into a tomato stake. He still had the scar. He remembered being up at the lake with her where they played wild Indians—he always made himself chief—and at the beach where Jenny helped him build sand castles with Timmy the Truck. And swimming in the ocean with her—that, too, remembering being terrified when a wave toppled him over into the surf, and he hadn't known which way was up and thought he couldn't possibly hold his breath a second longer, that in a moment he was going to be gulping in all that green water. Until he was suddenly standing upright and sputtering for air, and his kid sister, Jenny, was there hugging him, or maybe it was his dad, he couldn't remember. Just that he was alive and he hadn't drowned after all. He remembered retreating into a deep, dark hole the day she disappeared, and never really making his way out.

This is what she was like, he wrote me. This and this and this. And not just words, but pictures. A shot of Ben and Jenny, circa 2005—the kind of photo moms used to drag their kids to the Sioux City Mall for, the whole family getting to sit in front of an imitation Christmas tree wearing ugly reindeer sweaters. Jenny squirming in her big brother's lap in this particular shot, a bunch of oversize holiday candy canes in the background. And there was a picture of Jenny with her grandfather on the Kristals' front lawn, standing in a dripping-wet bathing suit as if she'd just been running through a summer sprinkler. *Do you remember him?* Mom had asked, pointing to a white-haired man holding just-born Jenny in the hospital. Grandpa, I'd answered, and Mom's eyes had gone all misty at that thought—twelve years of living in abandoned houses and wrecked trailers with the Mother and Father from hell and I'd managed to hold on to her dad. Ben had too. I remember my grandfather making Jenny guess which hand the Tootsie Rolls were in and she'd always guess right, Ben wrote on the page, evidently unable to figure out how I'd managed to pull off that amazing feat, which didn't exactly take rocket science. Maybe it was all that weed Ben was toking—he wrote how it helped him remember stuff, though my experience was pretty much the opposite, that grass was good for kissing memories good-bye, at least when you were sky-high.

Now and then Ben would ask me to share memories of my sister, and I'd just borrow things from the different sisters I'd been reunited with over the last two and a half years. Mousy Allison Greer for one, whose sister Karen disappeared when she was three years old, and who solemnly promised me after our tearful reunion that she would never, ever, not on pain of death, ever let me out of her sight again—*sisters forever*—until things soured, of course, and I had to get out of her sight pretty damn quick.

Sometimes I wasn't fast enough. I'd let my guard down and start thinking I was home free and stop believing I was who I *said* I was. I'd start going outside the role and begin fucking up my lines. I'd mistake those funny looks from Dad for being just funny looks from Dad, and completely miss that I was in serious shit. Twice I'd been sent to juvie hall, where they'd pretty much thrown up their hands—I'd been fostered out the first time (two lowlifes who stockpiled foster kids for the government assistance checks) and jailbroke out the second, pilfering the keys to the front door and sneaking out in the middle of the night. I was a serious puzzlement to the various authorities I came in contact with, not to mention a major pain in the ass. What to do with me? It wasn't like I'd attacked anyone or committed a break and enter, though, okay, there was one social worker who thought that's pretty much what I had done. *You assaulted this family, Jobeth,* she lectured me. *You played on their hopes and dreams; you devastated them. How does that make you feel?* She should've asked me how it made me feel before the dad began giving me funny looks—which was safe and warm. And maybe she should've asked them, too—those devastated parents who couldn't keep the smiles off their faces those first few weeks. Besides, as far as I knew, devastating dreams wasn't exactly listed in the penal code.

Why do you do this? the social worker had asked me. Good question. But I didn't provide a good answer. I just shrugged, which didn't earn me any brownie points with her. I suppose I could've taken her back to that morning by that dog-shit motel, when someone else's hopes were pretty thoroughly devastated, but I didn't bother. I didn't like going there, no, thank you, because before I knew it I'd start getting the stupid quivers again. Not going there was the whole point, wasn't it? The answer the social worker was really begging for. I didn't want to be *her*—the little girl pissing all over a fucking pervert who'd just traded Grade B meth for me. Would you? Would anyone?

I walked out of a house of horrors as Jobeth. Then I became them:

Karen Greer.

Alexa Kornbluth.

Terri Charnow.

Sarah Ludlow.

Jenny Kristal.

In case you're counting, that's five different girls in two and a half years. Five sets of parents whose names I'd needed to memorize, five different schools, groups of relatives, nosy neighbors, best friends. Five different *lives*. Sure, that's a lot—but here's the best part. Not a single one of them was mine.

Think of it as *my* meth, Mommy, keeping the helpless heebie-jeebies at bay. Whatever gets you through the night, and trust me, it can get pretty damn black out there.

A few times I'd thought it might really last, that I'd wormed my way in good and tight. I could see family vacations and college graduations—okay, a bit of a stretch since I'd never actually graduated high school, but still—I could even picture me being walked down the aisle one day by a beaming Mr. Charnow, who once started sobbing at the dinner table when I said, *Can you pass the salt, Dad?* I could visualize it clear as day. Then that guard I couldn't let down would turn into Mr. Hammered, and it would be just a matter of time.

There were shorter stays, too. The last one with a family in Le Mars, Iowa, Becky Ludlow and her husband, Lars—who seemed so dumb-assed at first that he might've been from the planet Mars—only it turned out he had more going on than I gave him credit for, since about two seconds after I walked through their front door, he was mentioning my three least-favorite letters in the English language. *Would it be okay, not that I don't believe you or anything, but just so we're all on the same page here and there's not the slightest doubt, would it be all right if you took a DNA test, Sarah?*

Well, now that you mention it, Lars, it might not actually be okay if I took a DNA test. I said, *No problem, can I just have a few days to settle in?* In a few days Sarah was gone, and Le Mars was on my growing list of places I must not come back to.

Truth be told, I wasn't crazy about dashing that mom's hopes and dreams, because Becky, who was dead set against me having to take any test—probably because she was afraid of what she'd find—had seemed like the kind of mom you'd pick from a catalogue. Apple-pie sweet, but with just enough Granny Smiths in there to make her interesting. When she came down to the station to get me—I usually presented myself to the nearest police station, though once I'd walked right up the front walk and said, *Ding-dong, I'm home*—it was as if she'd lost ten years in ten minutes. Seriously, she seemed to be one age when she walked into the room, and then an entirely different one when we headed home. That night I heard her weeping through her bedroom door, and Lars saying, *It's okay, honey* . . . and Becky saying, *That's just it, Lars, it is okay. Finally* . . .

Sarah, who'd let go of her dad's hand in a Home Depot ten years ago and was last seen holding someone else's hand as she walked out of the store in grainy security camera footage, had been a real daddy's girl, Becky confided. That's why he'd gone ahead and asked for a DNA test—because even with all those lost years, something just hadn't felt right to him, even though it had felt right to her. When he dropped that little bombshell on me and I took off one day later, I thought more than once about Becky doing a different kind of weeping through their bedroom door.

That's when I thought about maybe finally stopping the whole thing for good, breaking the pattern, so to speak. Just two days later I was combing through the net in search of missing children again—or to be one hundred percent accurate, searching for the parents missing them. It wasn't hard . . . America's got tons of them. The missing girls needed to be the right age, of course, the right eye and hair color—and they needed to have been kidnapped young enough so that no one would accuse me of not looking like them. And I needed some general info, too, but all that took was searching Facebook and the local papers, which would usually spend the week after a kidnapping writing about nothing else— telling the world about the missing girl's family, her friends and classmates and neighbors and teachers, all of whom couldn't believe that she was gone, and writing lots of highly useful stuff about the victim herself.

That's it. That's all.

Of course, once in a while you got stupendously lucky and stumbled across a memorial page created by the stoned-out brother of a missing victim, where all sorts of juicy tidbits were there for the taking. Add that to the hundreds of articles that came out when Jenny first disappeared and a virtual thesis in *Vanity Fair,* written years after Jenny's kidnapping. A real artsy-fartsy piece called "A Meditation on Loss" or something like that.

> *The first poster was put up within a day of the disappearance. In the end, there'd be over 1,500 of them, plastering what seemed like every available inch of the village. All of them mass-produced by the owner of a local printing company who barely knew the scared-out-of-their-minds parents but figured it was the least he could do.*
> *It was nail-gunned to a telephone pole in front of Fredo's Famous Pizzeria. . . .*

Gracias.

There were pictures in the article. Jenny sitting on a gym mat wearing a pink tutu. An eight-year-old Ben standing next to Jenny by a lake. Her parents at a rally they'd held at the local gym after Jenny disappeared, standing behind a podium with Jake holding Laurie around the waist as if he were keeping her from falling down.

There was something about Laurie's face I liked—a little Becky in there, and someone paying attention might've noticed that most of the moms I walked out of police stations with looked a lot like my real one. Before the meth got to her, when she could still manage to turn some heads, though God knows she ended up turning all the wrong ones.

Jenny Kristal. Jenny Kristal. Jenny Kristal.

I began practicing it in front of the mirror. And maybe it made me remember that pipe my mom couldn't let go of, too, the one I'd said looked like crystal. I'm not saying it did or it didn't—I'm just saying there's a chance it crossed my mind. And then I was trading Facebook messages with Ben and starting to think like Jenny Kristal, too.

I became Jenny Kristal.

When I washed my face every morning in the rat hole I'd ended up in after Le Mars, I looked up and saw Jenny Kristal staring back. My memories were her memories. My past was her past. I ate and slept and walked and talked her. And when I finally walked over to that telephone pole and up to that faded missing-child poster, that was my face on there. It was mine.

And I was home.

Where Becky Ludlow had just shown up, banging on my front door and telling me to please stop.

FOURTEEN

"You seem a little jumpy tonight, Jenny," Dad said.

That was because every time the phone rang, that's what I did. Jump. I was praying the landline was still in lockdown mode, but what if it wasn't? What if Mom needed to take a call from a client, or Dad from his mother in Florida, or what if Ben decided to pick up the phone just to be an asshole? And the voice on the other end said, *I have news for you. That lost and found headline in the paper was only half-right.*

What then?

And there was the front door.

It was growing bigger, just like the door in the police station, capable of letting in all sorts of people I didn't care to see, number one being someone who'd last seen her daughter going off to Home Depot with her husband, Lars.

Halfway through a pretty silent dinner—Mom asked Dad how work was and he said fine, then asked Ben how school was and he said, *Fucking fantastic,* and Mom said, *Can you please not curse,* and Ben said, *I'm not sure*—halfway through all that scintillating conversation, someone rang the doorbell.

I dropped my fork, which would've been okay if it was onto my plate, but it was smack onto the floor, and it had spaghetti all over it.

For a second, no one said anything.

Maybe because they were still treating me like I had HANDLE WITH CARE stamped on my forehead. So, no one was going to say *Jesus, Jenny, eat over the fucking plate,* or even *Can you please be more careful?* Everyone just looked at the floor instead, where the spaghetti sauce had splattered in ten different directions. I could see some on the bottom of the picture frame that held the four of us—Mom having scoured the family archives to produce a photo of the Kristals BTK—before the kidnapping. It looked like blood.

"Sorry," I said.

"It's fine," Mom said. "Accidents happen."

One of them was about to happen now. The doorbell rang again.

"I'll get it," I said, Mom already heading to the kitchen to clean up the spill, Dad edging out of his seat, Ben leaning on his elbows and warily eyeing me as if I'd just upchucked all over the table.

I was thinking this:

If she's standing there, I will slam the door in her face and tell everyone it's a reporter. Then we will all huddle in the living room like last time and outwait her.

Dad had stopped in mid-rise—looking like a kid who's afraid the music's about to stop in a game of musical chairs.

"Seriously, I'll get it," I said.

"No," Dad said. "If it's one of them we don't need you answering the door."

Them being a reporter. I couldn't think of a good reason why we would need me answering the door if it was a reporter. I sank back down in my seat.

I will deny knowing her.

I will say she's crazy—one of those loony tunes Detective Mary warned us would start coming out of the woodwork.

I will say, Who you going to believe—her or me?

Dad peered through the eyehole. He hesitated, then swung the door open.

"Come on in," he said.

"I'm going to my room," I said. "I feel sick." I lurched off the chair and headed for the stairs.

"Wait a minute," Mom said—she'd made it back from the kitchen with a dripping dishcloth in her hand.

I wasn't waiting a minute. It was Le Mars all over again. And Peoria. And Duluth. And Wichita. And . . .

"I really feel sick."

Someone was walking through the front door.

"Look . . . ," I said. "Look . . ."

But I wasn't looking. I was refusing to look. Instead I was staring at that picture of the four of us. Which reminded me of a different picture, the one that had given me the whole idea in the first place—a story in an old *People* magazine about a kidnapped girl who'd been rescued somewhere in Texas after ten years or something like that, and the parents saying they'd never given up hope even after all that time and other parents shouldn't either. And something else— that they'd hardly recognized their daughter at first because she'd been so young when she was kidnapped, they could've passed her on the street and never known it was her. And this picture of the four of them going to church and playing in their backyard pool and saying grace at the dinner table and they looked like a family you wouldn't mind being part of—okay, that you'd *kill* to be part of. Which is when I started looking for those other parents they'd talked about, the ones whose daughters hadn't come back.

And found the Greers.

Who'd kept a night-light on in their daughter Karen's upstairs bedroom every single night since she'd disappeared. So she could find her way home. Karen Greer was blond and blue-eyed and fair-skinned like me, which got me to thinking that it could be me, why not, why couldn't it? Why couldn't I have had a best friend named Samantha and a cat called Puss and a knack for drawing flowers and a crazy love for trampolines and all the other stuff I read about her? Why couldn't it have been me at the neighborhood pool with the rest of my day camp that morning when the counselor took one of the other kids to the nurse for five minutes and the lifeguard was too busy staring at the counselor's ass to notice some perv ushering me away? Why not?

And the Greers were only two states away, two little states that on the map looked small enough to almost walk across.

I am Karen Greer.

I am Karen Greer.

I am. I am. I am. I am. I am. I am. I am . . .

Saying it and saying it until I finally believed it.

"What do you want?" Dad said to the person who'd walked into the house.

"I cleaned up the leaves this morning," the landscaper said in a thick Spanish accent. "Eighty-two dollars."

"Sure," Dad said. "No problem."

There was another reason I'd been jumpy at the dining room table.

I should've mentioned. I'd created my very own Facebook page.

Counting my friends made everything *realer*.

Jenny Kristal's friends.

Currently at a whopping *1,372* and counting.

Sure, okay. I'd basically friended everyone who'd friended me. Most of them the same people who'd barraged the house with phone calls—the ones Jake had told to screw off.

Reporters. TV people. PR people. Agents. People with companies attached to their names, trying to make an end run around the Kristal palace guards.

Some regular people too.

Welcoming me home. Praising the Lord. Asking me to marry them.

And then there was this one:

Be careful.
You're not safe in that house.

FIFTEEN

The next morning, I played a game.

It was called "How long can I sit here without checking to see if Becky's back?"

Mom and Dad had left in two separate cars—Mom creaking open my bedroom door to see if I was still sleeping—I wasn't but managed to pull off a good imitation. *She's out like a light,* Mom whispered to Dad, who must've been standing behind her.

I was picturing something: Becky waylaying them—planting herself right in front of their cars and saying, *You need to hear something.* And I pictured Dad not stopping to hear something, because he was in the middle of checking his work texts—pulling out from the driveway and absolutely flattening her. A tragic accident, the papers would say—some crazy lady obsessed with kidnapped girls, who'd maybe gotten what she deserved.

But when I remembered her crying through the door—*That's just it, Lars, it is okay now*—I felt ashamed, and she magically unfolded herself back into Becky.

I listened as both cars pulled away, the sound of their engines—Mom's nice and smooth, Dad's hybrid kind of ragtag—becoming part of other sounds, a rumbling garbage truck, a garage door closing, a school bus jerking to a stop.

I felt relieved on two counts. She hadn't waved them down. They hadn't run her over.

When I went to the bathroom, I heard Ben slam the door on his way to school. High school. I'd gotten the lowdown from Mom, who said Ben had some issues after I was kidnapped and needed more than a year of treatment. That's why he was so behind in school.

Speaking of which.

A refresher course in Jenny Kristal, JK 101, was in session.

I'd fucked up at least three times already. I needed to bone up.

Ben hadn't written any Facebook entries since I'd shown up, which made sense, since coming back from the dead had to be a real buzzkill for a memorial page. I went back to the beginning to see if there was anything I might've missed.

My sister Jenny disappeared when I was eight.

That was the very first line he'd written.

This page is dedicated to her was the second.

One of my last memories of her was at a Fourth of July party in our backyard, he continued. My uncle Brent blew off bottle rockets and cherry bombs, and Jenny and me wanted sparklers, but he wouldn't give us any because he said we were too young. Maybe he was right about that, 'cause the next summer, he let me light a firecracker and I didn't let go fast enough. I still have the scar.

Then Ben started talking about the scar on his knee, from when Jenny pushed him into something in the backyard, which led him to talking about the *scars in my heart*. You needed to play "guess that segue" with Ben, because he insisted on jumping all over the place.

He wrote about shooting BBs at Goldy, and his sister finding out about it, and the two of them getting into a huge fight. Mom had to put us in different rooms, he wrote, and we had to play by ourselves the rest of the day. I'd completely forgotten about that . . .

Jenny stayed in her room the whole day, Ben wrote. Not even coming down for dinner. When she finally ventured out the next day, Ben snuck into her room and found the pictures she'd been hard at work on—all of them of Ben with his head cut off, or shot dead with a big bloodred crayon mark on his forehead where an imaginary bullet had blasted into his cranium.

Sometimes brothers and sisters don't get along, Ben philosophized. One of his last entries was about the day she disappeared. Apparently, they didn't get along that day either.

> I was upstairs in bed cause I had this humongous cast on my arm—I'd done a real 360 on the stairs and broken it, and I couldn't scratch it and it was driving me nuts. Me and my sister had started getting into it about something the night before—don't remember what—just something—and this time my dad made her leave MY room. But what I remember was going into her room that next morning, because I was still pissed at her I think, or maybe I went in there to declare a truce—it's all kind of hazy—but what I really remember is opening her door and then like completely freaking out— because she wasn't there, I guess. And then my mom came in looking for her—for Jenny, because she was supposed to have been down the block or something, only she wasn't. The rest of the day is still kind of a blur, with the police

coming and everyone starting to lose it, my mom going
absolutely nuts, and me too—literally nuts, I guess . . .

I tried to keep reading, but I was having difficulty multitasking. Studying up to be the best Jenny I could be, but wondering if the woman who knew I was a cheap imitation was or wasn't lurking behind the rhododendron bushes, patiently waiting for some kind of acknowledgment from me—an apology? A solemn pledge I would never, ever do it again?

Please, you have to stop . . .

I was losing this game—the one where I had to outwait the impulse to go outside and find out.

I opened the door by degrees—first taking it off automatic lock, then inching it open, then standing there on the front mat for a while before stepping out.

The coast was clear.

No sign of any woman hiding behind the hedges.

I put my foot out the door as if testing the water, then slowly eased the rest of me outside. So far, so good. There didn't seem to be any harm in strolling down the front walk, in crossing the sidewalk to the curb.

An older woman was dragging her empty garbage can back from the street.

A guy was raking a lawn.

A kid was thumping a basketball in his driveway.

I was strolling down the block.

Okay, negotiating my way down it, fiercely bartering for each step—*If you don't show up, I will take one more step, if you still don't show up, I'll take another . . .*

This is the block I walked down that day.

It was summer and I was on my way to my best friend Toni

Kelly's house, and I was taken. *Did he come up behind you and just grab you, or did he stop you? Maybe he said something to you first?*

He said, *Hey there, sweetheart, we'll get you to the bathroom real soon . . .*

I am not Jobeth, I said to myself. *I am Jenny Kristal.*

He said, *Your mom asked me to pick you up.*

Wait a minute. He said, *What's your name? . . . Jobeth, right?*

No. He did not say that. He did not say Jobeth. He didn't say anything. He grabbed me and he pulled me into his car.

Did you scream, Jenny?

Yes. I screamed.

I was screaming: *No, Mommy, I want to go home . . .*

I was not screaming that. He had his hand around my mouth. He pulled me into his car.

Was it just Father? Or both of them?

Both of them. He handed me over to her and he said, *She pissed all over me.*

No, just him.

I was on my way to Toni Kelly's house and I was taken. He stopped me and said, *Your mom said I should pick you up.*

Then he drove me to their house.

Was it a house . . . an apartment . . . ?

A house. With a locked front gate that people needed to be buzzed through, 'cause the only people who ever showed up were customers.

An apartment. It was an apartment, I think . . .

Get your story straight.

I'd borrowed from the truth to create the lie—it's easier that way—but sometimes it got all tangled up. The real Father and Mother were meth-dealing pervs who kept me in a locked house.

The *made-up* Father and Mother were transient pervs who squatted in abandoned apartments and junked trailers. Get it?

Not one person ever knocked on the front door?

I told you, I don't remember anyone in particular.

Okay, *one* person in particular.

A policeman.

He came into the house because someone had passed him their names. *Some skank bartered us for time served—we'll need to give her a visit,* Father said later. The real Father. I was standing in the corner of the living room even though they'd told me to stay in my room. The policeman smiled at me and tousled my hair. *Help me,* I thought, *help me, please help me,* and that was the first time it happened, where I was just thinking something and it came out of my mouth.

What? The policeman had turned away, was surveying the living room for places to stash drugs maybe, but he turned back and peered at me.

What did you say?

I was frozen solid—picture one of those Scooby-Doo ice pops they'd give me when I was the little girl with the curl and did all the stuff they asked me to—because I could see them staring at me behind the policeman. *Don't you dare,* their faces were saying, *don't you . . .* a double dare with real consequences.

So, I didn't dare.

Nothing, I said.

The policeman did that thing adults do when they want to make you feel that they're on your level—just one kid to another, so they make it literal—kneeling down eye to eye.

Now, honey, is there something going on here you need to talk about?

No, I said.

You just said . . . I could swear I just heard you say, "Help me." Is that what you said?

I shook my head. Father and Mother had inched closer, right behind the policeman, so when I looked into his face, I could see their faces too.

There's no reason to be scared, honey.

Yes, there was. I could see the reason to be scared, plain as day.

If there's something . . . if something is bothering you here, you need to tell me.

She's kind of shy, Officer, said Father. *She's being punished for lying, so she's none too happy with us today. You know kids. She has to learn that's the one thing we won't tolerate.*

The policeman kept looking at me. He had light blue eyes, the kind of color you paint on Easter eggs.

Is that right, honey? Are you being punished?

Sure I was. That's why Mommy had left me and hadn't come back. I was being punished for being bad.

If you keep moving, it'll hurt worse . . .

The first morning I woke up there I didn't know where I was—rows of pink baby bunnies had somehow hopped off my wallpaper, leaving wet brown stains instead. My crayon drawings of sunflowers and Grandma and Hannah Montana were gone. The empty cage where I'd kept Peanut until Mom forgot to feed him—it was missing. I screamed.

I was terrified.

I screamed.

Until the pillow covered my face. Both of them running into the room—red-faced and grunting like pigs, and stuffing the stained pillow over my mouth and saying, *Shut up shut up shut up.*

I couldn't. I knew where I was, why my room didn't look like my room. I kept screaming, even with the pillow over my mouth, I kept screaming and screaming and screaming.

You know what happens to bad girls who won't shut their mouths, Father said.

They showed me.

Mother put on the radio. Loudly. *I wanna dance with you . . . romance with you . . .*

They carried me into the bathroom and forced my head up over the sink. It had a brown rust stain.

Mother said, *If you keep moving, it'll hurt worse . . .*

She was pulling something out from under the sink. A metal box. She was opening the box and taking something out of it.

We told you to shut up, Father said. He was pressing down on my head. *We told you . . .*

Mother was shimmying her shoulders in time to the music.

Go 'round with you . . . get down with you . . .

Moving to the music even as she was trying to concentrate on something else. A gleaming needle in her hand. She was pulling a black thread through it.

I tried to squirm out of Father's grip—one hand forcing my chin up, the other pressing my head down over the sink. I tried. I tried. I know I did.

If you keep moving, it'll hurt worse . . .

Mother took her time.

Fathers work, and mothers sew.

Stitch. Stitch. Stitch. Stitch.

Carefully stitching my mouth together with shiny black thread. In one lip and out the other.

Father keeping my head locked in a vise as I shrieked and shook and bawled until I couldn't. Until nothing came out.

The brown stain turned startling red.

They made me stay like that for one entire day—my lips sewn closed, so I had to breathe through my nose and talk in whimpers. Squint and you can still see the scars—lip rings, I'd tell anyone who asked me later.

I kept my mouth shut the morning the policeman came because I could still feel the sewing needle going in and out and in and out of me. I could still see my Raggedy Ann mouth in the streaked bathroom mirror. I can still see it today.

After the man left, they locked me in the punishment place.

NO . . . please, please . . . I'm sorry . . . I'll be good . . . please, I'm scared, Mother, please . . .

I'd made it to the end of the block without knowing how I'd gotten there. Like when that woman found me leaning against the car and called the police. It had magically rained on both cheeks.

Behind the rhododendron bushes were two squirrels and a dog's un-picked-up shit.

I suddenly wanted to get back inside.

I returned as slowly as I had come—not because I was waiting for Becky to jump out and yell boo anymore, but because it felt like I was learning to walk all over again, like in those dreams where you've forgotten how. One foot, then the other, then the first foot again, and there I was, walking back down the block, up the front walk, and into the front door.

Up the stairs, down the polished wooden hallway that smelled of lemon Pledge and into my room, which used to be the den, which is why the family computer was there. The computer I hadn't bothered to switch off or, worse, the one where I hadn't even bothered to log out of the Facebook page sitting in plain view on the screen. Ben's Facebook page. I'd forgotten.

His school backpack was in plain view too, slumped onto the chair.

How was that *possible*?

Then I heard music. A guitar riff that seemed to lift me right off the floor and up against the screen where Ben—who'd obviously decided to cut school and come back into the house—had left a Word document blocking some, but not all, of the memorial page entry about the day Jenny disappeared . . . The rest of the day is still kind of a blur, with the police coming and everyone starting to lose it . . .

The big brother who hardly said two words to me had managed to type three.

WHO ARE YOU?

I stayed in my room the rest of the afternoon, the way Jenny had after the fight over Goldy. I was drawing my own pictures—in my head, I mean. Ben talking to Mom and Dad when they got home, sitting them down and explaining the reason the girl upstairs knew all about Disney World and Grandpa, and playing Indians and the Fourth of July.

Because she'd read about them.

She hadn't recalled things. She'd memorized them.

And another picture. The doorbell ringing halfway through Ben's little speech—*ding-dong*—and Becky Ludlow striding in to join the party. And maybe a phone call from Hesse and Kline, who'd finished digging around and were ready to put me back on the hot seat.

You're not safe in that house.

No kidding.

There were enemies within and enemies without.

Then I remembered something kind of odd.

About that Fourth of July Ben wrote about.

I thought I'd screwed up three times. That's why I'd been boning up and left the computer on where Jefferson High School's number one truant could come home and see it, leaving his backpack and a brief note.

But it wasn't three.

It wasn't.

It was four.

> One of my last memories of her was at a Fourth of July party in our backyard. My uncle Brent blew off bottle rockets and cherry bombs, and Jenny and me wanted sparklers, but he wouldn't give us any because he said we were too young. Maybe he was right about that, 'cause the next summer, he let me light a firecracker and I didn't let go fast enough. I still have the scar.

One of his last memories of me. The summer when Uncle Brent refused to give us sparklers. The summer I disappeared on the way to Toni Kelly's house.

When Mom asked me about Dad's stepbrother, about Uncle Brent—I'd said, *Oh, sure. I remember. Uncle Brent. You got mad at him because he let Ben light a firecracker once. On the Fourth of July, and Ben's hand got burned and you got real upset at him.*

But the summer Ben got his greatest wish—a real honest-to-God firecracker placed into his eager little hands—that was the *next* summer, when Uncle Brent was probably feeling sorry for him,

Ben having been tragically transformed into an only child. His sister long gone, almost a year by then.

I hadn't read Ben's entry carefully enough.

I'd fucked up and made his memory my own.

I'd pictured that time of night when the lightning bugs start to blink on and off like loosely screwed-in porch lights, and I'd smelled the sticky orange ice on my hand and seen Ben and Brent leaning over by the dark hedge where Brent was going *Shhh . . . shhh . . .* before using the end of his cigarette to light the fuse. I'd heard the sharp pop against my eardrums, seen bits of blue fluttering into the air like confetti, and Ben trying to hold it in before the hot tears took over.

I was careless and I'd fucked up.

That was not the odd part.

Pay attention.

Not that I'd forgotten. That was not the odd part.

It's that she had.

Sure I remember Uncle Brent. You got mad at him because he let Ben light a firecracker once. On the Fourth of July, and Ben's hand got burned . . .

And she'd said, *Yes, that's right, Jenny, I was. Ben still has the scar . . .*

Already missing one child and her second one almost gets his hand blown off at the Kristals' annual Fourth of July blowout, where they're finally trying to get things back to normal—*trying* being the keyword here, because how will things ever be normal again?—and Mom said, *Yes, Jenny, yes . . . that's right . . . yes . . .*

Agreeing with me, as if I'd really, truly been there.

Something she had to know in her sleep couldn't possibly be true.

SIXTEEN

I should've mentioned.

I'd written back to Facebook friend number 1,371. The profile was pretty much a blank slate. No hobbies. No photos. No interests. No playlists. No age, occupation, or hometown. Just a name—a first name, anyway. Lorem. Was that a boy's or girl's name?

Who are you?

Your Facebook friend. Who do you think?

Is this a reporter?

No. I'm NOT a reporter.

Is this you, BEN? Are you fucking with me?

I'm NOT Ben. I'm not fucking with you.

So who are you?

Your FRIEND. I told you.

Not after I go ahead and DE-friend you. That makes you an EX-friend.

I wouldn't do that. You're in danger.
You need to be careful.

You said that already.

Are you? Being careful?

Soooooo careful. I'm staying away from black cats and not walking under ladders.

You need to keep your eyes open. You need to watch everyone.

Why's that? Oh yeah. Because I'm not safe in this house. WHY's that again?

Let's just say they don't have a very good track record keeping Jenny around, do they?

SEVENTEEN

I should've been thinking about bouncing.

Mentally packing up, saying so long to Mom and Dad and Ben and Uncle Brent and Aunt Trude and Sebastian and Melissa and Goldy and my new Sealy extra-comfort bed.

To the entire Kristal house, which someone was warning me I wasn't safe in.

Lorem.

Who was three fries short of a Happy Meal. Your average internet troll taking time off from *Fortnite* and the latest rant from PewDiePie.

That's what I kept telling myself, when I wasn't telling myself the opposite.

That he knew something.

And was warning me for my own good. (Yeah, I'd decided Lorem was a he, after basically flipping a coin.)

Your friend, he swore.

My grandma used to play this game with me before she became

persona non grata—tracing letters on my back and making me guess what she was spelling. I L-O-V-E Y-O-U being her go-to phrase, even as the sharp tip of her fingernail triggered wrenching chills up and down my spine. That should've been a lesson—love hurts.

The words on Facebook Messenger had the same effect.

You're not safe . . .

I couldn't shake the chill long enough to get warm.

I could hear Mom and Dad whispering about something in the kitchen.

I knew what that something was.

I'd heard them come home—Mom first, walking in sometime after five, then Dad about a quarter to seven—and I'd heard Ben down there being Chatty Cathy. Ben, who spoke about six words a week to them, and it was just like I'd pictured it, minus Becky Ludlow walking in, even though I knew that was just a matter of time—it wouldn't be the landscaper walking through the front door next time.

Yeah. It was probably time to bounce.

Only I wasn't going to.

I refused.

For one thing, Mom was making chicken and mashed potatoes again.

"I'm making your favorite tonight, Jenny," she said cheerily. "How about helping me cook?"

You're correct. I'd been expecting something else. Something along the lines of:

We need to talk, Jenny . . .

Or:

How could you do this to us, Jenny . . . ?

Or:

We're calling the police, Jenny . . .

I'm making your favorite hadn't made the list.

"So how was your day, hon?" Mom asked, taking a frying pan out of the cupboard.

"Yeah, what'd you do all day, Jenny Penny?" Dad said, staring at his iPhone on his way out of the kitchen.

I looked up Ben's memorial page to get my facts straight and then forgot to log out, and Ben walked in and left a note for me: WHO ARE YOU?

"Not much," I said.

"I worry about you," Mom said. "Being by yourself all day."

"It's fine."

It was fine. Everything was fine.

Mom was putting on an apron that said WORLD'S BEST MOM on it, a Mother's Day present from Ben, I guess, before he began toking weed and leaving threatening notes for me. I was standing by the stove, having been given the job of peeling potatoes and dropping them into the pot of boiling water. When I picked up the first potato—it had those gnarly eyes on it, which makes you wonder why someone ever tried eating a potato in the first place—something even uglier flashed into my head, and I dropped the potato straight onto the floor.

"Sorry," I said, as I gingerly picked it up.

The closet.

I was suddenly back inside it.

The one off the kitchen, which really made it a pantry.

No.

It wasn't a closet. It wasn't a pantry.

It was a cell.

The punishment place.

It's so dark . . . I'm scared . . . please, I'm so scared . . . please let me out . . . please . . . I won't misbehave . . . I won't . . . I promise I won't . . . Mother, please . . . PLEASE . . . I promise . . . I'll be good . . .

The day I left, I counted the scratch marks on the back of the closet door. After fifty, I gave up. There was a ripped bag of moldy potatoes sitting on the floor. In the light of day, they looked like things you peel and eat and mash, instead of things you fear. But it was the smell that got me. I associate it with raw terror now. It smells like raw potatoes.

"You okay, hon?" Mom asked me.

I knew how I must've looked, which was not okay.

"That time of month," I said.

"Sorry," Mom said. "Can I get you some Midol?"

"I'm fine." My hands were shaking. I hid them behind my back.

"Maybe this wasn't exactly the best day to ask you to cook. Why don't you go in the living room and lie down."

"Honestly, it's just cramps."

"You sure?"

Mom was flouring the chicken, dropping the pieces of chicken into egg batter and then gently rolling them into the soft mound of white. Dad was in the living room watching a basketball game—I could hear the play-by-play. I needed to leave this room.

Only I needed to ask a question first.

"Where's Ben?" I asked.

Mom stopped. She had white flour all over her hands, making it look like she was wearing gloves, the kind women used to wear in pictures from the fifties. "At his friend's," she said.

"Everything . . . okay with him?"

A mist of flour was drifting over the center island like a passing cloud.

"You know Ben . . . ," she said.

Mom and I were cooking dinner. Dad was in the living room watching TV. *How was your day, Jenny?* they'd asked me. Another normal night in the Kristal house.

"Maybe I will go lie down," I said.

I had to flee that stench. And the place it'd dragged me back to. Dad was lying on the couch staring at the Knicks game. I needed him to stare at me right this minute. To break down the closet door and rescue me.

"What's the score?" I asked.

"Knicks down by a thousand," he said morosely. "It might as well be."

"Are they any good this year?"

"Not much."

"Did that guy make a foul?"

"Yeah."

He remained glued to the game.

I'm here, Dad. Me. Right here.

I'd stretched out on the orange love seat. I hadn't been aware that my legs were splayed out in a right angle, but something I *was* aware of is that most times when I wanted attention—from men at least—this is how I got it. It was subconscious, or *un*conscious, not sure what the difference is exactly, only that it wasn't something I set out to do but would somehow find myself doing. Like some weird blind reflex. That social worker who'd lectured me in juvie hall had asked me if I knew I was being *provocative.* Not to her— to Otis, the ancient black guard who'd escorted me into her office. I *didn't* know it until she mentioned it. The way I'd slowly saun- tered over to the chair, giving Otis a good long look at my ass. She'd thrown in my *provocative behavior* at the Charnows' just to prove her point. Mrs. Charnow ratting me out for leaving the bathroom door wide open when I took a shower, just as Mr. Charnow passed by.

It's understandable, she told me, *you were sexualized at a very early age. But it's not excusable. What happened to you as a child wasn't your fault,* she continued. *But acting on it now is.*

That's what I was doing now, I guess, legs wide open enough to provide a peek. *Acting* on it. Falling into old habits I couldn't seem to break.

"Did you *miss* me a lot, Dad?"

That got him to finally look over. And look.

I felt a sudden wave of nausea. *Stop.*

I quickly tucked my legs up under me, as Dad averted his eyes.

"Sure I did, honey," Dad said quietly, his gaze directed somewhere over my left shoulder. "*Of course* I missed you. Why wouldn't I?"

Fair question. Why wouldn't a dad miss his daughter, except that I could show him a mom who hadn't missed hers. I used to sit at the front window and wait for her. I know—real Little Orphan Annie of me—but I honestly kept thinking she was going to show up any minute. Even though they kept saying she wasn't—that she hadn't wanted to take care of me anymore, so this was it and I better get used to it. A pang of a memory: eleven years old and watching a TV ad for a silver charm bracelet being hawked for Mother's Day. *Give her a token of your love,* each charm something to do with your kid, like a soccer ball or a ballet slipper, and I was wondering what charms would be on *my* bracelet—a comic book, maybe—and I realized I was forgetting what she looked like, my mom, her actual *face,* and I asked them why she hadn't loved *me,* my mom, just blurted it out like that, and they filled me in, just in case I was still confused on the matter. *Oh, your mommy loved you, honey, she just loved Christy better . . .*

I'd thought Christy was another girl. They laughed and wrinkled a glassine bag in front of me. Christina, Tina, Chris, Christy, Crystal . . .

"How much?" I asked him, not liking that tremor in my voice, as if the shaking in my hands had spread to the rest of me, wanting to physically sit on top of it. To squelch it.

"What?" he said.

"I never asked you what was it like. How much did you miss me?"

An announcer in a paisley suit was droning away on TV: *He is swishing and dishing tonight . . . showing hustle and muscle in the lane . . .*

"Very much, sweetheart," Dad said, looking back over at me. "A lot."

Now it was my turn to look away. At the blank wall, so he wouldn't see me reverting into Jobeth. The version who hadn't been left in that motel parking lot yet. The one who'd grab onto a parent's leg and refuse to let go.

I wasn't going to take off.

Consider it a promise.

I'd bounced around long enough. More than a fucking basketball.

There'd been too many years out *there*. Squatting in junked trailers with roaches. Sleeping in motel beds with snakes.

This was my last stop. My last chance.

Where I had a mom who came in to comfort me in the middle of the night. A dad able to pull pennies out of my ears.

You're not safe in that house.

Shut up. Shut up. Shut up.

You're wrong. For once in my life that's exactly what I was.

Safe.

They don't exactly have a very good
track record of keeping Jenny around,
do they?

This one excluded.
I was staying.

EIGHTEEN

Jake

What was it like?

Like a void.

A void is a hole, an absence of, a vast and utter emptiness. There's no refuge in the void. There are no footholds or handgrips or guardrails. You're in free fall with no bottom in sight.

What was it like?

Like a rupture in the natural order of things. One of those things being when you give birth to a child, they get to grow up.

What was it like?

Like developing an inoperable tumor on your heart. So it grows and grows and grows and every single morning you can feel it pressing there.

Until you don't.

Did you miss me a lot?

And the answer was yes, of course he did. He missed the girl who took rides on his back, the one he could reliably amaze by pulling a penny out of her ear, or by transforming a yellow Splenda package—presto, whammo—into a blue Equal one at the Fairview Diner, she never asking to peek into the bottom of his fist where the Equal packet had lain scrunched and hidden.

He missed that girl, had been missing her even before she'd disappeared from their lives.

This twelve-years-older version of that girl—he didn't know her, so how could he possibly miss her?

How much did you miss me, Dad?

Very much.

He'd taken a Method acting class at the community college he'd been forced to attend due to the atrocious grade point average he'd garnered senior year—thank the steady source of LSD he'd had access to, courtesy of his second-best friend, Curtis. The Method's singular principle was as follows: Don't act, believe. You are who the script says you are. And so is everyone else. All the world's a stage and all the men and women merely players. Thanks, William. Here was proof positive.

Yes, I missed you. Of course I missed you. Very much.

Saying this to the eighteen-year-old nymphette auditioning for the revolving platform at FlashDancers on Forty-Fifth Street. Not that he was a regular customer—but clients being clients, he'd had occasion to pop in loaded down with a suitable amount of one-dollar bills.

Was she sitting like that on purpose?

This is Jennifer Morrow Kristal. Morrow for Laurie's father, who'd been saddled with an impossibly waspish first name even though he was half-Lutheran and wouldn't be caught dead in J.Crew. Jennifer for his own grandfather Joseph, taking the first letter being a kind of homage.

This is Jennifer Morrow Kristal, who when she asks if I missed her will be told *Yes, very much.*

She's a stranger now. But after a while, she won't be.

This is *Jennifer Morrow Kristal.* Jenny for short. Jenny Penny for fun.

The detective at the station had said, *You need to be prepared.*

And he'd thought, *We are,* having prepared himself the entire length of the clogged Long Island Expressway.

Embrace her.

Embrace her.

Embrace her.

Not meaning it literally, though literally was exactly how it played out, but, okay, not at first. Laurie had been the one to meet her halfway across the room—such neediness on the girl's face, but maybe that's what she was seeing on their faces, too; weren't they in need as well?

He staring at them clinging to each other like that as if he'd stumbled across an embarrassing intimacy, like the time he'd opened the bathroom door at a loft party in his twenties and seen his best friend's girlfriend with her legs wrapped around a total stranger.

They say—whoever they are—that the loss of a child will either bring you together or tear you apart. In their particular case, it had done both—bringing them together so they could tear each other apart. But that was mostly at first, when the wounds were still raw, gaping, and actively bleeding. Way before they'd developed the kind of scabs that masquerade as healing, even though each of them couldn't resist picking at them now and then.

She was a stranger, but soon she wouldn't be.

When she'd walked into the kitchen that first morning, he was about to ask her if she belonged to Ben. Until he remembered. *This is Jennifer Morrow Kristal.*

And they'd sat around the breakfast table and did what families do around breakfast tables, which is pretend things are fine. Which wasn't very different from sitting around a table with Ben. Pretending he was still the eight-year-old boy begging to kick around the soccer ball in the backyard or wash the car with him or traipse off to the computer games store, instead of the postadolescent stoner who'd broken away from his upstairs hibernation just long enough to down half a bagel before retreating back to his cave.

Ben. The crux where what you'd hoped meets what you've borne. Ben.

Hope it stays warm a little longer, he'd said to Ben's sister, playing the part of local meteorologist, because it was too early in the morning to play the part of Dad.

Or too late.

When Ben stumbled into the kitchen, blinking like someone who'd been trapped in a mine accident—remember those Chilean workers who'd subsisted on breath mints?—Jake thought Ben might want to take the stroll down memory lane with him, the kind of father-son talk Ben could actually relate to. My old drugs of choice versus his. Hadn't the therapist suggested finding areas of commonality?

My sister's where . . . she's home? My sister . . . ?

Thinking that Ben needed to get with the program. The Method acting one. Sympathizing that it must be hard to get your head around something like that when you had a head, were in a head, whatever the expression du jour was—even though Ben denied having been anywhere near a joint. Who, *me*? You going to believe me or your eyes?

When Jake told him Mom and Jenny were at the mall that morning, Jake could see Ben's face registering shock all over again. Maybe he'd thought he'd dreamed it.

Once upon a time, Jake had dreamed it too. Right after it happened, when he'd wake up and for just a moment, for that brief shift change when full consciousness relieved dull awareness, be ready to go and wake the kids for school.

Tell them to brush their teeth. To get dressed. And to please not fight this morning.

Kids *plural.*

That moment as fleeting as the brown mouse he'd once glimpsed scurrying underneath their fridge, when—and here's the kicker—he was really talking about the elephant in the room.

He let the smallest edge creep into his voice when Ben asked him where Mom was.

Mom took Jenny to the mall.

After which Ben trooped back to his cave.

Ben.

Oh, Ben . . .

NINETEEN

When I opened the door, it wasn't the landscaper.

It wasn't Becky Ludlow either.

I'd made sure of that, peering down from my bedroom window before trekking downstairs to open it. I'd been hunkering down in my bedroom these past few days—it feeling like a bedroom now since it had a real bed in it. I'd eaten my breakfast and dinner there—bad cramps, I told Mom.

Making it downstairs to open the door felt like an epic journey.

Blame it on curiosity. A girl who looked like me was ringing the doorbell.

When I opened the door, she stopped looking like me. She was wearing a tight pink T-shirt that bulged around the middle. Same with her jeans.

"Yeah?"

She stammered something I couldn't make out.

"What? Oni . . . ?"

She shook her head; her breasts jiggled. "Toni," she said.

"Toni? Okay. I'm sorry . . . what do you want?"

"I'm Toni Kelly. I thought . . . well . . ."

Toni Kelly. Toni Kelly. I didn't understand that was supposed to mean something to me, until it did.

I was on my way to Toni Kelly's house and I was taken . . .

"It's so amazing . . . ," she stammered, "I mean, really incredible to see . . . that you're alive and everything."

I didn't know if I should hug her or shake her hand.

"Hey," I said. "Toni."

We trekked back up to my room. Like a playdate.

We sat on my bed and didn't say anything at first.

She looked around the room.

"It looks different," she said. "I mean, I don't remember it that well or anything. Didn't you have a horse collection? You know, those Breyer ones?"

"Yeah. They're dog food now." It was a joke, but she didn't laugh. "I mean, my mom threw them out."

"Oh. Right."

More silence. The orange flower had fallen off the cactus—it was shriveled up on the floor.

"So . . . what's it like?" she asked me.

"What?"

"Being home? You know . . . after, you know, all you went through?"

"Good." I was fucking up my lines. She'd knocked me off-balance, her just showing up like this. I hadn't prepared for running through old times with my six-year-old best friend. "Really great," I said. "Unbelievable."

That was more like it. She nodded along to that—people expected certain words from you, a proper gratitude for your new-found existence. You needed to follow the script.

"I thought . . . you know, you being home, being back . . . that I should stop by and say hello."

"Right. Great. Thanks for coming."

Silence again.

"Was it terrible? I mean, you don't have to talk about it or anything. In the papers, they said . . . it sounds like it was really *awful*."

"It was."

"How did you . . . like, get away?"

"Look, I'd rather not . . ."

"Oh, sure. I mean, you don't have to. I was just wondering . . . 'cause of what I read. Anyway, great to have you back."

"Thanks." I was counting the rolls of fat under her T-shirt. Three.

"Is it weird being home with your parents? I mean, not seeing them for so long. It must be really strange, right?"

"It's okay."

"And all those reporters? Wow. You know, we moved. After you were . . . after you disappeared, I think my mom freaked. Like there must be a kidnapper or something in the neighborhood. We moved to Bellmore. Not that far. But I saw all the reporters around your house—on TV. It looked fucking insane."

"Yeah. It was crazy."

"I mean, one of them called me . . . wanted to know how I felt?"

"They called you?"

"Yep . . . you know, because you were headed to my house that morning. When you were . . . you know . . ."

"Kidnapped. I was kidnapped the morning I was headed to your house."

"Right."

I was starting to get this feeling. Like I needed to ask her to leave.

"You look . . . great, by the way. I mean, after all you've been through. You really look great."

"So do you." Liar, liar, pants on fire.

"Hey . . . can I take a selfie?"

"What?"

"You know, a shot on my phone. Of you and me."

"Why?" Yeah, it was definitely time to see her to the door and say thanks for coming.

"I don't know. Is it a big deal? Just a shot of us together?"

"I'm really kind of . . ."

When she pulled out her phone, it felt like she was pulling a gun on me.

"Just take a second," she said. "One little shot. Please . . ."

Okay, now I get it.

"Is that what he wanted?" I said.

She blushed. "Who?"

"The reporter."

"Reporter?"

"The one who called you? Who wanted to know how you felt?"

"I don't . . . huh . . . I mean, I don't really know what . . ." Back to stammering again.

Jake had told them no, but reporters don't take no for an answer. They find a way. Or they find a Toni.

"What did he say? Suggest you stop by for old time's sake? Welcome me back to the neighborhood? Tell me how fucking fantastic I look? And while you're there, hey, make sure you get a picture."

"Hey. No need to be a *bitch*. I thought you'd be happy to see me."

"I'm sure he was. When you said you'd do it."

"Like you're such a big fucking deal. Like anyone really gives a shit. Just because you were like raped by Daddy or Father or whatever the fuck you had to call him . . ." Her face was still red, but not from blushing. A vein in her temple was throbbing up and down.

"Nice seeing you," I said.

She stared at me with this truly venomous expression. Like if her phone was a gun, she would've pulled the trigger.

I didn't bother seeing her to the door.

Ever wake up from a nightmare and find yourself in a worse one? Almost giddy that it was just a dream, then wishing you could be right back in the middle of it.

Mom was there. In my dream. My real mom, looking okay, too, the way she did during her court-ordered rehabs, not so shrunken and jittery, but almost mom-like. I was curious what she was doing there, in my house—this house, some house, I wasn't sure whose. But I was surprised by her visit and asking her, *Why? Why?* The *why are you here* turning into a different why—it happens that way in dreams—turning into *Why did you leave me by the motel?* And she was getting real mad at me—the way she was that morning when I wouldn't get into the stroller and wouldn't stop hugging her knees.

She walked. Out of the house, out of the parking lot, out of the dream.

And I was screaming at her. Screaming bloody murder at her.

And then, suddenly, the screaming was at me.

Someone was screaming at me, and I had my head between my knees again because we were about to crash.

And die.

TWENTY

You can't go up there."

Where can't I go?

"I said stop."

Stop what?

"I'm not going to tell you again. I want you to leave."

Leave?

I wasn't dreaming I was in a house with my real mom.

I was wide-awake, in a house with my fake mom.

"Please get out before I call the police."

The police?

There was a woolly blanket over my head. No, my head was the woolly blanket. It was saying, *Let me go back to sleep. Please.*

"Please, I just need to . . ."

Another voice. Two voices now. One yelling at the other one to leave and threatening to call the police. The other one pleading that she needed to do something, so don't.

One of them was my fake mom.

The other one was my other fake mom. Two fake moms.

Becky Ludlow was in the house.

"I just need to talk to her. Make her tell you . . ." Becky again.

I got off the bed. I crawled over to the door and wedged my back against it. A hundred fifteen pounds of fear against a hundred forty or so pounds of anger. Put your money on fear.

I was dressed in Laurie's blue Costa Rican T-shirt, which I'd since appropriated. My tattoo was saying *VIDI*: I see you.

If I make a break for it out the window, I will (a) break my ankles; (b) break my neck; (c) break Laurie's heart.

The one whose heart I'd broken before was still pleading to be let upstairs.

"I promise you. If you just let me talk to her, I'll go. I promise. Just give me five minutes and after that—"

"You're trespassing. You invited yourself in under false pretenses. I want you out."

"I told you my daughter was kidnapped too. She was. Sarah was kidnapped."

"You said you needed to talk to me—one mother of a kidnapped child to another. That's what you said. I thought you were looking for a little . . . I don't know what I thought you were looking for, but it wasn't this."

"I do need to talk to you—one mother of a kidnapped child to another. One mother of a kidnapped child who came *back*. Only she didn't. Mine didn't. And neither has yours."

"Are you really going to make me call the police?"

"Listen. Do you know what it's like? What a stupid question. Of course you do. Having to go on living? After your daughter . . . after the person you love more than life—because you do, it's an expression people like to throw around a lot, but it's true, you do love them more than life. I'll tell you how I know that—because when my daughter disappeared, I stopped wanting to *live,* that's how. I took sleeping pills. I woke up in a hospital having my stomach pumped and I still didn't want to live. It's twelve years later and I still feel like killing myself every day. You know how that feels? Opening your eyes every morning and wishing, wishing really hard, that you were dead. But there's your husband and there's your other child—yes, Sarah has a brother—and even though it kills you that you'd rather be dead than be a mother to your other child, that's how you feel. That's who you are. That's what it's done to you."

"I'm sorry about your daughter. I am. But coming here and making these crazy—"

"Crazy? Yes, I'm crazy. Guilty as charged. You know how many times I saw someone—walking down the block, in an airport. Once we were at the movies, and I saw this little girl turn around in the front of the theatre. I jumped up and screamed, *Sarah, Sarah,* and this little scared-out-of-her-mind seven-year-old, she turns and looks at me—her mother was with her—and both of them, I saw it in their faces, they were looking at this crazy person. This lunatic. *Crazy?* Sure, I'm crazy. But not about this. Not about her . . ."

Her being *me.*

Me being wedged up against the door wishing it was thicker, not only because that would make it easier to keep her out of the room, but because it would make it easier to keep that voice out of my head. I didn't want to listen to the voice talking about how Becky wanted to kill herself. What losing Sarah had done to her. Because she was getting to the part where she'd lost Sarah twice. And I knew what that had done to her. It had put her on a plane from Le Mars, Iowa, to here. To hiding out in bushes, chasing me down the sidewalk, talking her way into this house.

"I'm picking up the phone now," Laurie said again. "I asked you nicely. I asked you to please, please, leave my house. You're still here."

"Let them come. I don't care. I don't. You know how I felt the day I got the call. You pick up the phone and there's this man on the other end saying he's a detective down at the police station, and you think it's happened, finally, they've found the body, they've found her remains, isn't that what they call it on all those police shows? And your heart stops, for a second it just stops, and then he tells you something entirely different than you were expecting, something so utterly impossible that you ask him to repeat it, please just say it again, because you couldn't have possibly heard it right, could you? And he does, he does say it again, and your heart that just a second ago was stopped, was absolutely frozen, it melts, it bursts, and suddenly you're screaming out loud, you're on your knees and you're screaming. For joy, for Sarah, for the mother you stopped being. Was it like that for you, Laurie? Was it the same? Did you get down on your knees and thank God, thank the police, thank the kidnapper even, because he kept her alive. Did you?"

"I'm not going to talk to you. I'm not going to share my feelings and my life with you. You're making a horrible mistake here. This is a terrible intrusion and you're making me call the police to have you arrested and I don't want to do that to you, I don't, but I've asked you nicely, and you won't listen."

"I have a picture," Becky said.

I have a picture . . .

We'd been sitting on the back porch.

I have a picture . . .

Becky and me, cradling two glasses of homemade pink lemonade, dead quiet except for the faint sound of buzzing insects, because we were all cried out.

I have a picture . . .

Slowly swinging back and forth on a wooden chair suspended by two rusty chains that creaked every time I pushed off the porch with my naked toes. And Becky calling into the house, telling Lars to please get his camera and take a picture to record my first day home, *please,* because Becky said she still couldn't believe it, she could not believe it, and maybe seeing it sitting there right in her hand would make it one hundred percent real. And Lars probably already fighting doubts of his own about what was real or not, walking out onto the porch and snapping a photo.

Click.

"A picture . . . ?" Laurie repeated dully.

"Before she left. Before Lars asked her to take a DNA test. *No, I told Lars. Don't be silly.* All those memories she has. All the things she remembers from when she was a little girl—before it happened. Before he'd decided to take her to the Home Depot that Saturday morning. I never blamed him, by the way—not to his face, not once—even though I wanted to, God, I wanted to, but he took that away from me, because he couldn't stop blaming himself. You understand? And then suddenly it didn't matter anymore, did it, because she was back. Some sort of miracle had taken place and she was back home and all those memories that kept coming out of her—our camping trip to Yosemite, watching *Finding Nemo* a thousand times in her room when she had her tonsils out, the winter we built a snowman together and the crows ate the snowman's nose—we used a big carrot and the crows ate it and she wouldn't stop crying about it until we performed an operation and gave him a new one. *Why on earth do we need a DNA test? I asked Lars, why? . . . Doesn't she know things only Sarah would know?* And Lars said it doesn't hurt to be sure, does it? I mean, a lot of that stuff was in the papers back then. *I'm just saying let's be one hundred percent sure here,* trying to be gentle with me, because he knew,

knew what losing her again would do to me—even though I hated him, absolutely hated him for bringing it up. But Lars knew something was off, knew that something wasn't right, and maybe the reason I hated him was because I knew it too, I did, somewhere I did. And this girl said okay, sure, I'll take a DNA test, and one night later she was gone. No note, no nothing. Gone."

"I'm sorry for you. I really and truly am sorry, but this has nothing . . . absolutely nothing—"

"I read about you in the papers. About Jenny. You've read articles like that, right? Articles about other children who've been found. Part of you thinking, well, if it could happen to them, after all this time, if their daughter can be found alive, then maybe, just maybe . . . only there's this other part of you, this awful part, that hates reading about those other girls—about those other parents, their happiness, their ridiculous insane joy. Then I saw her picture. The picture of Jenny. My heart stopped again. It stopped. I have the picture Lars took of her. Please, just look at it . . ."

Laurie was going to look at it. At Lars's picture. Becky and Sarah on a summer day. On a summer swing. Curiosity would make her look at it. Or maybe just wanting to get Becky out of the house. *Please look, and I'll leave.* So Laurie would. She'd look.

And one look at Becky's picture and she'd get the bigger picture. The one that had Ben telling them how he'd found his Facebook page sitting open on the computer screen in my room—all my memories in plain sight. And my slip-up about Ben scarring his hand on that Fourth of July I couldn't have been anywhere near—that would be in the picture too, something she'd managed to turn a blind eye to so far, maybe for the same reason Becky had turned a blind eye to things she had no real desire to look at. And this bigger picture would contain a smaller one: a girl sitting on a summer porch who'd once said she was *Sarah* but was now saying she was someone else.

I have a picture.

"I don't need to see it," Laurie said.

"I'm just asking you to take one second and . . ."

"The day we picked Jenny up we took her to a doctor. Your husband was right. He was right about needing to know. We wanted to be a hundred percent sure. So we took her to a doctor and he performed a DNA test. She's our daughter. She's our daughter with 99.9 percent certainty. So you coming here, making these accusations—I was trying to tell you. I'm sorry the girl who came to you was a fake, I am. But Jenny isn't. Our daughter's back. *Now* will you leave . . . ?"

There was a sudden silence; there was a soft, stammered apology—there was the sound of the front door being slammed shut. There was the sound of Laurie slowly trudging back up the stairs and stopping outside my door. And then, with me lying back in bed with my eyes squeezed shut, the sound of my door opening and Laurie walking in and standing there for a while, confirming that I must've slept right through it without hearing a word.

Then this other sound.

After Laurie tiptoed out of the room, this other sound that seemed to be coming from the direction of my bed.

Crying.

For just one moment, I'd thought: *We did go to a doctor and get a DNA test that said I was 99.9 percent their daughter?* Really? We did . . . we did . . . we did?

No.

We didn't.

Of course we didn't.

No.

TWENTY-ONE

I met Tabitha because she wouldn't stop staring at me and I returned the favor—like let's have a staring contest and see who blinks first.

Let's call it a tie.

I'd gone to the library to draw my very own Bizarro comic book. Because it felt like I'd been transported there—to the planet Bizarro. I needed to get out of the house so no one could peek over my shoulder. Besides, libraries felt like home to me—that's what I'd used them as between families, ratty crash pads, and the occasional hour-rate motel (sorry, not going there).

Maybe it was that shitty teen job at the mall that taught me it was actually possible. To walk out of Father and Mother's house and never come back. Or maybe it was Father getting sick—not sick enough to die, but sick enough to spend more than two weeks in bed and suddenly look frail, like he'd lost his superpowers. Like from now on he couldn't ever hurt me again. Or maybe it was something else—the day Father offered a customer something besides crystal meth.

That day.

When my bedroom door swung open and there was a sweating man in a tracksuit standing there who asked me if I'd like to keep him company.

They'd stopped locking the outer gate a long time ago, but it still felt like I was locked in—like those invisible fences used to shock dogs. On the day I knew I wouldn't be coming back, I stood staring through the iron slats at that world on the other side of it, the way you stare at the moon and say to yourself there's no way anyone could've actually made it all the way there. I walked through the gate holding my breath, convinced it was going to slam shut in my face. That I was going to be dragged back inside and locked in the closet for eternity.

When I finally stopped running, I found myself in a place that stayed open late, where nobody bothered asking why you were spending every single second there. Where an old *People* magazine and a Google search of missing kids on the library computer led me straight to Karen Greer.

I was drawing my comic on the sketch pad Laurie bought me. She'd noticed me scribbling on a stained napkin and asked if I'd like one.

Sure.

I'd started drawing comic books for the same reason I'd started reading them. To be somewhere else besides that house. Tiptoeing downstairs late at night after Father and Mother fell asleep and strolling into the Daily Planet. Where super-evil villains were persona non grata, and help was just a phone booth away. The first comic I ever traced—over and over until I could just about draw it by memory—was the one where Superman saved this little girl from a burning house, crashing straight through the roof with the girl tucked safely into his arms.

Don't worry, Jane, my cape will protect you from the flames.

When I came up with Super Invisible Girl, I decided to draw my own comic book. The girl no one could see. Or catch.

Or touch.

One day Father discovered some pages shoved deep in my drawer and said, *Stick to your day job.*

I was putting the finishing touches on the last frame of my new Bizarro comic when I noticed Tabs staring at me. I didn't *know* she was Tabs, of course—not yet—just this odd-looking girl peeking at me from behind a computer.

I was at a table directly facing her—that's what I saw when I looked up. Her staring face. When I said she was curiously put together I mean she borrowed from different stereotypes. She looked kind of like a Goth cheerleader. Like she couldn't decide which personality to wear so she decided to wear a bunch of them. Or maybe she was saying she was *none* of them. Or saying *Go ahead, good luck figuring it out.*

The staring contest ended when our eyes began watering. Later, she told me she was ready to say *no más,* when I quit at exactly the same time. She thought that meant something. The simultaneous finish. Tabs was like that—finding meaning in random things.

"Boo," I said.

"Boohoo," she answered.

She'd recognized me, she told me later. The poor little kidnapped girl. She'd felt a kind of kinship right then and there. Not because she'd been kidnapped. Because she often wished she had been, since her parents were *soulless dullards,* she said, and it would've been nice if she'd really been born to two other people—

parents less concerned with material crap and keeping up with the Joneses—which was, like, *their only reason for getting up in the morning.*

"That's so fucked-up," I told her.

"What? Wishing for other parents?"

"Wishing you'd been kidnapped."

"Sorry. Not trying to diminish what you went through. Just being honest."

Apparently that was Tabs's thing. Being honest. It made me want to be honest too—as honest as I could be given the circumstances.

Eventually we ended up splurging on skinny vanilla lattes at Starbucks, where Tabs admitted she didn't have many friends. Since she didn't fall into any discernable group, she existed out in the nether regions, neither one type nor another. Yeah, I noticed, I told her. Not that she was complaining exactly—most people were soulless dullards like her parents—but still, it was nice to talk to someone else who kind of fell between the cracks.

Step on a crack, break your mother's back. When I was about seven, I'd tried. To break my mother's back. Both mothers. Duck walking down the sidewalk searching for spidery fissures to stomp the shit out of.

One of the nice things about Tabs was she didn't ask me all the obvious questions. I couldn't tell if it was because she was being polite or because she just wasn't interested. Maybe both.

I was grateful, because I was able to talk more like Jobeth and less like Jenny. As if I'd been let out of a cage.

Tabs was taking a gap year, she said. A year you spent after one thing and before another. A limbo year.

"Yeah. I had twelve of those," I said.

She was using her gap year to pretty much do shit. She was pretty good at it. Hanging at the library, where she hacked into various websites on the library computers—she was a hacktavist, she confided to me. Meaning she liked to fuck with organizations whose principles she loathed—like the local NRA branch, whose website she'd managed to sneak into and plant pictures of school gun victims on—those little kids from Newtown.

"You got away with that?" I asked her.

"It helps if you don't use your own computer." She circulated among five or six Long Island libraries—never going to the same one twice in a row.

Tabs was an outlaw like me. That probably solidified it. Our new palship. We exchanged numbers and talked about maybe hooking up later that week.

"What were you drawing?" she asked me just before we split in opposite directions—we'd walked at least twenty blocks together and hadn't shut up once. "Back in the library?"

"A comic book," I answered shyly.

"Like Spider-Man?"

"Kind of," I said.

"Cool. Can I see it?"

"No," I said, tucking the sketchbook tightly to my chest. "I mean . . . it's not finished."

TWENTY-TWO

Bizarro characters are cracked—not just in the loony-bin sense. Their bodies have actual *cracks* in them, which is how you know that they're not the *real* Superman and Lois Lane and boy reporter Jimmy Olsen. The Bizarro Superman, Lois Lane, and Jimmy Olsen live on Htrae, which is *earth* backward . . . get it? The Bizarro code states: Us do the opposite of all earthly things. For example, in one unpleasantly moldy issue I'd read and reread down in that basement—the heater had sprung a leak and saturated everything—a successful Bizarro bonds salesman proudly used this slogan: *Guaranteed to lose money for you!* Being called stupid was a compliment in Bizarro world. So was being called ugly, greedy, and lazy.

Things were upside down and inside out there.

In my Bizarro comic the main character was Hteboj. That's *Jobeth* spelled backward if you're dense—remember, *dense* is a compliment. Hteboj had cracked skin and a smart mouth—which means dumb in Bizarro world.

Eirual and Ekaj were Hteboj's Bizarro parents, faithfully following the Bizarro dictum and cheerfully doing the opposite of all earthly things. So when Hteboj slipped up and told Eirual a story about her brother Neb nearly blowing his hand off that could in no way have come from her own memory, what did she do? She gave Hteboj a shopping trip to Tlevesoor Llam (Roosevelt Mall, spelled backward). When Eirual and Ekaj were informed by their son that he'd caught Hteboj pilfering memories from Neb's Koobecaf page, what did they do then? They made Hteboj her favorite dinner of chicken and mashed potatoes, that's what. And when Ykceb talked her way into the house on Elpam Street and told Eirual—one mother to another—that the daughter sleeping in their upstairs bedroom was the very same girl who'd pretended to be hers—even offering to show Eirual actual proof of it—*I have a picture*—what then? Huh . . . huh?

Eirual told the mother of all whoppers.

She took a DNA test. She's our daughter with 99.9 percent certainty.

Upside down and inside out.

That's the way it is in Bizarro world.

TWENTY-THREE

Downstairs with Laurie before she left for work in the morning, asking me what I'd like for my birthday, which was just around the corner.

Remember my third birthday party at Chuck E. Cheese? I asked.

Yes, Jenny . . . , Laurie said.

Remember how Dad kept playing Skee-Ball again and again, just so he could get me the cutest stuffed animal in the place?

Yes, Jenny.

That's how I got Goldy, right?

Yes, Jenny.

Later that night, watching *Vanderpump* in my bedroom—and Laurie coming in to ask about dinner. And me casually mentioning that pony ride I saw in the photo album, the picture of me—not me—of Jenny, being led around a dirt ring in a neon pink cowboy hat.

I just remembered something, Mom. That pony ride when I was a kid. I asked you if we could take the pony home with us, remem-

ber? *I wouldn't stop crying about it, I think I drove you crazy—so you stopped on the way home and THAT's when you bought me Goldy.*

I think you're right, Jenny . . . Yes, now that I think about it I think that was when I got you Goldy . . . Now, how did I manage to forget that?

Good question.

Something was happening here.

Another thing that should've made it into my comic—stuff reversing itself the way things do on the planet Bizarro. No longer Mr. Greer and Mrs. Charnow and Lars sniffing something foul and starting to dig around to see where the odor was coming from.

I was doing the sniffing this time.

I'd always known when it was starting. Sometimes the funny faces wouldn't register on my radar, but the funny questions would. Innocent sounding at first, if you were willing to ignore they were coming out of left field. Mrs. Charnow suddenly bringing up my first Halloween costume even though it wasn't close to Halloween—*Remember what you dressed up as?* Mr. Greer staring at the floor and plucking a memory out of thin air—the first time he'd taken me fishing on Lake Winowee. *Remember how many fish you caught, honey?* I didn't remember how many fish I'd caught, it was so long ago, I was barely five, and they'd say of course, don't worry about it. But that's exactly what I'd start doing, worrying—because I knew more questions were coming, and more after that, insistent-sounding questions, with Mrs. Charnow and Mr. Greer and Lars becoming more and more insistent that I answer them.

I didn't know when Jenny had gotten Goldy.

I didn't.

Odds were good it wasn't after that pony ride.

I'd made it up. About me crying. About me asking for a real pony. About everything.

My third birthday party was at Chuck E. Cheese. According to Ben's memorial page it was. I'd invented Dad playing endless games of Skee-Ball there.

Remember the day stupid Ben . . .

I was thinking about that time . . .

I'll never forget the time Mrs. Colletti sent me home with . . .

Maybe she's confused. Maybe she's just not remembering correctly. Maybe she has her head up her ass. Maybe she is remembering correctly, but she doesn't want me to know that I'm not.

Maybe she didn't really lie to Becky.

On the way to D'Agostino's to shop for groceries, I told her I'd been thinking about the summer we all went to Montauk to go digging for clams.

That was on Ben's page too. The family going to Montauk and digging for clams. And playing miniature golf. And going whale watching. All right there on Ben's page.

And all taking place *after* Jenny was kidnapped.

A stupid-as-shit effort to keep their minds off it—those were Ben's words—stupid-as-shit, picking a place Jenny had never been to, instead of heading up to the lake, which is what the Kristals usually did in the summer, back when they were still the Kristals. Not wanting to be where Jenny and her brother played Indians, fished for minnows, and roasted marshmallows because the idea was to stop thinking about her and not be reminded of their missing daughter every minute of their entire fucking vacation.

So they went to Montauk and went clam digging.

A whole year after Jenny disappeared. Ben already licking the wounds on his burned hand. Jenny already on her way to the cold case file.

Laurie said: *We're five minutes away.*

Remind me to pick up pears for Dad.

Do you like Dolly Madison ice cream?

Dad showed us all how to shuck the clams there, I told her. In Montauk. You made spaghetti and *clam* sauce with them. Isn't it amazing I can remember that?

Her hands blanched white around the steering wheel. The blood had run right out of them.

Yes, Jenny, she said. *Yes . . . it sure is.*

She knows.

TWENTY-FOUR

They were playacting.

Why were they playacting?

It didn't matter if they were playacting.

This is what I'd wanted. This.

Mommy, Daddy, and Big Brother. A house with a front walk instead of locked gates. *Want to go shopping with me, Jenny? Want to help me cook dinner, Jenny? What's the Knicks score, Dad? Ben's being an asshole, Dad.*

They want their daughter back. That's all.

Even if she's not their daughter.

They want her back so badly it doesn't matter if she's not their daughter.

It totally makes sense.

It makes no sense.

It was senseless.

Okay, sure—almost forgot. There was one member of the family who didn't want his sister back.

I once saw this show called *Ghost Hunters* where this guy visited haunted houses looking for cold spots. The rest of the house might be ninety fucking degrees, but behind a certain door, upstairs in the attic, it felt like the middle of January.

You could actually see this guy's breath coiling upward like one of those spirits he was supposedly hunting for, as he'd stare straight into the camera and solemnly proclaim: *This house is haunted.*

So was this one.

Haunted by someone who'd walked out the front door one day and never came back. One morning I'd caught Laurie staring at a picture of Jenny on the kitchen wall. When she heard me behind her, she'd quickly turned away, like she'd been caught cheating.

There were two Jennys in the house.

And it had its very own cold spot.

Ben.

I was looking for something to read.

Let's be clear about that.

When I say something, I mean anything. A *People* magazine, a trashy romance novel, a grocery list.

Anything.

The goal being to get my mind off this merry-go-round it was on—spinning round and round and always ending back at the same place: Why?

It was making me dizzy. I wanted off.

Dad had left.

See you tonight, Jenny Penny.

Sure, Dad . . .

Laurie had left.

Have a great day, Jen.

You too, Mom . . .

Ben had left.

Bye, Ben . . .

Door slam.

The merry-go-round was beckoning. I already had the ticket in my hand. Cue the calliope.

TV wasn't an option. There was only so much of Kim, Kourtney, Khloé, Kylie, and Kendall I could take before it all became white noise.

The downstairs bookcase contained actual books. The bookcase in Father's house had contained superhero comics and places to stash drugs.

The Norton Anthology of English Literature. Leviathan by Thomas Hobbes. *Of Suicide* by David Hume. These particular books looking as if they hadn't been opened in decades and had been possibly used as doorstops.

A bunch of Alex Cross novels took up most of one shelf, with Morgan Freeman's face peeking out on one of them.

Stuck behind the Alex Cross novels, a thick manila envelope.

Let me be clear again. Just for the record.

I was just looking for something to read, and since that manila envelope was addressed to Laurie and Jake Kristal and the return address scrawled in the top left-hand corner said J. Pennebaker, Bakersfield, Georgia, I wanted/needed/desired to read more.

Pennebaker. I knew that name.

I carried the manila envelope to the couch and sat there staring at it.

Pennebaker.

The guy who'd called the house just before I'd decided to take a walk and run into Becky.

Tell Mrs. Kristal I won't be calling again.

Someone calling to say they wouldn't be calling.

Pennebaker. Joe.

Only it seemed to me that even then the name had sounded kind of familiar—just like Maple Street had, and Forest Avenue, and this house.

When I opened the envelope and looked inside, when I took the stapled-together sheaf of papers out and began perusing them—no, really reading them, the way I'd once read Ben's Facebook entries, as if my life depended on them, my new life, because, well, it had—I remembered why.

TWENTY-FIVE

Interview. Mr. and Mrs. Kelly. July 12th, 2007. 10:24 a.m.

L: I'm Detective Looper of the Nassau Police Department. I'd like
to ask you a few questions about Jenny Kristal if that's okay.

Detective Looper.

July 12, 2007.

Mrs. and Mrs. Kelly.

They were like clues on that game show—the one where you get
to see the consonants but you have to buy the vowels if you're going
to put it all together. Like staring at half a thought. Or half a poster
on a telephone pole by Fredo's Famous Pizzeria, where you only get
the G from MISSING.

Detective Looper. The detective in charge of investigating Jenny's
disappearance. In all those articles I'd read and reread, when a
policeman was quoted on the case, it was always him. Looper.

July 12, 2007. Two days after Jenny went missing.
But who were Mr. and Mrs. Kelly . . . ?

L: Let's start with two days ago. Mrs. Kristal sent Jenny on her
way here to play with your daughter, Toni, is that right? She
called and set up a playdate?

Of course. Toni Kelly's parents. Back when Toni didn't have
three rolls of fat under her T-shirt.

This was the *transcript* of Detective Looper's investigation into
Jenny's case. J. Pennebaker of Bakersfield, Georgia, had sent it to
Laurie and Jake. Jenny had been on her way to see Toni Kelly that
morning, so that's where Looper had started.

MRS. KELLY: Yes. Well . . . she didn't specify a time or anything.
L: What did she specify?
MRS. KELLY: She asked if Toni was home and I said sure and then
she asked if she could send Jenny over sometime to play.
L: And you said okay?
MRS. KELLY: Yes.
L: But Mrs. Kristal didn't say when?
MRS. KELLY: She said sometime in the morning. I mean, I was
home all day, so I said sure, whenever.
L: Is that the way it usually works?
MRS. KELLY: Usually . . . I don't . . .
L: When she sends Jenny over to play? Mrs. Kristal usually doesn't
specify an exact time? Just says it'll be sometime in the morn-
ing or afternoon?
MRS. KELLY: I don't know . . . I guess . . . I mean Toni. . . . my daugh-
ter, Toni, and Jenny . . . they don't play together all that much.
L: They aren't friends?

MRS. KELLY: Sure. Well . . . more neighborhood friends, you know . . .

L: So this wasn't a usual occurrence? Jenny coming over to play?

MRS. KELLY: It wasn't unusual. I mean, it used to happen a lot more . . . when the kids were younger. I think Ben . . . her brother, Ben, he has a broken arm and Jenny was maybe getting on his nerves, you know the way kids fight, so I think Laurie wanted to get Jenny out of the house. She asked if it would be okay.

L: And you said fine.

MRS. KELLY: Yes.

L: But Jenny never came.

MRS. KELLY: No.

L: So did you call Mrs. Kristal? Ask where Jenny was?

MRS. KELLY: No.

L: Why?

MRS. KELLY: I just figured . . . I don't know . . . that she'd changed her mind. Like I said, it wasn't an exact time or anything. It was kind of indefinite. I just assumed plans had changed.

L: Okay. So when did you realize they hadn't changed?

MRS. KELLY: When Laurie called.

L: When was that?

MRS. KELLY: Around three.

L: And what did she say?

MRS. KELLY: She wanted to talk to Jenny.

L: Were you surprised?

MRS. KELLY: Of course. Because I hadn't seen her. I thought she . . . that Laurie hadn't sent her over.

L: And what did Mrs. Kristal say when you told her Jenny wasn't there? I assume you immediately let her know that was the case?

MRS. KELLY: Yes, of course. She got, well . . . kind of hysterical. She said she'd let Jenny out of the house at ten thirty in the morning.

L: To come over to your house?

MRS. KELLY: Yes.

L: Let me ask you something. Mrs. Kristal said she opened the door and watched Jenny walk to the sidewalk. Then she went back inside.

MRS. KELLY: Uh-huh . . .

L: Does that surprise you at all?

MRS. KELLY: Surprise me? Not sure I understand.

L: Parents don't walk their kids over to someone's house around here? For a playdate? I mean, is it normal to just let them walk there by themselves?

MRS. KELLY: It's a pretty safe neighborhood. We're just two houses away.

L: So Jenny always walks here by herself?

MRS. KELLY: Always? There isn't an always. I told you . . . my daughter and Jenny . . . they don't really play together very often anymore.

L: Okay. But when they do play together?

MRS. KELLY: I'm not sure . . . it's not like I keep track. Jenny's older now. I'm sure I've let my daughter run down the block to her friend Mandy. I'm sure I have. Like I said, this is a pretty safe neighborhood. Or was.

L: Okay. Let's go back to the phone call. Mrs. Kristal asked to speak to Jenny and you said she hadn't shown up.

MRS. KELLY: Yes. I said maybe Toni had let her in and I just hadn't noticed. I mean, it's possible, right? I jumped off the phone and ran upstairs to take a look.

L: That's where your daughter was?

MRS. KELLY: Yes. But Jenny wasn't there. Toni was watching cartoons. She hadn't seen Jenny all day.

L: Okay. What happened then?

MRS. KELLY: I got back on the phone and told Laurie. And by now, I was, you know, scared to death, I mean I was almost starting to cry too, I probably was, because I knew . . . well, I knew that it wasn't good. That something really horrible may have happened.

L: And how was Mrs. Kristal?

MRS. KELLY: How do you think? She was screaming. "We have to find her! We have to go look for her!"

L: So what did you do?

MRS. KELLY: Ran over there, of course. To Laurie's. I took Toni with me naturally . . . no way I'm leaving her alone now. And Laurie was calling the police and then, well . . . that was it. The start of everything. I mean, you guys came, two patrolmen I mean, is that what you call them? And then all the parents, me and Cindy Mooney and Nancy Klein and Amy Shapiro, we all went searching the neighborhood. Jake came back from work, and I called Brian, and he came back too.

MR. KELLY: Yeah, my wife kind of lost it. The Kristals too, of course. We were all half out of our minds.

The questioning went on for a while. Some questions directly for Mr. Kelly, like where he'd been when he'd gotten his wife's call. At *work*, he said. Morgan Stanley. And questions for the both of them—like did they know anyone who might've wanted to hurt Jenny, which seemed kind of ridiculous, since if Toni Kelly's parents knew someone who wanted to hurt a six-year-old, wouldn't they have told someone about it?

No, both Kellys confirmed.

The Kellys' house had been thoroughly searched that day—I knew all that from the online articles. Maybe Jenny had let herself in, the police thought, and got trapped in a closet or a crawlspace or behind a radiator? They'd looked underneath the backyard deck, inside the attic, underneath the brick barbecue. Nothing.

L: What can you tell me about Jenny? Anything at all that might be helpful.

MRS. KELLY: I'm not sure . . . what do you want to know exactly?

L: Like I said, anything at all. What's she like?

MRS. KELLY: Jenny . . . what's she like?

L: Yes.

MRS. KELLY: Normal. Just a sweet, adorable, six-year-old little girl.

Looper asked them if he could speak with Toni, but Mrs. Kelly said Toni wasn't there—they'd dropped her at her grandmother's while they helped man *Jenny Central*—the command center Jake and Laurie had set up on Maple Street. A place to take calls and hold hands.

Interview. Mr. and Mrs. Klein. July 12th, 2007. 1:34 p.m.

Looper asked them about the day Jenny disappeared.

MRS. KLEIN: It was horrible. I mean, just all-around hysteria, I'd say.

L: When did you first hear about it? About Jenny being missing?

MRS. KLEIN: Sandy called me.

L: Mrs. Kelly?

MRS. KLEIN: Yes.

L: Remember what time that was?

MRS. KLEIN: About three fifteen, I think. Something like that.

L: What did she say?

MRS. KLEIN: That Jenny was missing. That Laurie . . . her mom, Laurie, had sent Jenny over to play with Toni, but she never got there.

L: Were you surprised?

MRS. KLEIN: I was devastated. I mean, you never think something like that's going to happen to someone you actually know. It's awful. Kind of surreal, really.

L: Were you surprised Mrs. Kristal hadn't taken Jenny over there herself?

MRS. KLEIN: I don't know. I wasn't thinking about that. I was thinking about Jenny.

L: I'm sorry, according to Mrs. Kelly, you said, wait a minute, let me check my notes . . . you said you didn't understand how Jenny couldn't have gotten there? You asked if someone had snatched her away from Laurie on the way over?

MRS. KLEIN: Maybe I did. I don't remember. I was confused . . . about how it happened.

L: So you were surprised Mrs. Kristal hadn't walked Jenny over to the playdate?

MRS. KLEIN: I didn't say that. Look, every mother's different . . .

L: But it's something you personally wouldn't do?

MRS. KLEIN: What's the difference? What's it have to do with Jenny being kidnapped? That's what's happened here, right? Someone's taken her?

L: I'm trying to get a sense of how things work in this neighborhood, Mrs. Klein. Regarding playdates.

MRS. KLEIN: Why?

L: Look, if this was unusual, letting your kid walk to her friend's house—then, okay, maybe someone just happened to be there. Wrong place, wrong time. Someone got an idea. A crime of opportunity. If kids do that all the time around here, someone could've planned it—understand? On that subject, have you noticed anyone around the neighborhood lately who didn't seem to belong?

MRS. KLEIN: No . . . I mean, not that I've noticed. Honey . . . ?

MR. KLEIN: No. Don't remember anyone like that.

L: Okay, if something occurs to either of you later—some car you saw that seemed to be going a little too slow or someone you noticed loitering around—you'd be surprised how these things lay on the brain and then suddenly, pop, you remember them—call me. Jenny disappeared in broad daylight—somebody's likely to have seen something.

MRS. KLEIN: You mean that morning?

L: Yes, that morning. But I'm interested in other mornings too. It's possible that person—whoever might have taken her—was here before. You live almost perpendicular to the Kristals, right? On the opposite side of the block?

MRS. KLEIN: Almost. They're actually one house over. On the other side.

L: Right. So how often do Jenny and Jaycee play together?

Jaycee Klein—I remembered now. Another one of Jenny's friends.

MRS. KLEIN: You mean like playdates? Oh, I don't know . . . I couldn't say exactly. You know, now and then.

L: Now and then. Okay. We asked Mrs. Kristal for a list of Jenny's friends and Jaycee's on it.

MRS. KLEIN: Yes. They're in the same class.

L: But they don't play together that often?

MRS. KLEIN: They're really school friends. They played together more when they were younger. As far as playdates and everything. You know how kids are. Especially girls. Friendships are pretty transitory at this age.

L: Right.

Looper asked the Kleins—though Mrs. Klein seemed to have been doing most of the talking—the same thing he'd asked the Kellys. What was Jenny like?

MRS. KLEIN: Normal. Just a sweet, adorable, six-year-old little girl.

L: Thank you. If anything else occurs to you, please contact me.

The Mooneys went next. Tom Mooney owned the realty company Laurie worked for now. His wife's name was Cindy. They'd shown up at the house around the same time Mrs. Klein had.

Halfway through, something began nagging at me. What? I didn't know exactly. I flipped all the way back to the Kelly interview where Looper asked them about Jenny.

L: What's she like?

MRS. KELLY: Normal. Just a sweet, adorable, six-year-old little girl.

Then back ahead to the Kleins, where they'd been asked that same question.

MRS. KLEIN: Normal. Just a sweet, adorable, six-year-old little girl.

Weird, right?

I flipped ahead to the end of the Mooneys' interview, the very end. And there it was.

The same question Looper had asked everyone else. *What's Jenny like?*

And there was the answer.

MRS. MOONEY: Normal. Just a sweet, adorable, six-year-old little girl.

You didn't have to be the FBI to smell something fishy.

It wasn't just an answer. It was the same answer. And it wasn't just the same answer. It was exactly the same answer.

Word for word.

TWENTY-SIX

Looking through the photo album felt different this time.

Before it was like a surprise pop quiz—let's see how well I'd studied up on Jenny Kristal. I'd graded myself a solid B—having nailed Grandpa in one try—with deductions for missing on the stepbrother.

Now I wasn't supplying the answers anymore—I was looking for some.

Jenny's First Day.

There was me in the hospital again, nestled up against Laurie's throat. Okay, not me . . . her. Newborn Jenny. There was Jake, cradling Jen by the hospital window, looking like he'd just won the fucking lottery. And Ben forced to sit next to this thing called a sister and looking frankly bewildered by it all. And there was the Tootsie Roll dispenser himself, planting a kiss on Jen-Jen's bald head. And cigarette-smoking Brent, who looked like he couldn't wait for someone to relieve him of his baby-holding duties.

Then there were shots of Jenny back home. *Welcome Home*

Jenny, said the paper cut-out strung across the front hallway. Jenny being cradled in my upstairs bedroom, which had once been a nursery with pink elephants on the walls before turning into Goldy's pasture.

Jenny had that startled baby look in every shot, probably because everyone and their uncle—that's you, Brent—were sticking their faces in her crib, when they weren't sticking their cameras there instead.

There was Jenny on her back in the middle of a blanket somewhere in the Kristals' backyard, dressed just in diapers—pink for a girl—looking like a turtle who'd been flipped on its shell. Or that woman in those annoying ads they used to run a hundred times a day. You know, *I've fallen and I can't get up.*

Jenny posed next to a Christmas stocking that had her name sewn on it, wearing a teeny-tiny Christmas hat—the first in a series of "let's see how many stupid things we can put on Jenny's head and then take pictures of it." That cone-shaped birthday hat with a big fat *1* on it, for example, which is what she was wearing on the *Jenny Turns One* page. Looked like she was suffering from some kind of skin disease, since gobs of chocolate cake had turned her half-black and half-white.

There was the standard opening-the-present shot, a pile of crepe paper, ribbons, and wrapping paper littering the floor like cheapo torn-off lingerie—and Jenny still wearing that traffic cone on her head and looking even more startled than usual. Why not? Most of the birthday gifts seemed to be baby clothes instead of the kind of loot a one-year-old really wants—rattles, I guess?

I had a memory. A real one, as opposed to the ones I force-fed myself in preparation for a new starring role.

One of my birthday celebrations, let's say around four or five. My present from Mom was a scratch-off lottery ticket—it could be worth a *million dollars,* she'd breathlessly proclaimed, no doubt hoping it would stop her from having to beg Grandma for hand-outs. It wasn't so much the terrible littleness of the gift that had bothered me; it was that she'd already gone and scratched it off—much to her disappointment, since we hadn't won one cent.

Jenny seemed to have done a lot better. By birthday two she had her first Breyer horse—not Goldy—a black-and-white-spotted stallion she seemed to be chewing on. Not to mention a plastic corral to keep it in, assembled by Jake, I guess, since there was a shot of him staring at an instruction manual with a WTF expression.

The cake was different this time around—they must've discovered vanilla frosting washed off a lot easier than chocolate—but the guest list looked pretty much the same as Jenny's first birthday. There were the grandfolks, each of them posing with Jenny plunked down in their laps, and Aunt Gerta standing next to a smiling man who must've been her now-dead husband. And Jenny and Ben sprawled out on the floor next to a toy train—hello, Thomas. And wasn't that a teenage Trude sitting sullenly over there on the orange love seat? And what would a birthday party be without stoned-looking Uncle Brent grinning goofily by the cake—nice to know Ben was upholding the family tradition in that regard. Another grandmotherly woman was present too—Jake's mom, I decided—the one mothballed down in Florida. *This is Nanny. Do you remember me . . . ?*

I couldn't resist skipping ahead, wanting to see what cool shit Jenny had raked in for birthday number three. This time all the presents were assembled on a table in what looked like the Chuck E. Cheese Ben had mentioned on his memorial page—a fuzzy shot of Jake trying to lift a sorry-looking bear out of a pile of stuffed animals with a pair of mechanical tongs. The table was piled with several boxed horses—the rest of the family must've gotten the memo: everyone had to pony up with Breyers from now on. And wouldn't you know it—Goldy was in one of them.

I wouldn't stop crying, so you stopped on the way home and got me Goldy, remember, Mom?

Yes, I remember, Jenny . . .

Liar, liar, pants on fire.

A loud squeak. I shut the album.

I should've mentioned that it was the middle of the night. I'd woken up in the middle of a dream—okay, *nightmare,* since Mother was in it, cheerily threading a needle while I watched her and peed myself, literally. After I shot up out of the bed, I rolled up the stinky sheets and threw them in the bottom of the upstairs hamper.

I couldn't get back to sleep, so I went downstairs. Right to the photo album. After reading the police transcript that morning about the day Jenny disappeared, I thought I should take another look at her life *before* that.

I felt like I was breaking and entering, a housebreaker about to be caught red-handed and hauled off to jail. Except the happy homeowners didn't seem to mind that they had an intruder in their midst, did they?

Footsteps were padding across the upstairs floor.

The first night I spent in the house with the locked gate, I thought my mother was going to show up any minute. Honest. I refused the greasy KFC they offered me for dinner and bided my time sitting on their ratty couch in front of the TV. Until they pulled a dirty nighty out of the plastic bag Mom had left with them and told me to get ready for sleep. I just sat there. Mom was going to come get me so I needed to be awake for that. I might've *kept* sitting there, except my new mother, the woman who'd smiled at me from the front seat of a car, walked over and backhanded me across the face. I ended up upside down on the floor, seeing stars, and not the kind in Ben's upstairs diorama.

You'll learn, she said.

I did.

A toilet flushed upstairs, followed by the sound of padding footsteps and then the soft creak of a sagging bed. I waited a minute, then opened the album again.

Where were we . . . ?

That's right, loading up on presents at Chuck E. Cheese, enough horses by now for the sixth at Pimlico. One of Mom's meth-smoking buddies had liked playing the horses—I only remembered that because he'd blown all their drug money at the racetrack and Mom had screamed and thrown things at him before collapsing in a sobbing heap in the middle of the floor.

I'd never been on a horse, or even seen one up close.

No Breyers for little Jobeth's birthdays either.

I galloped ahead to birthday number four, passing a few Jenny-at-the-playground shots—mostly her sitting alone in a sandbox, Jenny wearing that pink cowboy hat during her first pony ride, Jenny in what looked like preschool, playing with Legos over in a corner, Jenny standing in the middle of one of those plastic backyard pools, Jenny sitting morosely on Santa's lap.

Birthday number four was back at the house and depressingly similar to the previous three. The only thing that seemed to change was the cake—a pumpkin-colored thing—and, of course, Jenny herself, who'd left babyhood behind and was on her way to blond and pretty.

I wondered—for just a moment I did—what I'd looked like at that age. Mom had packed kind of light the last day I saw her—no mementos included. The kind of photos Mother and Father took of me later weren't of the keepsake variety. *Okay, sweetheart, move your legs apart a little, that's a good girl . . .*

I turned the page.

There was Jenny dressed up as an Indian with a seven-year-old Ben, feathered headdress and everything. Somewhere upstate, I guessed—Ben had written about it on his page, that place they'd stopped going one summer in favor of Montauk, where they would dig for clams and bury memories.

We all loved Montauk, didn't we?

There were other shots of Jenny upstate—holding a fishing pole with a sorry-ass minnow attached to it, sitting cross-legged by a campfire, standing by a cliff staring off into space with a curiously disinterested expression. And then Ben standing next to her in the very same spot looking like he wished he was pretty much anywhere else on earth, which is how he looked most of the time.

There was a whole year to go, I knew. Only soon enough, I'd be coming to the end of the movie.

But not before a trip to that place where dreams come true. There was Jen-Jen hugging it out with Mickey himself, and a shot of Mom and Dad mugging at the camera on some kind of raft.

Maybe it was on its way to Tom Sawyer Island—that's what the fake wooden sign said in the next picture—Ben and Jen sullenly posing beneath it. Mostly Ben, who looked really pissed now— that's where he'd gotten himself lost in that cave, right? I'd made sure to mention that to Detective Mary when I was recounting my precious childhood memories pre–falling off the face of the earth, dropping just enough of them to close the deal.

Ben had that still-traumatized expression on his face, as if he'd been led out of that dark cave and into the blinding Florida sunshine just a second ago. Maybe he had. Jenny had her arm around him—pals forever—only it looked like Ben was trying to shrug it off and get to that humongous ice cream cone he'd been promised.

There were a couple of shots of Ben and Jenny taking Dumbo for a spin. *We waited for like two hours to ride the Dumbo, and it only lasted like six seconds . . .* and something called the Country Bear Jamboree, where the bears were dressed like a bunch of inbred white trash. Then the whole gang—Laurie, Jakey, Jenny, Ben, Grandma, and Grandpa waving from a choo-choo—well, five of them were waving; Ben, who might've still been reliving his near entombment, was resolutely resisting the temptation. Who was the picture taker? I wondered. Some other dad who'd wished upon a star and ended up waiting two hours for some shitty ride. Probably grateful to be taking pictures of somebody *else's* family, instead of staring at all those fat asses in front of him.

We were quickly getting there. To the end.

One more ho-ho-ho Christmas—Jenny back on Santa's lap looking as disinterested as she had on that upstate cliff. Then the requisite Jenny-by-Jenny's-Christmas-stocking shot—complete with a couple of striped candy canes peeking out over the top. And some more horsies under the tree.

Enjoy it, Jenny . . . , I thought, only I heard myself say the words out loud.

Please, I hope you enjoyed it . . . I do . . . I really, really do . . .

I'd been racing from birthday to birthday out of sheer jealousy, I think. Looking at everything Jenny got to remind me of what I hadn't. The Breyer horses and the nice parties and all those Xmas celebrations. And one other thing she'd gotten that I hadn't—a mom who didn't lavish most of her attention on a meth pipe.

I wasn't feeling jealous anymore.

I knew what was coming. I could feel it beginning, like creeping nausea.

Maybe she wasn't going to be strolled to the parking lot of a decrepit short-rate motel and dumped like trash. But she was going to walk out the front door to oblivion. The movie was ending.

Her last birthday.

Six years old now and the surrounding cast quickly thinning out. Maybe Jake's mom had already hightailed it to Florida. Aunt Gerta was a no-show. So was Trude. Maybe that's what happens when it's not your first or second birthday anymore—the guest list gets cut. No one's obligated to make the trek to Maple Street laden with presents. They just dump checks in the mail and call it a day. I wouldn't really know about that.

Still, something more than people seemed to be missing in her last happy birthday. The *happy* part. Or maybe I was just imagining that—everything colored by what I knew was about to happen. Jenny wasn't just blowing out six candles; she was breathing her last breaths. She was ripping open presents she'd never get to play with. Still, why did it seem like every smile was forced? Like they were all playing a part in this thing called Jenny's last birthday? Maybe because it was the middle of the night and I was in the middle of something I didn't understand.

There was that one beach shot left.

Kristals' Castle. Mom and daughter making up the palace guard and casting these crazy-long shadows on the sand because the sun must've been going down any minute. Jenny's shadow like the phony promise of a future that would never come. There'd be no getting bigger for her—she'd be eternally stuck at kid size.

I knew what was missing in Jenny's last birthday.

I knew.

It wasn't a lack of happiness.

It was the lack of something else. Not just in Jenny's last birthday, either. In the whole fucking photo album.

I flipped through it again just to make sure I wasn't making it up.

Jenny standing in playgrounds, in classrooms, in swimming pools, and in backyards. In crowded malls, on summer sidewalks, on ponies and on people's laps, and in her own room surrounded by fat pink elephants.

Jenny here, Jenny there, and Jenny everywhere.

Except never with even one other kid.

Ever.

Jenny, Jenny, Jenny.

And always, always alone.

TWENTY-SEVEN

Ben

They'd driven to Hunter Park to blow off steam, but Ben was still fuming, so good luck with that.

"What the fuck's wrong with you?" Zack asked, having just taken a humongous hit from his custom vape.

Darla asked him the same thing—Darla was someone Ben was hooking up with on a semiregular basis, which made her think she could ask him things like what was *wrong* with him? She'd been crowding him the whole night—in the car, at the park, grabbing at his hand, when she wasn't begging for a hug or, okay, promising him an *amazing* BJ, which he knew wasn't exactly her favorite activity since she had to be really baked to even consider it—all this lovey-doveyness probably having to do with the fact that he was suddenly some kind of celebrity by proxy, or was it *proximity* . . . due to his *sister* being all over the fucking news.

Only she, of course, wasn't his sister, which meant he was a doubly phony celebrity. Which only made him more pissed off every time Darla grabbed his hand or whispered in his ear—and Ben let her know that by shaking her off, the way he flicked off those creepy caterpillars that spun themselves down from the maple trees every summer. Which is when she'd asked him what the fuck was wrong with him.

"Nothing's wrong with me," he told her. "What's wrong with *you?*"

Darla got offended by that, striding off to the group of girls who were hanging by the hookup tree—they called it that not because you hooked up there, but because kids had been carving their names into it for forever—you know, *Jimmy loves Shari, Tony loves Maria.* He wouldn't be surprised if there was a *Darla loves Ben* on it somewhere too, courtesy of Darla, no doubt, who was right now talking to the girl he used to hook up with—Jamie—who was probably using this opportunity to rag on him with righteous passion, so there'd be two of them out there saying what an amazing asshole he was.

So all in all, he didn't need his best bud, Zack, cranking on him too.

"You need to chill," Zack said, which was something Ben usually said to girls, which made it even more annoying.

"I need different parents," Ben said.

"Like I don't?" Crappy parents were something Zack could relate to, since his dad had moved to Scottsdale, Arizona, and only saw him once a year in the summer—*seeing* being kind of a misnomer because he'd leave Zack sitting in the apartment all day with nothing to do, while he went off to work. And his mom—don't get him started on that—was always out gallivanting around with her newest boyfriend, who was a major asshole with a Mercedes convertible and a comb-over, which didn't exactly mesh.

"They're fucking *certifiable,*" Ben said. "I mean . . . seriously."

"Huh?" Zack said. "What'd they do?" While Zack could relate to shitty parents, he thought of Ben's as light-years ahead of his own, so he was understandably perplexed.

Ben had half opened up to Zack about his long-lost sister, first not saying anything at all about her, then finally acknowledging her presence when they'd seen her all over the TV news that morning. Then sharing his growing doubts about whether she really *was* his sister, which Zack had thought was kind of cool, even though Ben wasn't sure Zack entirely believed it—that his sister wasn't his sister—but the possibility that she might not be was kind of cool.

"Why do you think she's not your sister?" Zack asked him.

"I just do," Ben said, which, granted, maybe wasn't the most persuasive answer in the world. Especially mumbled from the back seat of a pot-smoke-filled car.

"Doesn't she remember all this shit about your family, like who everybody is and everything? If she's not your sister, dude, how the hell would she know that stuff?"

Which is when Ben saw it—when it crystallized for him.

"She read it."

"Huh?"

"On my page."

He'd never told Zack about the memorial page and all the shit he'd unloaded there, how all the trivial and nontrivial stuff he kept remembering about Jenny ended up there—everything—and so how all the stuff this girl might seem to remember wasn't remembered. It was memorized.

That revelation made Zack a semibeliever.

"Wow, so she's like a fake or something?"

And when Ben got home, what did he find sitting on his computer—sitting right there out in the open like some sort of cosmic joke, or cosmic reckoning—but his previously mentioned

Facebook memorial page, which she'd obviously been poring over while everyone was out of the house.

He waited for his parents to get home so he could deliver the coup de grâce—which is French for fucking nail to a cross.

His mom came home first, and Ben contemplated maybe doing this in two stages . . . first letting her in on the secret, then Dad. But since his mom was going crazy over Jenny these days—just over-the-top stupid—and since she seemed kind of distracted when she got home, not even acknowledging his cheery hello, but disappearing into her room with the door closed, he thought it better to wait until his dad got back and do it simultaneously. His dad was the more logical one anyway, and this was all about the facts, which were fucking inconvertible . . . or was it *incontrovertible*, something like that . . . pretty black-and-white, that's for sure.

He was downstairs waiting when his dad came through the front door, looking kind of rumpled and tired, but Ben had just the thing to wake him up—wake them both up—out of that delusional dream they were both living in.

"Hey, Dad," Ben said.

"Hey, Ben." His dad dropped his shoulder case on the alcove table, then nearly tripped over one of Ben's sneakers. "Jesus, Ben, how many times have I told you to put your sneakers away?"

"Hundreds. My apologies on the matter of the sneakers."

His dad peered at him. "Are you okay?"

"Affirmative. Can you ask Mom to come down?"

"Huh?" His dad was still peering at him as if he didn't quite recognize who he was.

Your only child, Dad. That's who.

"I have something of grave importance to talk to both of you about."

187

"*Grave* . . . ? Any particular reason you're talking like that, Ben?"

Yes, there was a particular reason he was talking like that. This was a matter of grave importance, and of grave consequences, so he was using language suitable to this grave occasion. They'd understand soon enough.

"Did you get suspended, Ben? Is this about smoking pot again?"

"No, I did not get suspended. I did not smoke pot again." Okay, he was lying about one of those things, but now wasn't the time for truth telling, or actually it was the time for that, but only about the much more grave matter of the imposter living upstairs in the den. Where was she, by the way? He hadn't heard a peep out of her since he'd left her that little note on the computer.

"Okay, so what's so *grave* that you need to talk to both of us?"

"Oh, you'll see. Can you get Mom down here?"

"Sure, Ben. Can I have a minute?" His dad walked upstairs, where Ben could hear him enter his parents' bedroom. Ben sauntered into the living room and sat down on the settee in front of the couch—which is where he usually put his feet up when he watched *The Walking Dead*—which is what the girl sitting upstairs was. It was the strategically perfect position for him, face-on to both of them, whom he'd ask to take seats on the couch. They'd need to be sitting down for this.

He was getting, all right, a little nervous, cursing himself for not fortifying himself with a little of that leftover Skywalker OG. This was momentous news he was about to break to them. Kind of heart wrenching and everything. But nothing compared to what *she'd* done—pretending to be his dead sister—something that was monumentally crazy, even sacrilegious, maybe even something you could get locked up for. He didn't know about that, but he'd see.

The bedroom door opened and he heard his parents start down the stairs.

So, Mom and Dad, I know this is going to be a shock to you . . .

Mom and Dad, I need you to brace yourself . . .

Guess what . . . ?

He was trying to choose an opening line. In debate class—which he personally sucked at—they said your opening line was the most important one, next to the closing line, which was even more important.

His parents walked into the living room.

"Okay, Ben," his dad said, "what is it?"

"I think you both should sit down for this."

"That's okay, Ben," his mom said. "What's the matter? Is this about school?"

"No, it's not about school. That's what Dad said. School's just fine. It's just fantastic. Amazing."

"Great to hear," Dad said. "So, what's the problem?"

"I really think you should sit down for this."

"Jesus, Ben." His dad sighed and shook his head. "Fine, we'll sit down. Laurie, would you care for a seat?" He motioned toward the couch, which Mom promptly sat down on, but he himself dropped onto the love seat in the right corner of the room.

"Here," Ben said.

"What?" Dad said.

"Here. I think you should sit down here. With Mom."

"For chrissakes. Why does it matter where we sit?"

Ben coughed. He fidgeted. He looked down at the floor. His heart was doing that tom-tom thing, and he suddenly felt sweaty all over.

"The thing is," he said, "Jenny isn't Jenny."

He looked up expecting to see shock and awe on their faces, but instead what he saw was pretty much nothing. The same expressions they'd walked downstairs with, which, if they registered any emotion at all, seemed to be minor annoyance.

"Come again?" Dad said.

"Jenny isn't Jenny. Hate to break it to you, 'cause I know . . . well, how much you miss her and everything. I know. But that's not her."

Now their faces did seem to show a little bit of alarm. Cool . . . he was getting through to them, and he felt some of his nervousness ease. Like his heart wasn't trying to break out of his ribs anymore.

"Listen, Ben . . . ," his mom said. "I know you're having a hard time dealing with this . . . Who wouldn't? It's totally natural to feel like you've been, well . . . usurped. But this is taking things too far . . ."

Huh? The alarm he saw on their faces wasn't for the fact that some crazy-ass imposter was sitting upstairs in the den. It was for him. It took a minute for that to register, and then another minute for the anger to start welling up in him, as his mom shook her head and his dad sighed as if this whole thing *had* been about him fucking up in school.

"Are you guys *hearing* me? I mean, seriously . . . are you fucking hearing what I'm saying?"

"We can do without the cursing, Ben," his dad said.

"Oh, really? How about this, then? The fucking girl sitting upstairs in the fucking den is not your fucking daughter. Am I making myself fucking clear here?"

"*Enough,* Ben." His dad again, looking truly pissed off. "I'm not going to tell you again, understand?"

"Well, I'm going to tell you again. She's not *Jenny.*" He pointed up to the ceiling, more or less in the direction of where the den was. "That girl up there is not your daughter. She's not my sister. She's not fucking anybody. She's a fake. She's some crazy bitch. Am I getting through to you?"

"First of all," his mom said, "keep your voice down. It's bad enough you're saying this to *us*, but I don't need Jenny hearing it. You're upset, Ben, I get it. You've been an only child for a long time, and suddenly you're not, your sister's back, and you're confused and angry. And, okay, I grant you, this isn't an everyday occurrence. You have a right to be confused. And, okay, you're having a hard time dealing with it and accepting it. But I can't have you making horrible accusations, and I can't have you screaming them where Jenny can hear it. Am I getting through to you?"

"Jenny is not hearing it. Because Jenny isn't *here*. Get it? Sorry if that sucks for you, but there it is. Okay, listen . . . all the stuff you think she knows, about our family and Disney World and all that crap. She read it. Understand? She fucking read it."

Dad sighed. Mom sighed. They both sighed.

"I'm not kidding," Ben continued. "Listen, I'm not making this shit up . . ." He noticed the distinct whine in his voice, which is how he sounded whenever he'd gotten busted by them over the years and tried to avoid one of their stupid punishments, which is decidedly *not* how he wanted to sound now, since he'd generally been lying when he'd attempted to weasel out of being grounded for smoking pot or some such shit, but he certainly wasn't lying now. "I never told you guys . . . but I put up this kind of . . . memorial page to Jenny. On Facebook."

Two blank expressions staring back at him.

"It was . . . I don't know . . . something I just did because I've always felt weird about it . . . about my sister being kidnapped. I mean, you guys never talked about it that much and I had a hard time remembering things . . . remembering *it*. And remembering her. I mean, I know I freaked out about it back then and everything and you put me in that fucking asylum—"

"For God's sake, Ben," Mom said, "it was a Catholic school. We didn't put you in a mental institution."

"Oh yeah? So why was everybody zonked on shit? I had to take pills every day. I remember. I don't remember a lot, but I remember that. I couldn't swallow back then, remember? I couldn't swallow pills, so the nuns had to mash them in applesauce, which pissed them off, like I was making them work too hard or something."

"*Depakote*, Ben," his mom said. "It was . . . just something to help snap you back. The therapist we took you to after Jenny . . . after she was kidnapped said you were suffering from trauma. You don't remember this—you don't remember a lot about back then— but you wouldn't go to school. You literally refused. I had to drag you there, and then I had to go back one hour later and drag you home. You were disruptive—you were fighting with other kids. You wouldn't go, and when you did, you wouldn't stay. I'm not blaming you, Ben, I'm not . . . Jenny's loss was devastating for everyone. I was a major mess back then. You wouldn't remember that either. But I was. A big one. Maybe if I wasn't, I could've helped you more than I did. I'm sorry . . ."

"I'm not asking for *sorry*. I'm sorry for you . . . and Dad. That's what I'm trying to tell you. I put up this page, on Facebook, 'cause so much of that time seems to be missing for me, like somebody erased it or something, it's . . . not just my memories of Jenny, but everything. So I put up this page, okay? . . . And I just wrote down anything that came to mind. You know, about Jenny and me . . . about us. Just all kinds of random shit. Whatever, you know like Jenny wouldn't let me play with her stupid horse, and how I got lost in Disney World . . . anything that popped into my head, right? And that Facebook page has got like a thousand followers now. Mostly people who've lost sisters and brothers like me, but other people too. And she's read it . . . that girl upstairs read it, and that's what she's been playing back to you. That's how she was able to fool you. And the police too, I guess. Okay? So now you know . . ."

He was looking for this to register on their faces. To see some kind of realization there, for his dad to stop looking like he was about to wallop him and his mom to stop looking like she thought he needed to be carted back to that asylum—because he didn't care what they said, that's what that place was . . .

"Look, Ben," Mom said, leaning forward on the couch, the way the guidance counselor at school leaned forward when she was try-ing to *empathize* with him. "Maybe it's wishful thinking," she said. "That you could lose your sister like that, get absolutely trauma-tized by it, and then come out of it and be just fine. And that she could come back into our lives now, and you'd be just fine with that too . . ."

"Did you hear what I just told you? Both of you? About her read-ing my page? I caught her *doing* it. That's how she knows. About all our stuff . . ."

Only his mom was giving him that smile, the kind you give to Special Olympics kids when they cross the finish line—they'd held regionals at his school last year and Ben had helped out for extra credit—the smile that's half *Attaboy* and half *I feel really fucking sorry for you.*

"Ben, what I'm telling you, what I'm saying, is that you obviously have a lot of . . . unresolved issues, honey . . . with losing your sis-ter, and with getting her back. And I understand that, I really do. We need to work through them. We need to work this out together, and we will. We're both here for you."

Ben couldn't actually believe what he was hearing. He'd laid it all out for them, like one of those stupid crime shows on TV, when they take you step by step through the murder and everyone nods and says you solved it. But his parents weren't nodding; they were shaking their heads; they were giving him pitying smiles and telling him how they all needed to work through this. He felt like he was in that sci-fi movie he saw as a kid, where the aliens came down and took over these parents' bodies and they all became smiling dummies.

"Are you guys fucking delusional? Am I speaking Chinese? I . . . caught . . . her . . . reading . . . my . . . page," he said, laying out each word for emphasis. "I went upstairs when she was out of the house and saw my page on the computer. I busted her. Red-fucking-handed. What part of this are you not understanding?"

"Well, wouldn't you be curious if you were her?"

"What?"

"Wouldn't you be curious if you were Jenny? About what her brother wrote about her?"

"Huh . . . ? What's that got to do with anything? I'm telling you that all the stuff she's told you—it's *on* there. On my page. Because I fucking wrote it. All of it. About Uncle Brent and Nanny and going to the beach and blowing off fireworks on the Fourth of July, and . . . and everything else. She's just memorized it."

"All the things on your page are things that happened, Ben." Mom again. "Of course Jenny would remember the same things—they happened to her too. I understand you're upset . . . I understand what an enormous . . . adjustment this is for you. But give it time, honey. We just need time . . ."

Which is when Ben had had enough. Right there. Because they didn't need time. They needed the fucking director of this sci-fi movie to yell, *Cut*. So they could all go back to reality. So his parents could stop being alien dummies saying things like *We just need time* and open their fucking eyes. And now he felt hot tears coming out of his eyes—twenty years old and he was actually bawling in front of them, the both of them still sitting there with those moronic smiles on their faces.

"You're both out of your fucking minds!" Ben yelled, and then sprang up off the settee and literally ran to the front door, which he pulled open and bolted through, making sure to slam it shut on the way out, before jumping into his car and heading to Hunter Park.

TWENTY-EIGHT

What do you want?"

Good question.

"I wanted to say I'm sorry," I said, even though I didn't want to say anything close to that. I wanted to say *I have a word of advice for you: lettuce.* I wanted to ask how her newspaper pal, Max, was—if he was her pal anymore, given that she'd returned empty-handed and photoless from her visit to the kidnapped girl on Maple Street.

"Huh?"

Okay, fair enough. Toni Kelly clearly hadn't been expecting an apology.

"I'm apologizing," I said, gritting my teeth, discovering that wasn't some dumb expression but something you actually found yourself doing when uttering words you'd rather choke on.

"Oh." A hint of interest now—trying to remember the reporter's phone number maybe and exactly what he'd promised her.

"I'm still coming to terms with everything . . . ," I said. What had

Mom/Laurie said to me that first night home? "You know . . . coming to myself."

"Sure," Toni said, that fake sweetness positively oozing out of her again. "I understand."

"You do? I'm glad."

I'd looked up her number online. Checked out her Facebook and Instagram, where she'd milked her five minutes of fame for everything it was worth, and it was basically worth shit.

OMG, she'd posted the day I came back. The day *after* I'd come back, after I'd inadvertently blabbed to that reporter at one in the morning. Jenny Kristal is alive! My best friend when I was six. She was on her way to see me when it happened. I can't believe it. God is good!

She didn't look like someone who gave God much thought, given that her T-shirt said EAT ME in one of her pics from this year's spring break.

"So . . . um . . . you want to hang?" Toni asked.

"Sure." I couldn't think of anything I felt like doing less. But I was on a mission—let's call it code name: Jenny.

I'd spent the last few years frightened to death of being discovered—of that exact moment when funny looks would stop being funny, and I'd end up being called on the carpet in front of shocked parents and pissed-off social workers.

Put it this way.

There was this game show from the sixties called *Truth or Consequences*. How would I know that? Because I'd looked it up after reading about this New Mexico town that got itself named after the show by winning a contest—swear to God—Truth or Consequences, New Mexico. A six-year-old had been vanished from there back in 2007, and I was trying her on for size. I found episodes of the show on YouTube—a host in a plaid polyester suit asking dumb trivia questions and making everyone who flunked them do even dumber stunts. Only on this one episode I saw, it was more like a publicity stunt, where the girl who couldn't name the singer of "Don't Be Cruel" ended up reuniting with the mom who gave her up for adoption. Instead of everybody laughing their asses off at a girl who'd never heard of Elvis Presley, they'd cried their eyes out. Me included. Anyway, the point of the show was that if you didn't supply the truth, there's consequences.

I could write a book about that.

Those rules didn't apply in the Kristal house. I hadn't supplied the truth, but there were no consequences.

Why?

It was like being locked in a black closet again, desperate for a tiny crack of light. Picture the stupid quivers times a million.

Something had happened to Jenny.

I needed to know what.

When I opened the door, Toni was all smiles.

"Welcome back," I said, trying to match her smile for smile. Be the girl who couldn't wait to reunite with her old BFF. Speaking of best friends forever . . .

"How come you never came to my birthday parties?" I asked her back in my room.

"What?"

"I was looking through an old photo album. All my parties were family only. I was just wondering . . ."

Toni shrugged. "I mean . . . how would I know?"

"You'd think I'd have my little girl gang there. All my BFFs."

"Maybe I was busy. Another party or something."

"Sure. What about Jaycee?"

"Huh?"

"Jaycee Klein. She was busy too?"

"Wait . . . are you like *pissed off* I didn't go to your birthday party or something?"

"Of course not." I smiled. "That would be really lame."

"Right. 'Cause I was like six."

"Me too."

"It was twelve years ago. Who knows?"

"Exactly. That's kind of what I'm trying to do here. Know."

"Know? Know what? Why I didn't go to your birthday party?"

"Know whatever. Anything at all. I'm hoping talking to you maybe brings things back. That you can help me recover some memories . . ."

"Oh." She perked up at that. "Got it. Sure." Being my amateur therapist would probably make her feel less guilty about selling me out for a little cash and two minutes of fame. Maybe the reporter she was pimping for would even write a whole article about it. She leaned forward. "What do you want to know?"

"About you and me. About being friends."

"*Best* friends . . . ," Toni corrected me.

"Right. Best friends. But my best friend wasn't at my party. At any of them."

"Geez, Jen. Like I said . . . maybe I was busy. Maybe Mom was having a meltdown about Dad and forgot to take me."

I'd noticed there was no Mr. Kelly in the picture anymore. Literally. No family pictures on her Facebook page. A few of him and Toni alone, and one with him and a younger woman with fake boobs, poor Toni shunted off to the side.

"Maybe that's it. Did we play together a lot?"

"Sure. All the time."

"Really?"

Jenny and Toni . . . they don't really play together all that much: what Mrs. Kelly told Detective Looper. Maybe that's why Toni's mom hadn't given it two thoughts when Jenny didn't make it over that day. She'd never expected to see her in the first place.

"Yeah, really. Why?"

"I heard that maybe we *hadn't* played together that much. Not after we were really little."

"Who told you that?"

Yeah, who?

"Mom."

"Your mother said we didn't play together?"

"She alluded to that."

Ever let the air out of a balloon to make that fart sound? That was Toni—minus the sound. I was threatening her new status as a major player in the Jenny Kristal story. The loyal best friend. Maybe I was threatening all those dollar signs dancing in her head—the ones she'd get for her page-one exclusive.

"You were coming over that morning," Toni stated emphatically. "To play. We had a *playdate*."

"I think I was being dumped on you. To get out of Ben's hair. He had a broken arm."

"You weren't being dumped on Jaycee, were you?"

"Got me there. You were definitely the dumpee."

"What?"

"Forget it. Give me a memory, Toni."

"A memory . . . of what?"

"Anything at all. I thought maybe you could help me recover some memories. So, hand one over. About you and your best friend."

"Well . . . let me think . . ." Her face lit up. "I remember your Fourth of July barbecues. When your dad's brother would blow off those bottle rockets. Cool shit."

"Yeah. Those were with everyone, though. The barbecues. What about just me and you? A playdate. What we'd do? One little memory, Toni Baloney. Just one."

"Your horses," she said.

"What about them?"

"We . . . played with them."

"Great. Which one was my favorite—you remember?"

"Huh?"

"I had a favorite horse. Which one was it? Think I remember, but I can't be sure. Was it Flicka?"

"Right. Yep. It was Flicka."

"Actually I think it was Black Beauty."

"Right. Black Beauty. That's it."

"Wait a minute, now. How could I be so stupid? Goldy. That was her name."

Toni turned red.

"Okay, so I don't remember your favorite *toy horse*. How would I remember that anyway?"

"Good point. What about something else?"

"Like what?" Toni was starting to look uneasy, like those two-sizes-too-small jeans she was wearing were maybe crawling up her snatch.

"Favorite movie. Favorite cartoon show. Favorite color. You were my favorite friend. So maybe you remember some of my favorite things."

"I don't know."

"Right."

"I can't remember." Toni had begun fidgeting with the rope bracelet on her wrist.

"I'm thinking maybe Mom was right," I said.

"Huh?"

"That we stopped playing together."

Toni just stared.

"Why do you think?"

"Why do I think what?" she said.

"Why we stopped playing together?"

Her face was forming the same expression she had when I kicked her out of the house the other day. She was starting to worry I was kicking her out of the story. That she'd go back to being a Fatty Patty with pretty much zero on her social calendar.

"You were like . . . violent," Toni stated.

Suddenly it was my turn to clam up. I don't know why it felt like she'd slapped me. Like she was saying it about me instead of the girl I was pretending to be.

It just did.

"Violent . . . ?" I finally repeated. "What do you mean?"

"You need a definition? Violent. As in physically the fuck *harmful* to me. To Jaycee too. You pushed me off the monkey bars once. I cracked a tooth. Hey, you wanted a memory, didn't you?"

"You remember me doing that to you? Hurting you?"

"Kind of. My mom definitely does. She couldn't stop talking about it when you showed up again. You were like this dangerous kid."

And here I'd thought that was Ben's department, I wanted to say. I almost did.

"That's why we stopped playing together?" I prodded. "Why you weren't at my birthday parties—why *no one* was?"

Toni shrugged. "Guess so."

"Why did I push you off the monkey bars?"

"Got me."

"We weren't like fighting or something? Calling each other names. You know, little-girl stuff?"

"I was sitting there minding my own business. You just fucking pushed me. I broke my tooth. That's the kind of shit you began do-ing. Hurting other little kids . . . The story was, you even pushed . . ." Toni stopped and picked at a nail.

"The story? What story? I even pushed *who* . . . ?"

"Forget it."

"That's the problem. Forgetting is the problem. I'm trying to remember, remember?"

"Yeah. Well, maybe not this."

"Who did I push?"

"I told you. Let's forget it."

"Let's not. The story was . . . c'mon—I even pushed who, Toni?"

"Okay, since you asked. Ben."

"Ben? My brother? Pushed him where?"

"Down the stairs. He ended up with a *broken arm,* remember?"

"I pushed Ben down the stairs and broke his arm? Who says?"

"Everyone."

"Everyone. Who's everyone?"

"My mom and dad. Other people."

"Why would I do that? Why would I push Ben down the stairs?"

"I told you. You turned into this little monster. Like Chucky."

"They never told me that. My mom and dad. Even Ben. He didn't say I did that. No one has." I was about to say Ben never wrote it either—it wasn't on his memorial page. I remembered something about him flying down the stairs, sure, but nothing about me being the one who *caused* it.

Toni shrugged. "Maybe they don't want to upset you. I mean, with all the shit you've been through."

"So, if I asked Ben, he'd say, 'Yeah, you pushed me.'"

"How do I know what Ben would say? Ask him. Maybe he isn't sure. 'Cause you, like, did it from behind. It was *suspected,* though."

"So, people thought I did it?"

"My mom said you did it."

"How about my mom?"

"Your mom? How would I know? Look, it's not like your mom announced it to the neighborhood. I'm sure people, like, didn't bring it up to her on the street. *Hey, heard your crazy daughter pushed your son down the stairs.*"

I understood something now. I thought I did.

Something being spelled out in a flashing neon sign like the ones that cover the entire sides of buildings in Times Square—even as I showed a pissed-off Toni to the door, photoless again, but maybe with a story she could actually sell to somebody.

Normal. Just a sweet, adorable, six-year-old little girl.

Now, why would three moms of Jenny's friends go word-for-word the same when asked what Jenny was like? And why those words? Those words, in particular.

Normal. Let's take that word.

Try this.

Because your friends' daughter was just kidnapped.

And those friends—Laurie and Jake—were losing it. Freaking out with shock and fear and whatever else goes through parents' minds (mine not included) when their kids are stolen. And the community was in full support mode: Jenny Hotlines and Jenny Central and Jenny posters and Jenny Searches. So, when the local detective stops by (and maybe the local paper) and asks you what Jenny was like, you have two choices. Tell him she's bat-shit crazy and borderline homicidal, or tell him she's just a normal, sweet, adorable, six-year-old little girl. For the sake of her parents.

They must've had a little conference that day. Talked it over. *If they ask us about Jenny, we'll say this, this, and this. All of us. We need to keep it consistent.*

The same thing must've occurred to J. Pennebaker.

Who'd sent the Kristals that transcript. Where three different parents had said exactly the same thing. He must've been puzzled by that too at first.

I'd finally remembered why his name sounded so familiar. It was in that magazine article I'd found online while researching my new self—the one marking the ten-year anniversary of Jenny's disappearance. Detective Looper was in there, and a private investigator, and even some phony psychic the Kristals once threw money at trying to find Jenny. And someone else.

A cold case detective named Joe Pennebaker, who would scrupulously go over every single piece of evidence again. Which sounds more impressive than it was, since there really wasn't any evidence— not any physical evidence, anyway.

J. Pennebaker equals Joe Pennebaker.

But why was Joe Pennebaker still calling them two years later? Who knows?

But I knew why he'd called to say he'd *stop* calling. That one was easy.

Because I'd come home.

So, now it was my turn, I guess.

To be the cold case detective.

TWENTY-NINE

Maybe we can talk to Jenny privately this time?"

"Why?" Laurie asked.

Good question.

The comedy duo had returned for an encore. I'd kept making excuses like *Do I have to?* and *I told them everything the first time* and *I don't want to go back there,* but this was the *FFBI*—the Fucking Federal Bureau of Investigation—so you could only say no for so long.

"It might be easier for Jenny to open up without her mother sitting there."

That's okay, I felt like saying, *she's not my mother.* Which would only be news to two of the four people standing in the living room.

"That okay with you, honey?" Laurie asked.

"Perfectly fine," I said.

My antenna was definitely up. Mostly because Hesse and Kline looked more FBI-like this time, like they wanted to throw a raincoat over my head and offer me some new silver bracelets. Like they'd maybe left the kid gloves at home today.

"Do you know what DNA is, Jenny?" Hesse asked after Laurie had retreated to the kitchen.

"No. I haven't been living on planet Earth so I have no idea."

"Excuse me?"

"Yes, I know what it is." *Lars had been pretty familiar with it too,* I thought.

"We did some analysis of hair fibers found inside the trailer."

"Great."

"We matched yours, of course." That's right, I remembered. They'd taken a cheek swab after the first interview.

"No surprise there," I said.

"Not there, maybe . . . ," Kline answered. "We found male and female hair fibers in the rest of the trailer."

"No surprise there either."

"We tracked down the original owners of the trailer. It's theirs."

"Great."

"They're African American. And over eighty."

They were staring at me and waiting for a response. *Let 'em wait,* I thought.

"See, Jenny," Hesse said. "That's the surprise. Right there."

"Not following," I said.

She sighed. The way Aunt Trude did when Sebastian threw that mini-tantrum and cracked his sister's iPhone.

"We're trying to figure out how you could've lived in that trailer with your abductors when there's no physical evidence of them ever being there."

"Huh?" I was playing dumb.

"The previous owners, Mr. and Mrs. Washington, vacated the

trailer four years ago. Plenty of their DNA is scattered throughout the place. And then there's yours. But no DNA from Mother and Father. How do you explain that?"

Simple. They weren't *there,* of course. The deserted trailer was a grungy pit stop between the Greers and the Kornbluths, a good six months after I'd walked through the gate of Father and Mother's house. The idea was to keep *them* and Hesse and Kline as far apart as possible. You understand—there'd be the little problem of our stories not exactly matching up.

This is why they'd wanted to interrogate me alone today, I thought. So Laurie wouldn't tell them to stop badgering the witness. Who'd, after all, been through *hell*. So she wouldn't make them pack up their box of questions and go home.

"Mother and Father's DNA," Hesse repeated. "Why do you think there's none of it in that trailer?"

"I'm not a DNA scientist. I wouldn't know," I said.

"Don't think you need to have an actual degree to understand the problem here, Jenny. We just want you to help us understand. Maybe you got your facts confused. Maybe you can take us through the timeline again?"

"The timeline?"

"Yes. When you lived with them . . . your *abductors* . . . and when you left?"

The way Hesse said *abductors* was hard to miss. The way the supervisors at juvie hall—prison guards to you—used to say *ladies.* Something they didn't believe for one second.

"Maybe I took you through it ten times already."

"It's just not adding up, Jenny."

"They were in the trailer. With me. Doing things to me . . ."

I said don't move . . .

"I have no idea why you can't find their DNA," I continued, making myself sound righteously indignant. I could do indignant. "Maybe they did a really good job of cleaning it up before they left."

"So, they managed to clean all their hair fibers but somehow left the Washingtons'? Does that make sense to you, Jenny?"

"Sure. Why not?"

"Because it defies scientific possibility. It can't happen."

"If you say so."

"Yes. I'm afraid we say so."

I gave a Toni Kelly shrug. Like *What do you want me to do about it?* Even though I knew, of course, what they wanted me to do about it, which was tell them the truth. Sorry, not my strong suit.

"Then there's the lack of any corroborating witnesses," Kline jumped in again.

"Corroborating . . . ?" *Speak English,* I felt like saying.

"People who saw them around the trailer. They had to get out *sometimes.* To rifle through those Goodwill bins you talked about, or pick up food. Why wouldn't anyone have seen them?"

"The trailer was in a deserted lot," I said. "No one lives there. That's why they call it deserted."

"The lot, sure. But how about around the lot? Around the neighborhood even?"

"There wasn't a neighborhood. There weren't *neighbors.*" A corny joke I suddenly remembered: What did the filly say to the stallion when he tried to kiss her? Stop, the neighhhhhhh-bors might talk.

"Walk a few blocks and there are. Houses. Streets. People. None of those people ever saw anyone fitting your description of Father. Or Mother. They just saw you."

"Maybe I was the only one worth looking at."

I gave him the stare I'd practiced from Instagram—narrowed eyes, pouty lips, tilted chin—*Don't you agree?*

Kline smirked. I wasn't fitting the FBI profile for the victim of a child kidnapping. I wanted to tell them *victim* was my middle name—they needed to trust me on this. I'd earned my victimhood— I'd be happy to show them the slash marks in a pantry stinking of raw potatoes if they didn't believe me. We could count them together as a group project.

"Jenny, have you told us the whole truth here?" Hesse doing empathy, which wasn't as convincing as me doing indignant, but passable.

"And nothing but the truth," I said.

I'd had enough. I had things to do. People to talk to. One people in particular, I was thinking. And hadn't I been given a kind of immunity from prosecution here? Even if I didn't understand why.

I clammed up. *No, Laurie, not the made-up clamming we did in Montauk.* The kind that made Hesse and Kline begin shooting me stone-cold stares, especially Hesse, who dropped empathy like a hot potato and embraced tough love instead—mostly the tough part.

"We need answers, Jenny, and sooner or later we're going to get them," she said.

I stayed quiet.

"There are things we believe you're not telling us. Things that don't fit your narrative."

My *story,* I almost said out loud. My *story.* They always seemed to go for three syllables when two would do.

"We'll be back," Kline said. "And we'll be having a word with your mother."

Be my guest.

THIRTY

I met Jenny in a dream.

We were sitting on the front porch and it was summer. That very day, I think—the day she disappeared. She was dressed just the way the articles described her. In pink shorts and a white striped T-shirt.

We were facing each other, sitting Indian-style. I was thinking I ought to be scared sitting there alone with her—*like Chucky*, Toni taunted me—but here's the thing: I wasn't.

I felt calm and peaceful instead.

Jenny was just a little six-year-old girl. Who reached out and hugged me. And whispered something in my ear.

Save me, she said. *You can. You have to . . .*

When I woke up drenched in my own sweat, I jumped into the shower and scrubbed myself head to toe, as if I was trying to wash her off. No dice.

So I went looking for a number.

Whose number, you ask? The one belonging to J. Pennebaker.

Who'd said, *Tell Mrs. Kristal sorry, I won't be calling anymore.*

I thought maybe I should call him.

Finding that number turned out to be easy. I just looked through the mail.

West Elm, Target, and Victoria's Secret catalogues. Something from the board of elections. A solicitation from the Juvenile Diabetes Research Foundation.

The phone bill.

Mind if I have a look, Mom and Dad? No? Great.

I immediately spotted that weird 404 area code, which Google confirmed was from the state of Georgia.

There was something weirder.

There were at least thirty calls placed from J. Pennebaker to the Kristals.

I counted them.

Thirty in one month, which seemed like an awful lot. Unless you were a member of the family, say, as opposed to someone trying to find a member of the family. Or at least he had been, more than two years ago.

Pennebaker had been calling nearly nonstop.

Most of the calls lasting exactly one minute. Why's that? Probably because they'd gone straight to voice mail. He'd been calling, but the Kristals hadn't been answering.

Something else was bothering me—add it to the growing list. Not just that Pennebaker called to say he wouldn't be calling. It was that *sorry* he'd thrown in there. Why sorry? Sorry for what, huh?

The barrage of calls, probably. Sure.

Thirty of them, ending with the last one, the thirtieth—right after I'd come home.

And then I thought, *Hey, if all those calls went to voice mail—maybe they're still on there.*

See?

This cold case detective thing wasn't as hard as it looked.

THIRTY-ONE

mm . . . hello, Mrs. Kristal—this is Joe Pennebaker. As I was trying to explain to you and your husband on the phone. Yeah, I finally retired and moved down to the land of cotton. Still trying to get used to people saying please and thank you. Anyways, I still have this case on my brain. Your daughter's. The thing is, every detective worth anything has one like that. You know, the case that won't leave you alone. The one that keeps you up at night. Jenny's case . . . I don't know, maybe it's because I lost my daughter too—to cancer, I know, it's not the same thing, even if it eats at you the same way, but I know what it's like losing a daughter. Anyway, there's some things I've been digging into and I have just a few . . ."

Click.

The Kristals' answering machine looked like a relic from back when Jenny disappeared—waiting for messages from a daughter that never came. It had proclaimed: *Time's up.* Like the psych they'd made me sit down with at juvie hall, who'd grant you exactly fifteen minutes and not a nanosecond more. I used to spring some great revelation on her at exactly the fourteen-minute mark just to see if she'd cut me off in midsentence. *Let's pick this up next time,* she'd say in a pretty bored voice.

Next time for Pennebaker was just a few seconds later.

"Umm . . . this is Joe again. Sorry about that. What I was going to say is I have just a few questions for you, if that's okay? If you or your husband could give me a call back, my number is 404-672-8579. Thank you."

Evidently Pennebaker never got it. That call back.

"Hey there . . . this is Joe Pennebaker again. If you or your husband could ring me back, I'd really appreciate it. As I said, I've been doing some digging around and there are a few things I've come across—some things you could maybe help me clear up . . . one or two questions, that's it. My number is 404-672-8579. Thank you."

They hadn't answered that one either. By his next call, Pennebaker was sounding a little anxious.

"Joe again. Joe Pennebaker. I know I'm not officially on the case anymore. Your daughter's. But it'd really be helpful if you could answer just a few questions. Honest . . . all I need is a few minutes of your time. That's all. My number is . . . well, you have my number by now. Please call me back anytime."

I was downstairs in the living room—one ear to Joe Pennebaker, the other on the front door, which Long Island's number one truant might walk through at any minute. And wonder what I was doing with the home phone glued to my ear without my saying anything into it.

Pennebaker must've waited another few days before trying again.

"Pennebaker here. I was hoping I'd hear back from one of you by now. Look, since I can't seem to get either of you on the phone . . . understand you're busy and all, I do . . . but this is about your daughter . . ."

He was ping-ponging between pissed and polite and having a hard time deciding which. It was kind of funny—if I wasn't seriously on edge, it might've been. On edge regarding that front door. And on the edge of my seat (the orange love seat in case you're interested) waiting for Pennebaker to finally say something interesting. Okay, you discovered something—spit it out . . .

". . . just some questions about . . . I don't know, the family dynamic, let's call it. I mean, back then. It might have some bearing on what happened to your daughter. So, if you could just please call me back."

It must've worked. Finally. They did call him back. And left a message.

"Uhhh . . . Joe Pennebaker here. Got your message. Look, I understand your frustration with the lack of progress in this case. I'm including my own investigation in there, of course. Totally appreciate your feelings. I understand the two of you thinking you just want to throw your hands up and say no more . . . you're done, you're out, but—"

Click.

"These damn machines. I was saying I understand how you might want to give up and say I don't want to hear anything anymore, I've been talking to detectives for twelve years and where has it gotten us . . . I get that, I do . . . but that's the exact reason—"

Click.

"Jesus . . . can't these machines give you more time? I was saying that's the exact reason I'm calling. I can't give up on this case. I *refuse.* I went back and looked at everything with fresh eyes. The transcript of the initial investigation for one thing . . ."

The transcript he'd mailed to them. The one I'd read in the middle of the night.

"There's something in there that stood out. That I'd flat-out missed before—"

No shit.

I gave me, myself, and I a pat on the back. Pennebaker might have missed something his first time through the transcript. Not me.

"In the interviews with some of your friends in your neighborhood. I tracked back and *re*-interviewed them. Then did a little more digging after that . . ."

So Pennebaker had spoken with the neighborhood parents. Maybe that's why Mrs. Kelly couldn't stop talking about me after I'd come back. Because she'd been speaking about me before I'd come back. And so had the Mooneys and the Shapiros. Blabbing to Pennebaker. Telling him how that sweet, adorable, normal little six-year-old had really been the little bitch from hell.

He kept trying to get them after that call. At least ten more times—sometimes hanging up without leaving a message, sometimes leaving a long one that needed three different callbacks to finish. He was sometimes friendly and sometimes like a cop who needed his questions answered now, and sometimes both. On the last call he made to them—the last one before his call to me when he asked me to let them know he was sorry and wouldn't be calling them anymore, he'd finally come clean—what exactly it was he wanted answers on.

"Look, I need to ask you a few questions about your son," he'd finished. *"About Ben."*

CLICK.

THIRTY-TWO

I went to the Roosevelt Field Mall with Tabs.

I'd wanted to get out of the house and go somewhere with lots of people around. Because, okay—the house was beginning to feel a little like juvie hall. Minus the ammonia smell and the shitty food and the snitch of a roommate.

They'd leave the hall light on there 24/7. There was no escaping that sickly yellow light, because even with the door shut, it would seep through the cracks like something living.

It said: *I'm watching you.*

I'd woken up in the middle of the night because I'd heard a door close.

My door.

Just as I went and opened it, a light shut off. I couldn't tell whose light. But I caught its visual echo, I'd guess you'd call it, like the imprint of a camera flash that lingers in your eye.

Someone had been in my room while I was sleeping.

Watching me.

I'd never made it back to sleep.

I need to ask you a few questions about your son. About Ben.

Why wasn't Pennebaker asking questions about Jenny? Who liked to push her best friends off monkey bars and her big brother down the stairs? Only I was starting to remember other stuff from Ben's Facebook page.

Like that scar he still had on his leg from when his sister pushed him into a metal tomato stake in the backyard. That time he was in the ocean and remembered being pulled under by a wave. Or was it by *Jenny*? That's who he remembered being there when he made it to the surface after nearly drowning, wasn't it? His little sister. And then there was that time he got lost in the same cave Jenny had easily walked out of. Maybe she'd had a little something to do with the getting-lost part. And there were those crayon pictures he'd seen in her room after a fight—the ones with bloody targets drawn on Ben's forehead. At some point, other kids were being kept away from Jenny for their own protection. But not Ben. He was there. In the ocean. In the cave.

In the house.

"Wanna do a little vogueing?" Tabs said.

We were passing one of those photo booths you put a dollar into and walk out with stupid snapshots of yourself—probably a big deal before you could do exactly the same thing with your iPhone. The booth had probably been there forever and they just hadn't gotten around to junking it.

The whole mall looked about ready for the junk heap today. Old and faded. I hadn't noticed all those stores with RENT ME signs the day Laurie took me here. I must've been too busy loading up on skinny jeans and scoop-neck tops. It was like a pretty girl smiling at you and suddenly you see all these missing teeth.

No missing teeth for Tabs and me. We mugged for the camera

with our faces glommed together, changing our expressions between flashes. It reminded me of that day in the police station with Detective Mary.

Mind if I take your photo, Jenny?

We divided them up when we left the booth—one for you, one for me. Tabs was partial to the shots where we looked like complete idiots, sticking our tongues out, pursing our lips into exaggerated Os, squinting our eyes.

Your eyes . . . they used to crinkle when you laughed . . .

Personally, I liked the ones where we'd forgotten to mug, where maybe the flash had caught us by surprise and it was just the two of us being normal. Tabs and *Jobeth* at the mall.

That's how I felt with her.

Like Jobeth.

The one I might've been if my mother hadn't loved Crystal more.

"What are you going to do now?" she asked me, after we'd devoured two Ben & Jerry's cones and wandered back out to the parking lot searching for Tabs's car.

"I don't know. Nap."

"I mean the rest of your life now?" Tabs said. Cherry Garcia versus Cookie Dough had somehow morphed into a serious life discussion.

"Stay put," I said.

I meant it.

That psych from juvie hall told me I'd been continuously trying to recapture my stolen childhood by stealing other childhoods. Maybe so. But what happens when you *stop* being a child? What then?

This.

Jenny had asked me to save her in a dream. She'd whispered I was the only one who could.

Okay. I'm trying.

I owed it to her, I thought. To that dream Jenny in a striped T-shirt and pink shorts. The one who'd never gotten to grow up. And maybe I owed it to myself.

When I'd found her, fixated on the photo of this smiling blond kid who looked a lot like me, practiced her name in front of a cracked bathroom mirror—it hadn't sounded much different than mine.

Jenny . . . Jobeth . . . Jenny . . . Jobeth. See?

When I'd tried Jenny on for size, she'd fit.

We were members of the same stolen-childhood club. Maybe I was trying to steal hers back. For both of us.

I was getting close to something. To an answer. To what really happened to her on that morning twelve years ago.

I'd been staying for me.

Now I was staying for her.

Even with a knot that was slowly tightening in my stomach. As if I was back in that locked house dreading the sound of heavy footsteps coming up the stairs.

THIRTY-THREE

I forgot to give you a message," I said to Laurie.

"What's that?"

We were eating dinner—KFC instead of home cooked, one of those humongous buckets that come with different kinds of chicken, so everyone in the family can have their favorite—memo to the Colonel, that only works if everyone has different favorites. Me and Jake both reached for the Extra Crispy—and after a brief standoff, I let go and said, *All yours*. KFC was one of those foods that tastes good when you eat it but afterward makes you nauseous. Actually KFC generally made me nauseous even before eating it— because I associated it with the first night in that locked house, when I kept thinking Mom was going to come get me but I got smacked in the face instead.

Jake said, *Sure you don't want it, honey?* and I said, *I'd be happy to sign an affidavit*, then added, *Just kidding*, because he forgot to smile. Then I told Laurie about the message I'd neglected to give her.

"This guy named Joe Pennebaker," I said. "He called to say he was sorry and he wouldn't be calling anymore."

A look passed between them, the kind you probably wouldn't notice if you weren't making noticing your new hobby. Dad had stopped gnawing on his chicken bone. I should've mentioned, Ben was MIA again.

"Oh . . . ," Laurie said. "When was that?"

"Like last week. Sorry. Forgot to tell you."

"No problem." Jake.

"Who is he?" I asked.

"What?" Laurie again.

"Joe Pennebaker. Who is he?"

"Why?"

"Just curious. I mean, what's he so sorry about?"

Silence.

"I wouldn't know, honey," Jake said.

"You wouldn't know what he's sorry about? Or you wouldn't know who he is?"

"He's a policeman. That's who he is."

"You mean a policeman around here?"

"No. He's retired."

"So why was he calling you?"

Silence again. Mom shifted in her seat. Dad wiped the grease off his upper lip.

"He used to work on your case," Laurie said.

"My case?"

"He was the cold case detective put on it."

"Guess he didn't do a very good job," I said.

"Guess he didn't," Jake said.

"Did he have, like . . . a theory?"

"A theory?" Mom said, as if it were a word she wasn't familiar with.

"Yeah. Like what he thought happened to me?"

"Like you said," Jake said, "he didn't do a very good job."

Poker, I thought.

We juvenile delinquents used to play it after lights-out, for commissary food—Twinkies, Yodels, and Suzy Q's. I was good at not showing any emotion—I'd had a bunch of practice—so I pretty much ended up with my own personal commissary.

This was a poker game where we all knew one another's cards.

We were forbidden to put them on the table. House rules.

"I'm trying to remember," I said. "Did me and Ben fight a lot when we were kids?"

Laurie scraped her fork on the plate. It sounded like fingernails across a blackboard.

"I don't know," Laurie said. "The usual, I guess."

"The usual? Is that a lot?"

"Now and then."

"Who started them?"

"What?"

"The fights? Who started them? Ben or me?"

Laurie shrugged. "Who remembers?"

You, I thought.

"How did we fight with each other? Like those Rock 'Em Sock 'Em Robots Ben had?" (Thanks, Facebook page.) "Did we fight like that? Actually start punching each other?"

"I don't know, Jenny. Sometimes you fought. All brothers and sisters do."

"I'm just wondering why Ben doesn't seem to like me." I actually knew why Ben didn't like me—because he didn't think I was me.

But that was one of those cards I couldn't put on the table. That I knew he'd gone and blabbed to them about me. *I know that you know that I know* . . . My head was starting to throb.

"I think Ben just feels . . . pushed aside," Laurie said.

"That's it? That's all?"

"I'm sure he'll come around."

"I'm thinking maybe I did something to him. Back then, I mean. When we were kids."

"Did something?"

"Like maybe I was this little terror. Maybe he remembers that."

Silence again. Then: "You were a perfectly normal sister."

Normal. A sweet, adorable, six-year-old little girl.

"Who always fought with her brother. How did Ben break his arm?"

What's that expression—so quiet you could hear a pin drop? I could hear something else dropping. Almost. The pretense—as heavy as a beach towel you mistakenly leave out in the rain.

"He fell, honey," Jake finally said.

"Just like that? All the way down the stairs?"

"I thought you didn't know how he broke his arm."

"I wasn't sure."

"That's right. Down the stairs. He didn't look where he was going."

Jake looked like he wanted to ask me where I was going. Wanted to tell me to stop going there.

"What happened after I . . . went missing?"

"What do you mean?" Laurie.

"To Ben. You said he flipped out or something? That's the reason he's still in high school, right? You sent him away somewhere."

"Ben was traumatized," Laurie said. "By your disappearance. He needed help."

"Sure. That must've sucked for him. Not as much as it sucked for me. But I get it. Where?"

"Where what?"

"Where did he go? Where did you send Ben?"

"A school."

"A school? Like what *kind* of school? A school for traumatized kids?"

"Sort of."

"You mean like a mental hospital?"

"Like a school."

"What was it called?"

Can we please drop this? Jake's face was saying. *Drop the Hesse and Kline—like interrogation. Drop the playing pretend. Drop the "you're our daughter and we're your parents." Drop it. Stop it. End it.*

"St. Luke's Center," Laurie said.

She looked down at her plate, but when she looked back up, she suddenly looked like Laurie again, complete with that toothpaste smile. Asked me if I might help her clean the dishes? Was I binge-watching anything on Netflix? Did I need a warmer winter jacket?

I felt a sudden chill breeze, but when I glanced at the dining room windows, they were shut tight.

THIRTY-FOUR

My Facebook friend had messaged me again. Lorem.

Just this morning.

It'd been a while.

I'd briefly de-friended him.

Then wondered what if he wasn't some crackpot messing with my head?

And friended him back.

Then de-friended him again seconds later.

Because *of course* he was some crackpot. Who else would it be?

A friend. That's who.

The kind that looks out for you. One I didn't even know I'd had. But a friend.

Welcome back, he messaged.

Gee thanks.

Ask them.

Ask who?

Who do you think? Laurie and Jake . . .

It was the first time he'd mentioned them by name.

Sure. Ask them what?

Are you being careful?

Absolutely. Scout's honor. With a
capital C.

Ask them where they sent their son.

What . . . ?

The year you disappeared. Ask them
where they sent BEN.

So that's what I'd done.

THIRTY-FIVE

Never have I ever rubbed one out in school," Tabs said.

I picked up my vodka and orange juice halfway. Was juvie hall a school? Yes and no. I opted for no and put the drink down. We were in Tabs's room—a pretty nice-size one, meaning her *materialistic* parents must've been doing a good job of keeping up with the Joneses.

"Your turn," Tabs said.

"Never have I ever thrown up during sex."

Tabs took a swig of her greyhound. "Like who hasn't?"

"Me."

If you're trying to get to know new friends, this is a great way to go about it! What better way to get to know someone than by learning about their past experiences, no matter how trivial? Tabs's parents had the Never Have I Ever party-game edition—which provided the statements for you, so you didn't have to think of any yourself. Mostly of the pretty boring variety—like *Never have I ever double-*

dipped and *Never have I ever danced in the rain.* The raciest one was *Never have I ever gone commando.*

We'd decided to go off the reservation and make up our own.

"Your turn," I said.

"Never have I ever peed in my pants."

Mom was walking away from me in the motel parking lot. Turning the corner and then gone. *Dammit, what did you just fucking do . . . ?*

I downed my drink.

Tabs had a poster of Kurt Vile on her wall. Next to one of the Brooklyn Nets. Next to that ubiquitous one of Che Guevara. Her room an odd mix—just like her. We were the only ones in the house—her mom was a tax lawyer and her dad a *professional asshole* who both worked long hours, so we'd taken our sweet time raiding the liquor cabinet.

"Never have I ever used the same sanitary pad twice."

"Eww," Tabs said. "Really?"

"*I* didn't."

"Does anybody?"

Yes. A girl in the first juvie hall, where pads were hard to come by. I stayed quiet.

"Never have I ever sent nudes on Snapchat."

"Never have I ever been with two guys in one day."

"Never have I ever had a foursome."

"Never have I ever been with a friend's dad."

We veered into the sex stuff and stayed there. Maybe it was the vodka.

Confession. I might have been *sexualized* at an early age like that social worker said, but like most things with Jobeth, I'd been playing pretend. Starting way back then. Pretend you like it. Pretend you're somewhere else—back under the Billy Goats Gruff bridge in that kids' playground. Or out rowboating on Shanshaw Lake. Or circling Pluto.

Anywhere but in that house. In a bedroom with shit-colored water stains on the wall.

Sex was my personal bartering system. If I did it without trying to run out the front door, or down to the basement, quietly agreed to lie there without their having to strap me to the bed, I got to stay out of that pitch-black pantry. Thanks, Mom and Dad.

If I flashed Mr. Charnow in the shower, I got to live in the house a little longer. Or I would've, if his wife hadn't caught me and sent me straight to juvie hall. On the street, sex sometimes got me fed and clothed and out of the rain. It was something I used when I had to—IN CASE OF EMERGENCY BREAK HERE.

My head was starting to swim. More like a bad dog paddle, in clear danger of going under. I'd never been much of a drinker or a huge druggie—though I'd tried pretty much every one in the book and some that weren't. I had this fear of losing control—probably because I'd lost every single bit of it at the age of six. Couple that with one more fear. Getting kicked to the curb—it was hard to stay hypervigilant on eighty-proof vodka.

Things seemed safe with Tabs, though, safe enough to blow through two bottles of her parents' best.

"Never have I ever mixed coke and X." Tabs's turn.

I took a drink.

Tabs's text had suddenly popped up on my iPhone—courtesy of Laurie and the new Verizon Family Plan. Wanna hang?

I'd sent her back a thumbs-up emoji.

She gave me a house tour for laughs, making fun of the furnishings—like *My parents saw this in Martha Stewart's house in some magazine so of course they had to run out and buy it.* And *This is my parents' idea of humor*—pointing to the TIPS ACCEPTED sign above the liquor cabinet.

I provided a laugh track, but I actually thought the house was pretty impressive. Maybe because the ones I grew up in featured Naugahyde couches, dirty shag carpeting, and pitch-black pantries where you had to bang on the door to be let out.

After we'd tapped the liquor cabinet, we scoured the party-game drawer—Clue, Trivial Pursuit, Boggle.

Never have I ever played Never Have I Ever, Tabs had said.

"Whose turn?" Tabs, starting to slur her words.

"I forget," I said.

Tabs giggled. "Never have I ever been so drunken."

"That's not a word."

"What do you mean? Tabs got good and drunken."

"Good and drunk."

"Who are you, Alex Trebek?"

"I spent a lot of time in libraries."

"Why?"

"Somewhere to go where they wouldn't kick me out."

Tabs was lolling on the carpet in her skinny jeans and Alice Cooper T-shirt. "Jesus . . . the room's actually spinning," she said. "Like stop the merry-go-round, I want to get off."

"Want to stop playing?" I asked.

"No. Never have I ever wanted to stop playing."

"Okay. So, you go."

"Little old me?"

"Yeah."

"Okay, let's see. I got one. Never have I ever pretended to be someone I wasn't."

I almost reached for my drink.

"You sure?" Tabs asked. "Like you're absolutely positive about that?"

My heart was beating faster.

"Yes."

"Like you never, ever pretended to be someone you weren't?"

"No."

"Even when you were like six? You never pretended to be Ariel or Dora the Explorer? Really?"

"Sure. I guess."

"*Buzz*. If you're caught lying, you have to take two drinks. When I press the buzzer, you have to get more buzzed."

"Huh?" The game was starting to annoy me.

"Them's the rules."

"Okay. Fine." I took two swallows—two small licks of flame.

"What about when you weren't six?"

"What?"

"When you got older. You never pretended to be someone you weren't then?"

"I said no."

"I know what you *said* . . ."

"I want to stop playing. This game sucks."

"Never have I ever been a party pooper. Go ahead, you've got to take a drink. Because you're pooping on this party."

"I'm going home." I got up—the room was spinning crazily.

"Never have I ever pretended to be a kidnapped girl who came home," Tabs said.

And things went dark.

A cold compress.

When I was four or five, during one of my mom's "I'm getting straight" periods—which generally lasted only as long as my periods did later on—I'd come down with the flu. *Your forehead feels like I could fry an egg on it,* my mom said when she rested her hand on it, but her hand itself felt like cool water, like sticking your head in a playground fountain in the middle of August.

It felt like love. The closest thing to it, anyway. After that, I used to pretend to be sick in the hope I could get her to rest her hand on my head again.

Get up, you're fine, she'd say, having no patience for me in the middle of the heebie-jeebies or when she was spacing out on the couch with the crystal pipe practically falling out of her hand.

There was a cold compress on my head.

Tabs's hand was attached to it.

I was on the floor.

"Shit," Tabs said. "Sorry. Did I do that to you? You scared the living shit out of me."

I shook my head.

"Too much vodka."

"Really? Really and truly? It wasn't what I said to you?"

I shook my head again. My throat felt like sandpaper. I waited for the room to come into focus. I needed my brain to do that right now.

"How did you know?"

Tabs sighed. "I did a search. There's a face recognition app you can run with someone's picture—I used one of the pics we took at the mall. The app hits on anything similar. You know, sometimes it fucks up. Sometimes . . . bingo."

"Why?"

"Why what?"

"Why'd you run a search?"

"I don't know. A vibe. I'm sorry."

"It's fine."

"No, it's not. I . . . like you. I mean, we're friends. I'm an ass-hole."

"What picture came up?"

Had Becky put that picture online—the one of us sitting on the porch? Laurie had sent her packing with that bullshit DNA story—but maybe Becky had seen right through it. Maybe she'd gone home and posted my picture on some online site, like tacking a wanted poster on the post office wall.

No.

"It was from over two years ago. This family called the Greers? Some local news site."

The Greers. The ones who'd left the night-light burning in their daughter's room for more than ten years hoping she'd come back one day. Until she had. Kind of.

"I mean, you were younger," Tabs said. "But the more I stared at it, the more I realized it was you. And then there were the circum-stances . . . I mean, it'd be a super-colossal kind of coincidence that the app would find a hit with another girl who'd been kidnapped and made it home, right?"

I closed my eyes.

"What are you going to do?"

"What do you mean?"

"Give me a head start, okay? A day. That's all I'm asking. A day to clear out and then you can tell whoever you want."

"Why would I tell someone?"

"Because . . . 'cause . . . I'm a fucking imposter."

"So?"

"So when people find out about me, they usually don't keep it to themselves."

"I'm not people."

"So you're not going to tell anybody?"

"Why the fuck would I? I told you about hacking into the NRA, right? Are you telling anyone?"

"That's different."

"Why?"

"I don't know. It just is. I'm pretending to be someone's kidnapped kid."

"I'm pretending to be a law-abiding citizen. See, we're even."

I looked at her. At my first real what . . . confidante . . . coconspirator . . . friend?

I'd go with friend.

Other than the one on Facebook, that is.

Are you being careful?

"Don't you even want to know how it started? How many times? Why the fuck I do it?"

"Of course. Do I appear to you to be an unintellectually curious dullard? Why . . . you feel like telling me?"

"Yeah," I said. "Yeah, I do."

THIRTY-SIX

"oly fuck," Tabs said.

You ever look over at someone watching a horror movie with you? The way they try to look but not look at the same time?

This wasn't a movie. Not rotten tomatoes. Rotten potatoes. Rotten story. Rotten life. Rotten me.

It poured out like vomit.

I couldn't stop. I couldn't come up for air.

We're going to meet Mommy's friend.

Define *friend,* Mom.

Define taking your six-year-old to a motel parking lot and selling her.

Put a name to it. Say what you did.

Meet my new mom and dad, Tabs. Yours are soulless dullards. Mine were soulless baby fuckers.

I know, your lips are zipped. Great. Mine were sewn together with black thread. Stitch one, slip two.

Don't look away, Tabs. Do not. I'm the one who gets to do that. To look away. To bury it so deep it can't hurt anymore. Who gets to look in the mirror and see Karen Greer. Alexa Kornbluth. Terri Charnow. Sarah Ludlow. Jenny Kristal. Anyone but me.

You asked. You did.

"I'm sorry," Tabs said when I'd finished purging.

"About what?"

"Everything. What happened to you. It's fucking horrible."

"Some people think I am. Fucking horrible. I mean, when they find out I'm not their long-lost child."

"I can see how they might get a little upset about that."

"I mean, it's different at first. Before they find out."

"Define *different*."

"Like I just made their decade. Like I've just given them their entire lives back."

Why are you crying, Becky? It's all right . . .

That's just it. It is all right . . . finally . . .

"Is it like that now? Your new parents—they don't suspect anything? They think you're Jenny?"

I hesitated. Once a bunch of us gangstas had snuck into a water park shut down for the winter, all of us high on X, and I'd strolled out onto the top diving board—the kind hot-shit divers do backflips from in the Summer Olympics. The drained pool said, *Jump, Jobeth, jump.* I'd thought long and hard about it.

Jump, Jobeth . . . jump . . .

"I think they want me to think they think I'm Jenny."

"Huh? Why would they want you to think they think you're their daughter if they *don't* think you're their daughter? Jesus, Jo . . . Should I start calling you that now? . . . My head hurts just saying that."

Good question.

How good a hacker are you, really?" I asked Tabs.

This was later on, after we'd both fallen asleep from (a) the two bottles of primo vodka and (b) plain emotional exhaustion, then woken up blurry-eyed and disoriented—at least I had, like waking up on my first morning in whichever new house I'd laid claim to, and still believing it was the one I'd just been evicted from.

Tabs stared at me with one eye open and said, "I need a sheep-dog."

"What?"

"Hair of the dog. Sheepdogs are the hairiest."

I got up and took a pee. Tabs stumbled into the bathroom as I was finishing up and filled the vodka bottles with water. I heard her replacing them in the downstairs cabinet.

"They like to look at them more than drink them," she said when she made it back upstairs.

Which is when I asked for that hacker self-evaluation.

Here's my second confession of the day—just in case you're wondering why I'd told Tabs everything. It wasn't just because she'd figured out who I really was—or more to the point, wasn't. Or because I needed a good purging—I did, but no.

Call it a tactical decision. Or maybe just a massive leap of faith.

I was on a mission, remember?

We're friends . . .

Okay. A friend in need is a friend indeed.

"Where do you rank? Say, one to ten . . . ?" I asked her.

"Can't put a number to it," Tabs replied.

Che was gazing at me with that tilted black beret on his head as if he wanted me to sign up for the revolution.

"Try. Come on . . . one to ten?"

"Shit . . . eight."

"Okay."

"And three-quarters."

"Great."

"Make that seven-eighths. Eight and seven-eighths. This guy I know . . . he hacked into US Central Command. Not shitting you. He's a nine, easy."

"Eight and seven-eighths—that's good enough."

"Good enough for what?"

"Ever hack into a school?"

"A school?"

"Or a hospital?"

"Which one?"

"A school-hospital. More hospital, I think. Ever hack into one of those?"

THIRTY-SEVEN

Ben's middle name was Horace. Benjamin Horace Kristal. Good thing I remembered that because *Ben Kristal* turned up zilch. And we still didn't hit pay dirt until we typed in *Benjamin*. Things must've been pretty formal at the St. Luke's Center.

We'd gone to the Bellmore library—a new addition to Tabs's circuit. The woman librarian looked half-dead but sprang to life when we walked in—probably because she wasn't used to anyone under eighty being there. She stared at us like specimens in a zoo, until we made it past the thriller section to the completely empty bank of computers.

"You know Nancy Drew was my first girl crush," Tabs whispered.

Tabs used this thing called BackBox—*a hacker's best friend*—plugging a flash drive into the USB port.

"It should get me into the hospital system," she said. "Don't imagine they're worrying a whole lot about cyberpunks."

I pulled my chair up behind her.

Tabs's fingers flew across the keys—as if they knew where they were going before she did. Numbers and letters accumulated on the screen like bugs on the windshield of a dangerously speeding car.

"What do they mean?" I whispered.

"Entrance this way."

She wasn't bullshitting.

In less than ten minutes we were looking at a page with ST. LUKE'S CENTER PROVIDER PORTAL splashed at the top. She stopped typing, turned around, raised a needed-to-be-plucked eyebrow.

"*Now* what?" she asked.

"Patient records, I guess. We're looking for 2007–2008."

She punched at the keyboard a few times. Frowned.

"It's a little like being in a dark cave," she said. "You can go this way or that way and you don't really know until you go ahead and try it. You can get lost just like that."

Like Ben had. I pictured the seven-year-old Benjamin Horace Kristal wending his way through Tom Sawyer's cave. And then suddenly having no idea where he was—clawing at the blackness with both hands, surrounded by ghost chatter. Is this what it was like for my sister? Ben later wrote on his memorial page. Being lost in a deep, dark hole, but never being found . . . ?

It was taking Tabs a while to navigate through the dead ends. The librarian kept making the rounds like a sentry—probably checking to see if we were accessing porn.

Tabs looked up and flashed the librarian an innocent-looking smile—like *Do you think little ole me would ever do anything even semi-unlawful?*

Guess not. The librarian creaked on her way—her heavy orthopedic-looking shoes squeaking with each step, which would seem like a definite no-no in a library, but maybe not, since it had basically turned into a senior center.

"Here we go . . . ," Tabs whispered. "User list . . . word list . . . hack-me subdirectory . . ."

She was talking to herself now. Lost in the task at hand. Fingers dancing, eyes zigzagging up and down the screen. Sighing a lot. That too. "It's password protected," she muttered.

"What's that?" I asked her, pointing to words positioned directly beneath *St. Luke's Center* that were in a language I didn't recognize.

Sinite parvulos venire ad me et nolite eos vetare . . .

"Latin," Tabs said. "I was stupid enough to take it junior year. *Suffer the little children . . . and . . . and . . . forbid them not to come to me.* I mean, this *is* a Catholic hospital, right?"

Latin, okay, sure. Of which I knew one word—the one imprinted on my left hip in florid red ink: *Vidi.* I saw.

And suddenly I did.

That it just might be possible I knew *two* Latin words.

Another word besides *Vidi* that suspiciously looked and sounded a lot like those other words on the screen.

"What if it's in *Latin*?"

"*What?*"

"The password." I told her to try that word—the one that had just come to me.

"Huh?" Tabs shrugged, then turned and attacked the keyboard again. Ten seconds later, she cackled out loud. Too loud. The librarian shot us a dirty look.

"When I said I wanted to take Latin, my dad said, 'What the fuck is that good for? You planning on dating Marcus Aurelius?'"

"Were you?" Her head was blocking the screen.

"I was actually more into Sappho. Guess we just found out what

243

Latin's good for. The password for patient records. The word you gave me—it's Latin for *therapy*. That's it. It was that fucking simple. Okay, *how'd* you know that?"

I didn't answer her.

I was too busy staring at the screen. At the password that had just unlocked St. Luke's patient records.

L-O-R-E-M.

THIRTY-EIGHT

Okay, Facebook friend number 1,371. (Which wasn't a boy's name or a girl's name but, surprise, surprise, a password name.)

I'm here.

My stomach wasn't cooperating—I needed an airsick bag.

I felt like there was something in there I didn't want to see. Something I shouldn't be seeing. I'd been locked up twice for breaking and entering—breaking hearts, entering families hanging on by their fingernails—but this was the real deal. Like we'd smashed through a basement window at St. Luke's—cleared the sticky cobwebs off our faces, landed softly on a cold cement floor, then directed a flashlight onto the rusty file cabinets, where we ticked off the alphabetically listed names down to the *K*s.

Benjamin Horace Kristal.

Right you are, Tabs, St. Luke's was a Catholic hospital. That also happened to be a Catholic school (*like a school for traumatized kids?*). Or a Catholic school that was also a Catholic hospital.

Emphasis on *Catholic*—most of the doctors and teachers had

Father in front of their last names. Too bad for Ben none of those fathers were Jake. While the teachers were feeding the kiddies ABCs, the doctors were feeding them Depakote, Thorazine, and lithium—"Heavy-duty shit," Tabs whispered—the dosage was listed right there in Ben's file. Maybe I'd had it better than I'd thought in juvie hall—mystery meats, dykey roommates (sorry, Tabs), pissed-off social workers, and the rest.

Why a Catholic institution? The Kristals didn't strike me as religious—Laurie seemed to worship tanning beds more than Jesus.

Maybe not back then.

When your daughter's just been kidnapped, you probably want to hedge your bets. Grab some Muslim prayer beads, stick on a skullcap, pray to the Virgin Mary. Whatever it takes. I'd noticed a King James Bible in their bookcase that looked like it hadn't been opened in years, when it must've become clear this whole prayer thing wasn't working.

Ben's therapist was Father Krakow.

"Priests can be psychs?" Tabs whispered. "Talk about multitasking."

Krakow kept meticulous word-for-word records, starting from when a traumatized eight-year-old landed on his doorstep. As I began reading—as we *both* did—it was as if everything disappeared: the computer screen, the rows of tables, the library—the years.

SUBJECT: BENJAMIN HORACE KRISTAL.

I suddenly shivered—my whole body doing a kind of electric slide.

"Somebody walk over your grave?" Tabs asked.

"No," I said. "Over Jenny's."

THIRTY-NINE

SUBJECT: BENJAMIN HORACE KRISTAL.

BACKGROUND.

Interviews conducted with both parents. Patient's younger sister (Jenny age 6) disappeared outside the family home. Apparent abduction. She's still missing—no progress has been made by the police. Laurie Kristal (patient's mother) is exhibiting severe emotional distress and psychodynamic guilt. She states she allowed her daughter to walk to a neighbor's house by herself. "God will never forgive me." Jake Kristal (patient's father) shows symptoms of repression, withdrawal, self-isolation. Emotional fraying clearly evident between spouses.

Laurie Kristal relates that patient has been *disruptive* in school. Nonverbal in family home. Emotionally unresponsive. Frequent physical outbursts.

Incident: Parents discovered daughter's bed torn apart, with the mattress turned over and several of the wooden slats smashed. Some of the pillows had been ripped. Patient denied doing it.

Incident: Patient covered himself in red paint at school. Has been violent in schoolyard with other children—school board is considering expulsion. Patient offered no explanation for these behaviors.

Incident: Mother (Laurie) discovered the patient had neatly laid out his missing sister's clothes across his bed. She states this is the way *she* used to do it for her daughter every morning before school. Mother states the clothing was different color, but similar to the kind Jenny wore the day she was abducted. Father (Jake) disagrees. "Just some clothes he found in the hamper." (Dissociative Identity Disorder?)

Laurie states the patient exhibits almost no recall of the morning his sister was abducted—it's as if his memory of that day has "been erased." Patient is suffering a recurrent nightmare: being locked in a closet with poisonous snakes with the closet set on fire. Patient is terrified by this very specific and recurrent dream. He's resisted sleeping due to his fear of having to repeatedly undergo this clearly traumatic nightmare.

FIRST SESSION.

Benjamin exhibits markedly insular posture. Appears sleep deprived (nightmares). Notably underweight—mother (Laurie) says patient is not eating well since sister's abduction. Shows little eye contact. Nonverbal. Unresponsive.

Insight-oriented play therapy instituted.

Patient piles blocks up, then repeatedly knocks them down. Robotic motions. Monotone responses to questions. What are you building, Ben? Nothing. Or: Don't know. Why are you knocking the blocks down, Ben? I want to.

When offered animal play figures, he shows no interest. Noticeable aversion to the horse figures. Refuses to even touch them. (Follow-up) Don't you like horses, Ben? No. Why don't you like horses, Ben? (Shrugs) Didn't your sister like horses, Ben? (Silence)

Drawing is aggressive. Breaks two crayons. (Relaxation techniques?) His picture is indistinct—black swirls. What's that a picture of, Ben? Jenny's room. Why did you draw your sister's room? (Shrugs) Is your sister's room black, Ben? No. (Patient tears up the picture.) Why did you destroy such a nice picture, Ben? (Patient unresponsive.)

During puzzle play, patient chose family dinner scene. Patient noticeably leaves sister/daughter out of puzzle. Why did you leave out the sister, Ben? She's not there. Where is she, Ben? In school. Why is she in school when her brother's home? She's swimming up at the lake. Without her family? She went on a playdate.

What are you girls looking at?"

The librarian had walked into the room where I was sitting with Father Krakow and eight-year-old Ben.

What was *she* doing here?

Looking over our shoulders. It was as if I'd suddenly been sucked back through a time portal, from that room in the St. Luke's Center where a therapist/priest was wondering what's up with this screwed-up eight-year-old—not that different from the screwed-up twenty-year-old who enjoyed posting half-page sentences on Facebook—and I was back in the present day. Where a flash drive was noticeably sticking out of the USB port of the library's computer.

"School research," Tabs said, her hand strategically curled around it.

The librarian hesitated—trying to peek past our bodies.

"Okay."

"We're cramming for a test," she added. "A humongous one."

The librarian nodded as if she could relate to humongous tests, even though the last one she might've taken would've been with a quill pen.

She shuffled off.

"Whew," Tabs said, fake-wiping the sweat off her forehead.

"Maybe we should shut it down," I said.

I was hoping she'd say, *Good idea,* pull that little black drive out of the USB, and then the both of us would bounce. It was that feeling again—that I was going to see something I wasn't meant to. That I was being bad and there was going to be hell to pay. I was going to be put back into the punishment room and never, ever let out.

"Don't be a pussy," Tabs said. "She's blind as a bat. Say . . . why are we looking up Ben anyway?"

Because in Pennebaker's last message, he'd said *I have questions about your son. About Ben.* Because in a house that'd been warm and welcoming before warm and welcoming started to turn creepy, Ben was the cold spot. Because my faceless Facebook friend had told me to find out where Laurie and Jake had committed him twelve years ago.

Ask them where they sent their son.

Because.

"I need to know why everyone's playing pretend. To understand what happened back then. I think it's got to do with him."

"Ben? He was eight."

"The day I showed up—that night—he went past my door and he laughed. Like, *I know you're not who you're saying you are. I know you're not Jenny.*"

"So? You're not Jenny."

"How did he know that? I mean for sure? That was before I fucked up and forgot to log out of his memorial page. How did he know that first day? Why was he so sure?"

"I repeat. You're *not* his sister. And she'd been like *dead* for twelve years. It must've seemed impossible."

"He knew."

Ben's second session was even more unproductive than the first.

The patient was uncommunicative, unresponsive, uncooperative. One big *un*. Ben apparently sat with his hands in his lap staring out the window.

Don't you like it here, Ben?

(No response)

Wouldn't you like to play with something, Ben?

(No response)

What would you like to do, Ben?

(No response)

The patient was reacting to *exterior displacement,* according to Krakow's notes—a fancy way of saying he'd been dumped in a Catholic hospital for wacko kids and left there. The ward nurse noted signs of agitation, emotional distress, and possible night sweats. I could relate. I myself had tried screaming that first morning when I woke up in a strange bed. I had the lip scars to prove it.

Ben had it a lot easier. He just had to hang with an understanding therapist who kept begging him to play with blocks.

(Need to promote an empathetic, inquisitive, trusting, and thera-peutic alliance with patient.)

The patient wasn't jonesing for alliances.

Then or now. I remembered him marooned on that orange love seat on my first night home.

Okay, Ben, we can just sit here and not talk if that's what you'd like. That's perfectly okay. We can just sit here quietly together. Sound good?

It must've sounded good enough, because that's what Ben did.

No further communication with patient today, Krakow wrote at the end of the session.

There were a lot more where that came from.

A bunch of sessions where nothing much happened except Father Krakow asking questions and Ben not answering them. A lot of them about that dream of his—locked in a burning closet with a bunch of snakes. Ben kept up his mute act—he wasn't talking.

By this time, Krakow had ventured a diagnosis—Ben was suffering from childhood traumatic grief.

Avoidance of talking about the deceased (or missing) person, or doing things associated with that person (i.e., refusal to touch the horse figures). Disruption of learning (i.e., acting out in class—paint incident). Numbing (i.e., noncommunication and withdrawal). In-creased arousal (i.e., destruction of bed, fighting with classmates). Nightmares (specific and recurrent).

He ticked them off like one of those checklists Karen Greer's mom used to put together before family outings. Snacks. Tissues. Bug repellent. Fruit juice. Handi Wipes. Except we Greers were generally going somewhere fun like the Oky-Doky Amusement

Park, which had a ten-story water slide, while Ben was basically going off the deep end.

EMDR...?

Krakow wrote in capital letters. Then typed it again farther down, this time leaving out the question mark.

I googled it.

"Eye movement desensitization and reprocessing."

"Well, that clears it up," Tabs whispered.

"A psychotherapy treatment that facilitates the accessing and processing of traumatic memories to bring to an adaptive resolution. With successful EMDR therapy, affective distress is relieved, negative beliefs are reformulated, and psychological arousal is reduced. During EMDR therapy, the patient attends to emotionally disturbing material in brief sequential doses while simultaneously focusing on an external stimulus—the most commonly used one being therapist-directed lateral eye movements."

"Sorry," Tabs said, "not fluent in Greek."

No, just Latin.

"I think it's a kind of hypnosis," I whispered. "A way to take Ben back."

"*Back* . . . to what?"

"To that emotionally disturbing material. To what happened."

FORTY

This is the way I pictured it.

Noncommunicative Ben shuffling into Father Krakow's office with his eyes on the floor and his mind who knows where, plopping himself down on a kid's chair. Or maybe it wasn't a kid's chair—it was a perfectly normal-size chair that swallowed up undernourished Ben. The kind of hardwood chair that would make my ass start throbbing in the psych's office at juvie hall. Fifteen minutes was about all I could take—and maybe that was the point. Fast-food therapy depended on getting us in and out fast.

So, there's Ben.

And there's Father Krakow.

I googled him to see if there was a photo, but the only Dr. or Father Krakow in New York with a photo was a dentist on Madison Avenue who specialized in implants. I improvised. Made Krakow a male version of Becky—who when she wasn't chasing me down the block or trying to barge up the stairs had a sweet and sympathetic face.

Father Krakow told Ben: We're going to try a little game, Ben.

What kind of game?

A memory game.

(No response)

I know you don't remember a lot of what happened when your sister disappeared, Ben.

(No response)

Would you like to play this game so we can remember?

(Patient shakes head no)

See, Ben, I think the reason you don't remember is because your mind is trying very hard not to.

(No response)

Our minds—I know this might be hard for you to understand, but I'll try to explain it to you. Our minds are our "friends" most of the time. So, if there's a bad memory, something that upsets us, that makes us sad, our mind says I'll just go ahead and block that memory, so it won't make us sad or anxious or angry anymore. Understand, Ben?

(No response)

But here's the thing. Sometimes when we sleep, our mind, well . . . it lets down its guard a little bit. Because it's hard keeping those unpleasant memories locked up like that. Like trying to hold your breath underwater. So it lets things out in dreams— bad dreams sometimes. I know you've been having the same bad dream for a while, and I know you haven't been sleeping well because of it—you're afraid you're going to have that nightmare again. And I know you've been a little sad and a little angry and you've done some things in school and in your house to maybe let your teachers and parents know that. And maybe you don't really know why you're so unhappy and so sad and so angry, and that's why you're here, Ben. To help us find out. To help you be happier. To be Ben again. Can you understand that? At least, a little?

(No response)

That's why I want to try this memory game, Ben. To see if we can't find out what's upsetting you so much. I know maybe that's a little scary for you, Ben. I understand that. Have you ever been really sick and needed to go to the doctor for a shot?

(Patient nods yes)

I know shots, well, they aren't a lot of fun. They're scary, and sometimes they even hurt a little, and who wants that? But try to remember how that shot made you feel afterward. How it made your fever go away, and your throat stop hurting, and in no time at all, you were better? Do you remember that, Ben?

(Patient nods yes)

Okay. Well, this is a little like that. Like getting a shot. It can be scary looking at things our minds don't want us to. It can even hurt a little. But after a while, we start feeling better. We're not sick anymore. Doesn't that sound like something you'd want, Ben? To not be sick anymore? You're going to forget a lot of what you say to me during this memory game—I know, forgetting sounds kind of funny for a memory game—but just remembering it here—in this office—will start to make you feel a whole lot better. I promise. Sound good?

(Patient nods yes)

Okay, then. Here's how we play the game. It's called Follow My Fingers. I'm going to move my fingers back and forth in front of your face like this, Ben. And you—you just follow them with your eyes—that's good, great, just like that. See, that's all you have to do. Just keep following my fingers. That's the whole game. Think you can keep doing that, Ben?

(Patient nods)

Great. And while I'm moving my fingers back and forth—good, that's right, keep following them—I'm going to ask you to remember that dream you keep having. We're going to start there. Okay? And when you remember it, Ben, you're going to see it just like you saw it while you were dreaming. As if you're asleep and dreaming it all over again. And you're going to feel just what you felt then. As if it's happening right now, okay?

FORTY-ONE

BENJAMIN KRISTAL. FIRST EMDR SESSION.

It's dark.

Like up at the lake when it's night and there's no streetlights or flashlights or nothing.

But I'm not OUTSIDE.

I can tell.

I'm inside someplace.

There are old clothes in here. I can feel them against my face—like they're covering me. It smells really bad.

Like that stuff Mom rubs on my chest when I get a cold.

Like . . . MOTHBALLS.

Am I in the basement CLOSET? There's mothballs in there and old clothes and stuff?

I've got to get out of here. (mewling noises)

I'm scared.

When I try to open the door, there's NO knob. Like nothing's there.

I can't push it open either.

I'm locked in.

"LET ME OUT!"

I'm screaming for someone to open the door and get me out of here but no words come out. It's like I can't SPEAK.

I hear something moving.

Back in the clothing.

I can't see what it is. But I know it's there. I KNOW. I can hear it crawling around in there.

"LET ME OUT! PLEASE . . ." (mewling noises)

I'm screaming my head off—I am—but there's STILL no sound. Just quiet. Except for what's in the clothing. Something.

And then I SEE it.

A SNAKE.

Its big head slithers out of the clothing. It's staring at me.

Its eyes—they're yellow and glowing. It has this long black tongue it keeps flicking in and out at me.

I'm BANGING on the door.

"PLEASE, MOMMY. DADDY. PLEASE. LET ME OUT. PLEASE . . ."

The snake—it's crawling out of the clothes. It's gigantic—like the kind in South America that lives in rivers and can swallow a cow. It drops to the floor of the closet. It begins crawling to me. Its mouth is opening . . . I can see these two huge fangs.

"PLEASE . . . NO . . ."

I hear OTHER sounds now. MORE snakes. Back there in the clothing. Slithering around in there.

"I'M SCARED . . . HELP ME . . . PLEASE . . ."

The snake is wrapping itself around me. Around my neck.

Squeezing. It's cold and slimy and its mouth is wide open and I know it's going to eat me. It's going to swallow me all up.

I'm choking. I can't breathe.

The other snakes. They're crawling out of the clothes. Dropping to the floor of the closet. Coming at me.

I can't BREATHE . . . I CAN'T . . . I . . .

There's this other sound. It sounds like . . .

Someone lighting a MATCH.

I can smell smoke.

The snake's EYES are on fire.

The closet—it's burning.

It's lit on FIRE.

"PUT IT OUT! . . . PLEASE PUT IT OUT . . ." (screams)

Flames are all around me. Burning the snakes up.

Burning ME up.

"It HURTS. It HURTS. HELP . . ."

FORTY-TWO

I can hear him in the house. Ben.

He's in his bedroom playing something on his iPhone. A spooky riff of electric organ. One of those weird electronica groups.

When we closed our criminal hacking operation down, Tabs slipping the flash drive back into her pocket, the two of us strolling back down past the clueless librarian and out the door, we followed the rules for once and said nothing.

Outside, where the sharp chill seemed to squeeze all the air out of me, Tabs said, "That was some fucked-up dream."

There was something else fucked-up: The files seemed to stop there, right after that session. We'd had to sit through all the boring ones where pretty much nothing happened, then after Krakow finally puts Ben under with that hypnosis stuff and things get interesting—nothing. A brick wall.

"I have crazy nightmares too," I said softly. Like I wanted Tabs to hear me and didn't.

Ben's dream had hit a nerve.

The locked closet.

Feeling trapped in a closet is a symbolic manifestation of the patient's powerlessness, Krakow had written. *His sister is missing, his family in crisis and his trauma unacknowledged. He is, in a sense, trapped in a living nightmare, which manifests itself as a sleeping one. Fire is almost always a representation of great anger—anger at his perceived powerlessness. This anger has previously sought its expression in fighting with classmates, destroying his sister's bed, and now in this very specific and recurrent nightmare.*

"Why would the files just stop like that?" I asked. "He said they were going to *start* with Ben's dream. Where's the rest?"

"Fuck yeah—I want my money back. It's like yanking Netflix episodes midstream."

We stood for a minute blowing on our hands, our breaths commingling in a single wet cloud, as if we were wordlessly forming a secret pact. A secret pact about secrets.

Keeping them and solving them.

When I opened the door to the basement, I was hit with a musty belowground smell, the kind of stink I associate with dead things.

I descended the steps in slow motion. The light at the top of the stairs was thin and piss-colored, no match for the fathomless black of the basement.

When I made it off the bottom step, something smacked me in the face. A cobweb? Or worse . . . a real *spider*web? Ben might hate snakes—for me it's spiders. If you've ever seen a close-up of a spider's crazy eyes, you'd understand—like looking in a kaleidoscope where one picture morphs into eight.

I'd run into a light cord—it was swinging back and forth like a metronome.

I pulled on it.

The basement was half-finished.

The floor was faded linoleum, but the walls were gray pock-marked concrete. If it was heated down here, it was hard to tell. I could see my own breath.

Along with other things.

It looked like a garage sale with no customers. For good reason— like *who'd buy this stuff?* A collapsed Ping-Pong table. Two deflated footballs sitting on top of a torn volleyball net. Mildewed boxes piled high with household crap. Mounds of old clothing.

A big rust-colored boiler emitted deep belching sounds, and a table off in the corner was littered with tools—screwdrivers, hammers, and pliers that seemed to have been untouched in years— like some kind of museum exhibit: SUBURBAN DAD'S WORK TABLE, CIRCA 2000.

There was a basement closet to the right of the boiler.

The one Ben was locked in, in his nightmare.

My legs refused to go there. *Walk over to that closet,* I commanded, *chop-chop,* but they were suddenly on strike.

It was Mr. Hammered's fault.

He was lying down on the job again. Ignoring my explicit instructions and letting two psychopaths back onto the premises.

They used to make me walk into the closet myself.

Stuffing their faces with Domino's pizza. Laughing at some stupid sitcom on the kitchen TV.

You know where to go . . .

A million times worse than them dragging me there—kicking, screaming, crying, pleading . . . *No, please, no, Mother, no*—which is what used to happen before I learned that making them madder meant I'd be locked in longer.

You know where to go . . .

Into a closet whose door would always lock shut behind me— sometimes not right away, not till they'd taken their sweet time polishing off a slice, or until their show ended. Standing there waiting for that click of the lock and stupidly praying it wouldn't happen. That I wouldn't end up trapped in a place so dark I couldn't see my own hands clawing at the door. Maybe that's why I can't sleep much anymore—because being covered in darkness is being trapped in a closet I can never get the fuck out of.

You know those World War II photos that are always turning up on TV? Grainy black-and-white shots of Nazis forcing Jews to dig their own graves—the ones they'd soon be lined up and machine-gunned into. *Those* awful photos show up on TV too. But it's the ones taken before all those bodies lay naked and bullet riddled that made me nauseous. The Nazis exerting power that was total, complete, *casual*—shots of them grabbing smokes and cracking smiles while doomed Jews shoveled away in the background.

You know where to go . . .

Why use force when you can use fear?

I felt it now—it refused to go away. Just got stuffed in a basement smelling of dead things—and sometimes, no matter how hard you tried, you still had to walk down the stairs and face it.

The closet seemed five miles away.

Like I'd need to be some kind of power walker to get there— those bags of bones you see every four years in the Olympics who move like herky-jerky marionettes on speed.

Then I thought: This is Ben and Jenny's closet. Not yours.

There are no sacks of moldy potatoes sitting in it. No Jobeth in there either.

And suddenly, I could move.

But when I opened the closet door, I found myself searching for scratch marks. The ones caused by a little girl's fingernails. The ones I'd counted . . . *forty-one, forty-two, forty-three* . . . before I'd finally taken off for good.

They belonged to a different closet door.

In a different house. Belonging to a different girl.

None here.

The sickly fluorescent lighting only penetrated so far—I could make out the edges of bunched hung clothing, but I couldn't tell what kind. The closet reeked of old person's smell.

I flicked on the flashlight app on my phone.

I didn't know why I'd walked down here or what I was looking for. Dreamscapes, I guess.

Poisonous snakes?

An eight-year-old Ben huddled against the door?

No, Ben was upstairs listening to music.

I think I just wanted to see the closet of Ben's nightmare with my own two eyes. His nightmare. And mine.

Consider it anticlimactic.

It was a basement closet filled with closet stuff.

The kind of musty-smelling crap—old raincoats, faded blouses, a Boy Scout uniform (Ben's?) that wouldn't have made it into the Goodwill bins Mother and Father dressed me from—if you were willing to believe the just-resurfaced Jenny, that is, which Hesse and Kline weren't.

Not anymore.

We need answers and sooner or later we're going to get them.

Yeah, me too.

There was an orphaned black glove on the floor. A ripped scarf. An old leather belt coiled up in the corner.

That's all.

Except for . . . those.

Those . . . what?

I didn't know. I had to kneel down—something you don't really want to be doing in a basement, any basement, but especially this one—and eyeball them up close.

I'd thought they were shadows at first. Black puddles where the door met the closet floor.

Except when I moved the door, they stayed where they were.

The black flaked off in my fingernails. The kind of thing Lysol can't do squat about: spilled OJ, scuff marks, piss—the crap I had to wipe up when they stuck me on juvie hall KP.

This wouldn't be listed on the Lysol bottle.

Black and crusted particles of wood.

Scorch marks, I think you'd call them.

You know—the stuff that's left behind after a fire goes out.

FORTY-THREE

You up?"

"Huh?" The answer was, *Not really.*

I'd had a hard night.

Screwy dreams where I was chatting with my Facebook friend. Face-to-face with him. Who kind of looked like Dad, which made no sense except it was a dream, so why not? I was back on the couch in my loose cutoffs and splaying my legs out like when Dad had been trying to watch the Knicks but I'd wanted him to watch me—*please, Dad, ME*—and I felt that sickening nausea again, because maybe I was doing everything but selling tickets, but before he'd looked away, he'd looked.

Only it wasn't Dad—in the dream anyway. It was the Facebook friend who'd sent me down a rabbit hole. He wanted to know about the downstairs closet. About the fire. He asked me if I was being careful.

Then he'd whispered: *Shhhh . . . I hear something.*

So did I.

A door opening.

And because this was a dream where you can be one place and then suddenly another, we weren't in my room anymore—or maybe it was Tabs's room—but in the actual basement of St. Luke's. As if we'd broken in for real.

A door was opening and I was in a panic.

They were going to catch us.

I woke up sweating—jolted upright in bed, it taking me a second or two to realize that's where I was, in bed—and feeling this "thank you, Lord" sense of relief. Which didn't last, because a door had opened. It had. And I knew it was my door.

Just like a few nights ago.

I heard another door slamming as I stumbled out into the hall.

The wooden floor felt ice-cold on my naked feet, or maybe I was. As if I'd wandered into that cold spot and was about to pronounce this house haunted.

"Who is it . . . ?"

I hadn't decided if I should shout or whisper, so I'd compromised. A hush with real purpose.

Nobody answered.

"WHO IS IT?"

The hall was gloomy—just enough light seeping from the downstairs blinds to see that the other bedroom doors were shut tight.

I waited till I stopped sounding like someone's panting dog.

Till I could catch my breath.

I went back into my room, shut the door, crawled back into bed. I pulled the covers up over my head. I must've finally fallen asleep.

Till my cell rang.

"You up?" the person on the other end repeated through the fog.

It was Tabs.

She sounded rattled.

"Now I am. What time is it?" Early. The little light eking through my window was the color of dirty dishwater.

"Don't know. Think I've been up all night."

"Join the club. Why were you up?"

"Poking around St. Luke's."

"*Huh?*"

"I went back in, Jo. Couldn't help myself. Kept wondering why Ben's case file ended there like that. Seemed fishy."

"You hacked into the system again?"

"Pay attention. Yeah. I hacked into the system again."

She was speaking faster than normal, like when you're worried the voice mail you're talking into is about to cut off. Like Pennebaker.

"Ben's file didn't end there," she said.

"Don't understand. There was nothing there. We looked."

"Trust me. The rest of the file's in there. Just not there, there."

Either I was too tired to hear straight or she was too tired to talk straight.

Or both.

"It's filed in a different place, Jo. *Capisce?* The files we broke into were password protected. Five letters. L-O-R-E-M. Remember . . . ?"

Yeah, Tabs. I remember—it was my suggestion.

"Translation: therapy," she continued. "Okay, makes perfect sense, right. But they put the rest of his case file somewhere else. I had to go exploring, okay?"

"Why would they move it?"

"Because it doesn't belong. Because . . . look, follow me. There's this whole different section with a *different* password. *Latin* again, of course. It wasn't rocket science—I just needed to find out which word. I mean how many Latin words could there be for *psychiatric* terms, right? That's what I tried first—you know—treatment, trauma, grief—whatever. Nothing worked. So I went in the other direction."

"What other direction?"

"The *Catholic* one. That's when I found it. The other section."

"I don't understand. What kind of section?"

"The one no one was ever meant to see. You don't even have to know Latin to understand the password for this one: C-O-N-F-E-S-S-I-O. That's the password. That's where it was—Ben's second EMDR session. I just emailed it to you. It was in *Confessions*, Jo. Understand? Do you?"

Her voice sounded like a taut guitar string right before it snaps.

"Get the fuck out of that house."

FORTY-FOUR

I tried.

Promise I did.

Didn't pack a single piece of clothing. Just went.

It was predawn. Coast clear.

I would make it downstairs and out the front door and over to Forest Avenue. I'd grab a lift from your average horny truck driver. I'd fend him off till at least Albany. Or Pittsburgh. Or who-the-fuck-knows-ville.

I'd been staying put, but now I wasn't.

It was time to kiss the Kristal house good-bye.

And Jenny Kristal. Yeah, her too. The kid who kept plucking at my sleeve. *Save me.* It's too late, sweetheart.

I saw her walking down the block that morning in reverse, backward, through the front door and up the stairs and back into her room.

I needed to save myself.

The hall was still black. It felt like the house was holding its breath. A pall hung over it like at a funeral.

It was years overdue.

Amen.

Someone had fastened the chain lock on the front door.

I'd only seen it locked once before—the day the reporters turned the front yard into a rager.

That should've been my first clue.

Jake's open laptop sitting in plain sight on the kitchen counter was the second.

The download was sitting there on the screen.

The rest of Ben's file.

Tabs had warned me to create something called a hole-in-the-wall—a hiding place on the upstairs computer since I didn't have my own (next up on Jenny's wish list). Tabs had sent me directions how to hide it in Program Files—inside a picture or game file. I'd been too panicked.

Yeah, it was just like juvie hall.

They'd been watching.

Online. And off.

"Come in," Laurie said.

She and Jake were fully dressed—as if I was late for something. As if I'd forgotten we were supposed to be on our way somewhere right this very minute.

We were.

"We're going up to the lake," Jake said. "We need to talk."

Wondering why I went with them?

Why I walked into the back seat of their car like I used to walk into that closet? Out the door, down the front walk, using my very own two legs? Probably for that very exact reason—because I was conditioned to. Because they brought the fear.

When I discussed not going, they discussed calling the police.

I said, "Not if I call them first."

"Who do you think they're going to believe?" Jake asked calmly. "A con woman—excuse me, con *girl*—who's committed *fraud?* Impersonating someone for *monetary* gain—new clothes, new furniture, new rent-free life—someone who's been *locked up* before, who preys on people devastated by personal *tragedy?*"

Versus them.

The two parents who'd been *preyed* upon?

It was a rhetorical question.

Each accusation—con girl . . . fraud—landing like a hammer blow. Picture the hammer I'd spotted on that downstairs worktable. Jake bringing it down here, down there, and soon enough you're beat to shit. You're fractured.

Because that's who you are. Those things. They're you.

"Look," Laurie said, with the same too-wide smile I remembered from our strolls down memory lane—except now it gave me the trembles instead of the warm fuzzies. "We just want to talk things over, okay?"

That first day when she'd pulled out that photo album on the couch, I thought.

It wasn't to fondly reminisce with her newfound daughter.

It'd been a crib session.

To get me ready for all those relatives who'd be coming over the next day. *Remember who this is, Jenny? And her? And him?* And if I didn't remember, she was there to help. *That's your uncle Brent . . .* Prepping me for the FBI too—making sure to stop that first interrogation like a concerned mom who was not going to put up with them badgering her daughter. Not after the hell she'd been through.

We stayed mostly quiet on the trip up to the lake, as if the mournfulness of the house had decided to hitch along for the ride.

Except when Jake asked if I'd read all of that stuff on the upstairs computer—what Ben told the doctor about that morning in 2007.

"Yeah," I said. "Couldn't put it down."

FORTY-FIVE

BENJAMIN KRISTAL. SECOND EMDR SESSION.

Watch your back.

My arm woke me—it's itching like crazy.

Watch your back.

Itching under the cast where I can't scratch it. Mom says I'm going to have to wear it for FOUR more weeks. The teacher made the whole class write stuff on it with Magic Markers—like 'hope you get better' and 'sorry about your arm' and John wrote 'stop falling down the stairs ANUS'—but it weighs like two tons and the itching's driving me nuts.

Watch your back.

Dad said you got to be more CAREFUL going down the stairs. That I wasn't looking where I was going. Mom too. While Jenny was putting on this whole NICE act.

"Poor Ben, let me draw you a picture to make you feel better," and Mom and Dad saying AWWW, say THANKS to your sister, Ben.

The picture was ME falling down the stairs, and guess who she drew standing at the TOP of the stairs. Smiling. Standing right where I lost my balance and took a header all the way to the bottom. That's when I remembered. I'd FELT someone behind me.

Watch your back.

I tried to tell Dad. That it felt like someone, well, PUSHED me before I fell—and there was only ONE someone there. And he said what are you saying—are you blaming your SISTER for being a klutz? For not looking where YOU were going? And I said I WAS looking where I was going but maybe I should've been looking BEHIND me.

Not the FIRST time.

We were playing "Indian Trail" at the lake last summer and I was leading the scouting party and we marched up to Eagle Cliff, where you can look over the whole valley to see if settlers are coming, and I walked right up to the ledge because Jenny kind of dared me to. And I turned around to peek down, and suddenly she was right there behind me—like SHOVING me—and I grabbed a branch of this big dead tree and I said are you CRAZY, and she said she SLIPPED. But the ground wasn't wet or nothing, it wasn't—so how'd she SLIP, huh?

Watch your back.

Jaycee's brother told me Jenny isn't allowed at their house anymore.

Other kids too. Jenny like put Legos in Jaycee's mouth and Jaycee started choking, and she did something to Toni too—I don't know what, but SOMETHING, but when I asked Mom about it she said those girls are just being mean and making things up.

Watch your back.

One night I was dreaming I couldn't breathe—and I woke up and guess what—I COULDN'T breathe, because there was a pillow over my face and Jenny was there on top of me holding it. When I yelled at her she said she was starting a PILLOW FIGHT, but like I'd been SLEEPING, and it's not just that, it's the way she LOOKED at me when I finally got her off me, like she hated me or something. Like she wanted to kill me.

Watch your back.

I would've DIED if I went over Eagle Cliff—it's like a hundred million feet high—I could've died falling down the stairs too—that's what Mom said—that I could've BROKEN my NECK.

Jenny's younger and she's a GIRL, so good luck getting them to believe ANYTHING bad about her. They won't. They just won't. EVER.

Watch your back.

But this morning, I forgot.

FORTY-SIX

Ben

He'd come back from school and immediately sucked up the last of the blunt he and Zack had lit up behind the bleachers, stepping over used condoms and crushed Budweiser cans.

Weed helped him remember stuff.

He was conducting a kind of experiment.

Toking up and going back to the scene of the crime. Well, technically the crime had taken place outside, somewhere between their house and what used to be Toni Kelly's. The scene of whatever it was he couldn't remember.

Things had been poking through lately. Not anything he could actually get his head around. It was like finding those jigsaw pieces he'd forgotten to throw back in the box as a kid—the ones that'd turn up under his bed or mixed in with his plastic *Ice Age* characters. Scrat, Stu, and Diego the saber-toothed tiger. Was that blue puzzle piece part of the sky or the ocean?

After he'd been sprung from the loony bin—sorry, *school*—it had taken a while to defog. To come off those horse pills that had seriously screwed with his senses.

It was a little like that now—the fog lifting, so to speak. Ever since she'd shown up.

The experiment would go as follows:

He'd load his brain up on the last of the Skywalker OG—*check*—walk into his *sister's* room—*check*—then see if anything jogged the old memory bank.

Okay, he'd tried this before without the aid of illegal substances. *Shhhhh* . . . Peeking into the room at night while she'd been sleeping, as if looking at her on the bed would be like looking at Jenny. Would tell him something he desperately needed to know.

She was out of the house somewhere today—he had a vague memory of hearing them all leave early this morning—voices, doors closing, and the rumble of a car headed down the driveway—like at the crack of dawn, interrupting his dream early. Which maybe was *fortuitous*—one of last week's vocabulary words—since his dream sucked. Even though it seemed familiar, like those dreams everyone has of walking into school naked. This dream wasn't like that—it was all his—but he could swear he'd dreamed it before. Filled with snakes. And fire.

Let's see . . .

The thing is, the room was different than back then. Not just absent the wide-screen TV and cluttered work desk, but with a different bed that he was pretty sure had been in a different place. Yeah, Jenny's bed had faced the door back then—so when you opened the door she'd be staring right at you—but this new bed was kind of sideways to the door. Maybe that meant the experiment was working—he was remembering the way the room used to look, which was a start, setting the stage, so to speak.

He tapped his forehead as if he was knocking on a door asking to be let in.

It worked. Sort of.

He suddenly remembered . . . hiding.

Huh . . . ?

He was pretty much doing the opposite of hiding right this second—standing in the middle of the designated crazy girl's bedroom in broad daylight—but in this memory of his, he had the definite sensation of hiding from his sister, Jenny.

Hiding where . . . ?

Behind the maple tree in their backyard? One, two, three, get off my old man's apple tree . . . No. They used that tree for running bases, where you had to tear ass from one base to the other—the maple tree to the white fence—while trying like hell not to get tagged.

Underneath the back porch? No way. Ben used to avoid even looking under the back porch because who knew what was down there? Rats maybe.

Wherever it was, it'd been pure black. Not black as in the absence of memory, but black as in the absence of light. And it had smelled like ass.

Okay . . .

Dead leaves?

Peat moss—the dung-smelling crap his dad used to spread around the yard before winter?

Bird shit?

Mothballs.

The distinct odor of mothballs was suddenly front and center as if someone had rolled them out there onto the floor. Right under his nose.

A smell similar to if not exactly the same as dead skunk—which they used to catch plenty of whiffs of on the way to the lake every summer, rolling up their car windows and holding their noses till they were far enough away.

The basement closet.

Wait a minute. He was getting mixed up. His *dream* had a closet in it, didn't it? He'd been stuck in a closet in his dream.

So why did he remember hiding in the basement closet for real?

Because they'd been playing . . . hide-and-seek. Yeah.

Jenny and him.

He felt a sudden sharp pang under his ribs.

Why?

It felt less like hiding and more like, well . . . being trapped.

He'd once worn a real straitjacket for Halloween, which after a while he'd begged Zack to get the fuck off him, because he'd had trouble breathing. As if the straitjacket wasn't strapping his arms to his chest but literally crushing it. Like he was being buried alive.

This memory of hiding was like that.

His mind on pot was like a pinball machine, he thought, one memory kind of bouncing off another, its trajectory directed by that particular memory onto the next one. He had to trust the process.

Let me out!

He suddenly heard himself at eight years old, as if he'd inadvertently stumbled onto an old video locked on autoplay. *Hey there, little Ben.*

That's what he'd been shouting that morning.

In the closet.

Hearing it as clearly as if he were suddenly standing on the other side of the door.

And then he suddenly remembered.

What happened.

FORTY-SEVEN

Jenny's standing by my bed.

She says she can't sleep. "Get up, sleepyhead."

"Get lost, doodyhead."

She keeps standing there. She won't leave. She wants to play.

Play what?

Hide-and-seek.

I'm up already from the itching under my stupid cast and Mom won't be making breakfast for hours—it's still dark. Okay, I tell her.

We go down to the basement.

Tiptoeing. Jenny says we shouldn't wake Mom and Dad.

She says, "You're the hider"—we usually flip for it, but I guess she wants to be the seeker and hiding's more fun anyway.

Fine.

Jenny turns around and closes her eyes and starts counting.

I sneak into the closet. Into the back where I'm completely hidden by these old clothes.

I hear her count "eighteen . . . nineteen . . . twenty . . . ready or not, here I come."

It's creepy in the closet because it's completely dark and smells of mothballs, and I'm thinking I should've hidden somewhere else, like behind the boiler maybe.

At first Jenny doesn't know where I am—it sounds like she's looking everywhere but the closet, and I'll be stuck in here forever.

When I hear her outside the door—finally—I try holding my breath.

"Ben," she whispers, "are you IN there, Ben?"

She just keeps standing there and asking if I'm IN there, and finally she finds out YEAH, I am—I can't hold my breath anymore. I have to let it out.

"Got you," she says.

"Your turn." I start climbing out from the back. I hear this sound—like this metal clicking.

The door won't open.

I try it again. It STILL won't.

"Stop playing around, Jenny," I tell her.

There's this old latch on the closet because the people who lived in the house before us kept TREASURE there—that's what Dad said.

We were never supposed to touch it.

"Very funny, Jenny. I'm dying laughing."

She's locked it.

"Open the door, doody-face."

"No."

"I said OPEN the door."

"Got you."

"Want me to wake Mom and Dad? You're gonna get punished for a whole YEAR."

"Go ahead."

"HELLLLLLLLLLLLLLLLLLLLLLLLLPPPPPPPPPPP!"

When Mom yells at us to come up from the basement and we don't hear her she always says, "Are you guys DEAF?"

No. You just can't hear anything from all the way down here.

Jenny has started talking to her imaginary friend.

That's what Mom calls it.

"Shhhhh . . ."

Mom said she started doing it when her REAL friends stopped playing with her. She just made one up.

"He's in there . . . ," she whispers. Giggles.

"Open the door, Jenny! NOT kidding . . ."

"Locked in . . ."

"JENNY!"

"Uh-huh," she whispers. "Be right up."

She's singing something.

"Let's gather round the campfire, and sing our campfire song, and if you don't think that we can sing it faster, then you're wrong . . ."

The CAMPFIRE SONG.

The one we sing up at the lake every time we build a fire. You have to sing it faster and faster until you can't understand the words anymore. That's the idea. Keep singing it till the fire's really going and everyone's giggling and you can't understand a word anybody's singing.

"Let'sgatherroundthecampfireandsingourcampfiresong . . ."

"STOP SINGING, MORON."

"andifyoudon'tthinkthatwecansingitfasterthenyou'rewrong . . ."

I'm sweating. Banging on the door.

"gatherroundthecampfire . . ."

"What's THAT? What are you DOING?"

There's this other sound.

"gatherroundtheCAMPFIRE . . ."

"What are you DOING, A-HOLE?"

I hear it AGAIN.

I know what it is.

The sound.

The last time I heard it was when Dad stacked all the branches into this big pile and put little balls of newspaper in there and then pulled them out of his pocket.

The box of matches.

Taking one out and striking it against the side of the box.

"theCAMPFIREtheCAMPFIREtheCAMPFIRE . . ."

"Are you NUTS, JENNY?"

"theCAMPFIRE . . ."

"PUT the matches down! You HEAR ME, retard!"

The box of matches from the kitchen. The ones Mom uses to light the stove. She must've swiped them.

"roundthecampfire . . ."

"Please open the door, Jenny . . . PLEASE . . . I'm asking nicely . . ."

Something flicks through the bottom of the closet door.

A lit match. It burns the edge of my big toe before going out.

"singourcampfiresong . . ."

"ARE YOU CRAZY??"

Another match slides under the door.

"JENNY, STOP! PLEASE LET ME OUT . . . NOW!"

"ifyoudon'tthinkthatwecansingitfasterthenyou'rewrong."

The match has caught a piece of a sweater or coat or something. It's smoking.

"I'M GOING TO KILL YOU WHEN I GET OUT OF HERE. I'M GOING TO MURDER YOU. I SWEAR . . ."

Another match.

"YOU'VE STARTED A FIRE! OPEN THE DOOR!"

I hear her walking away.

Walking away and leaving me here.

"WHERE ARE YOU GOING? COME BACK HERE!"

Up the stairs. Slowly. One at a time. Like when Mom calls her in from the backyard and she drags her feet—does it for real, moving one foot, then the other in slo-mo, like a windup toy.

I hear the door at the top of the stairs shut.

"PLEASE! JENNY . . . JENNY, PLEASE . . . I WON'T TELL MOM . . . COME BACK! PLEASE!"

I'm coughing. Because of the smoke.

I stick my head down by the crack under the door. I need air.

I gulp it in as fast as I can. I take a deep breath and go back to banging on the door.

Then more air.

I keep doing that. Up and down. Banging and breathing.

Hitting the door with my good arm. The one that isn't broken. The one that doesn't have a cast on it.

A HEAVY cast.

As heavy as a BATTERING RAM.

When I hit the door with that arm, the pain shoots straight up into my head. Like a hundred times worse than when I first broke it.

I can't do it. I can't.

My arm—it's killing me.

No. Something else is killing me. For real. The FIRE. When I try to suck in more air under the door, there ISN'T any. I can't breathe.

You have to do it . . .

You HAVE to.

I start crying even before I hit the door with my cast again.

I hear myself shrieking from the pain. Like somebody else is doing it. It feels like I cracked my arm all over again.

You have to . . .

I hit the door again.

And again. And again. And again. And again. And again.

Screaming each time. Not just from the pain. I'm seeing Jenny's face there. In front of me. Like I'm smashing it in. "I'm going to murder you," I'm screaming at her. "I AM."

There's this sudden splintering sound.

I've made a tiny hole in the door. Just enough to put my mouth there and suck in some air.

I hit it again. Over and over and over and over. Smashing my cast into Jenny's face. Again and again and again . . .

My arm goes numb after a while.

I keep doing it.

I smash THROUGH. Right through the door. A hole big enough to WALK through now.

But I can still see Jenny's stupid face in front of me and I want to KEEP SMASHING it, just keep SMASHING it, and. . . .

Watch your back.

I'm thinking if I tell Mom and Dad, if I tell them Jenny LOCKED me in the closet and tried to light it on FIRE, they'd say stop MAKING things up, Ben.

Watch your back.

Be nice to your sister, Ben.

Nothing will ever happen to her. NOTHING.

She'll just keep TRYING.

Like on the stairs.

And in the backyard when she pushed me into a tomato stake and I had to get like THIRTY stitches.

And I know it wasn't a WAVE that knocked me under that day at the beach. I know it.

It felt like someone holding me down, not letting me up as HARD as I tried. 'Cause that's what someone was DOING.

The someone behind me on the STAIRS.

And on EAGLE CLIFF.

Watch your back.

When I walk up the basement stairs I can't feel my feet. Like I'm floating. Like when I'm playing Zombie Apocalypse and it's down to one shot. When it's me or them.

I'm in front of Jenny's door.

I shove it open.

FORTY-EIGHT

Ben

He'd heard about certain kinds of pot that could cause visions.

Laced with lysergic acid, or Mexican mushrooms, or some other hallucinatory shit.

So you saw stuff that wasn't real. That seemed real enough, sure, but was kind of a figment of your imagination. And of the pot. Just stuff your mind cooked up.

Please . . .

He saw himself going up the stairs. In his *Star Wars* pj's.

His eyes burning. His lungs aching.

He saw himself standing in front of his sister's door. Right there. It's shut tight. There's a picture of Goldy scotch-taped to it.

He rips the picture to shreds.

He slams the door open.

Jenny screams.

"No, Ben! No! GET OUT!"

But Ben doesn't get out. He doesn't.
God help him, he doesn't.
"PLEASE, Ben . . .
"Please, NO.
"PLEASE . . ."

FORTY-NINE

They took me to the clearing first.

Smack in the middle of tangled woods—the trees leafless now, dead vines hanging like brown rope curtains around a small open area of yellow grass. It'd be hard to find if you weren't looking for it. If you didn't know it was there.

There was no gravestone. They didn't dare.

In case Ben decided to tramp through here on his way to Eagle Cliff. Or someone else wandered someplace they shouldn't. The clearing was part of their property, they said—but you never knew. Someone could go hiking, get lost, take a wrong turn.

There was an old gray stone set into the middle of the clearing—but it might've been there forever, part of the landscape. You wouldn't think anything of it, give it any special significance.

Just a stone.

Unless you knew what was lying under it.

"We come out here from time to time," Laurie said. "Just to say a prayer."

Juvenile hall had automatic locks on both hall doors.

Meaning as soon as those doors closed, you were locked in tight. The guards had special door keys they kept in a gray lockbox. The lockbox keys they kept on them. Attached to their belts, mixed in with their house and car keys on NY Giants and Walmart key chains, or if you were Otis, who liked to doze off in his chair just to the right of the south entrance door, attached to nothing but his fingers. I think rolling that key back and forth in his hand helped put him to sleep.

That was the key to me getting out of that juvie hall.

Otis's key.

Tiptoeing down the hall barefoot, sneaks in hand, Otis's decibel-busting snoring doing a good job of covering up unintentional sounds, like me bumping into the wheeled cart that somebody had stupidly forgotten to store—then me gently lifting the key from the palm of Otis's brown, open hand.

It was almost like Otis was offering it to me: *Here, Jobeth, go ahead and take it.*

I was sitting in the lake house thinking about that. About locked doors. Back from the visit to the clearing. I didn't know if Jake had locked the front door or not. I'd heard a click.

"We had a choice," Laurie said.

The three of us were arranged around the living room—Jake and Laurie on the couch, me across from them on a hard Adirondack chair. The tone had changed since Jake called me names back in the house. Like we were back to being the happy reunited Kristals, and we were maybe about to break out the Game of Life. Or leaf through the family photo album. Or talk about a murder.

"We could lose both our children," she said. "Or just one. We had a choice. I don't expect you to understand it. What we did. The logic."

She was right about that.

"I found them that morning," Jake said. "He'd choked her—with that *cast* on his arm. I think that's what happened. He was out of his head. In shock—literally catatonic. She wasn't breathing—I tried CPR. She was dead."

That word hung in the air. *Dead.* Like it needed its own moment of silence.

"Ben's never remembered," Laurie said softly. "What he did to her. Trauma can do that—blot it out. Probably a blessing . . . I like to think it is. We made up a story for him. For everyone. I sent Jenny down the block to a playdate that morning. She never got there."

"She almost killed him. Ben. In the closet, I mean. She was . . . sick . . ."

"Not always," Laurie said. "It started somewhere around four. Her problems. One day she was a perfectly normal little girl—a really amazing little girl, our baby—and one day she wasn't. As sudden as that."

Normal. A sweet, adorable, six-year-old little girl.

"She just changed," Laurie said.

"Why didn't you uh . . . stick *her* in St. Luke's? Or somewhere? I mean, when she started hurting other kids?"

Jake sighed, cracked his knuckles. "Willful denial, I guess— know what that means? You don't want to believe what you don't want to believe. Maybe her friends were making things up. Maybe Ben was. They were kids. She was a kid. You don't want to think your daughter is . . . mentally unstable . . . dangerous even . . ."

"What would've happened if you'd told the truth?"

Sure, me asking someone else to tell the truth sounded kind of funny. Even to me.

"I mean after it happened. It was almost like *self-defense* what Ben did, wasn't it?"

"We saw the closet afterward. Saw the fire damage. Figured it out. Jenny had brought the box of matches up to her room. He must've smashed the door in with that cast—it was just plywood. It didn't matter. Two shitty choices. Admit to the world one of our kids was psychotic—and the other one a murderer. Have him sent to a psychiatric hospital till he's eighteen. And have him always know what he'd done. That he'd murdered his own sister. Have him go through life like that. Or make up a story. For him. For the world. Save him. Save us too, I guess. From people pointing fingers at us every time we went out for a coffee—the parents of two monsters. We picked the less shitty choice. We lived with it."

"But you did send Ben away. For a year . . ."

"He was acting out," Laurie said. "Violently. His school was about to expel him. We were stupid thinking he'd be just fine—that he'd lose his memory of what happened that morning, but that would be all. That he'd be perfectly okay. Play Little League, go to school, be a kid. We had to do something. We couldn't just leave him home. We needed to get him right."

"You picked a Catholic mental hospital," I said. "With priests as doctors. That was for in case . . . right . . . ?"

Jake squinted at me—maybe he was surprised I'd figured that one out.

What had Tabs said over the phone?

C-O-N-F-E-S-S-I-O.

They must've figured if Ben said anything—if anything came back to him during one of those EMDR sessions—no one would be running to the police. It'd be protected. What happens in confession stays in confession—right? Priests can't tell. Besides, the church was pretty good at keeping secrets—they'd had enough practice. Check out their latest sorry-ass apology on your favorite online news site.

"Look, you're talking about an eight-year-old kid," Jake said. "Zonked out on Thorazine. Ben said some stuff under hypnosis. His doctors held a staff meeting about it—was it true or not? Their diagnosis? Delusional wish fulfillment. Kids *wish* someone dead— their parents, their sister—because the dad didn't get them that new Xbox game or their sister got a bigger portion of ice cream. Then something happens—the dad dies in a car accident, the sister drowns in a pool. And they think they did it. They truly believe it. Jenny had been trying to hurt Ben. Worse. He wanted to hurt her back. Then she walked down the block one day and disappeared. He made up this story in his head. They convinced him to believe our story instead. It sounded more rational to them. When he came out, he wasn't beating up schoolkids anymore. Or ripping apart Jenny's room. He turned into your normal dope-smoking turd. The script stuck."

"Until Pennebaker."

Silence.

"How'd you find out about him . . . ? I mean that he was . . . ?" Laurie didn't get to finish.

Jake did.

"Yeah, okay. Pennebaker," Jake repeated, saying his name the way you spit out a particularly annoying particle of food— something you just can't seem to dislodge. "Like you said, he didn't do a very good job. At first. Two years ago, he told us the case was still cold as Alaska. His words. Then he retired down to Georgia and it began warming up. In a hurry. He just wouldn't let it go. He re-interviewed people. Went through all the files again— whatever cold-case detectives actually do. I'm guessing he didn't have a whole lot else on his plate now that he's officially retired. I imagine he's not into golf. Maybe he even got someone at St. Luke's to talk to him—dug up the same files you did. Don't know. He was relentless. Wouldn't stop calling. Three times a day sometimes. Wanted to know about Ben. Just Ben—he was zeroing in on Ben. We felt hounded, okay? Threatened. The story was threatened."

"Then me."

"Then you," Jake said.

Me. Who they'd brought up to the lake. Where they must've taken Jenny's body that morning. Before they'd raced back home to begin planting the lie.

"Kind of a gift from God you were. Obviously. We needed Pennebaker off our back. You showed up. Jenny's home. She's come back. A miracle. It was, for us. For Ben, too. Pennebaker stopped calling. The threat was over. Sometimes you just get lucky—did you *hear* that?"

It sounded like some wind through the trees. Jake went over to the window. Peered through it for a while, shrugged. Came back and sat down again next to Laurie.

"That stuff on the upstairs computer," he said. "From St. Luke's. How'd you get it?"

"I hacked it." After I'd downloaded the file, I'd erased Tabs's email.

"So you're the only one who's seen it?"

"Yeah."

Jake looked at Laurie. Back to me.

"Okay."

I'd asked a bunch of questions already. I had one more. The only one that mattered.

"So what now? Why'd you bring me here?"

"Ben's *home*," Laurie said. "We needed somewhere to talk about this rationally. Without Ben sitting in the next room."

"Seems like it's mutually beneficial we keep this to ourselves," Jake said. "I mean, no one has to hear about Ben . . . what he did to his sister. Not now. No one has to hear about you committing another fraud. You're not a kid anymore. You'd go to jail for this. So . . ."

"*So . . . ?*"

"It's not working out. I mean, you were away from us so many years and you've been through so much. And you don't just pick up where you left off and become a family again. You tried. We tried. It was just too hard. You aren't six-year-old Jenny anymore. It isn't twelve years ago. You're grown up. You decided to leave. Out to the West Coast maybe. You're not sure. You'll try and keep in touch. It's sad—but at least we know you're alive now. Maybe one day we'll be a family again. Maybe not."

Okay, the door was locked. But not forever. There was a way out.

"Those FBI agents. They more or less called me a liar."

Jake shrugged. "It won't matter when you're gone, will it? Don't think they're going to tack you on a wanted poster. For what? For being a little evasive on the details? For arousing some suspicions?"

"I think Ben knows."

Jake snorted. "Don't worry about Ben."

"Okay," I said. "Sure. I'll leave."

"And you'll keep your mouth closed. Sorry—want to be perfectly clear here. Quid pro quo, right?"

I felt every scar left by Mother's sewing needle. They burned.

"Sure thing."

See? Mouth shut.

FIFTY

I was upstairs killing time.

"I've got a few things to do around here," Jake said. "Amuse yourself. We'll drive you back later. Then we'll pack you up and get you to an airport."

Okey-dokey.

There was a computer in the upstairs loft.

I played *Candy Crush*—making it to level three before I lost all five lives. Though I had *already* lost five lives. Karen Greer, Alexa Kornbluth, Terry Charnow, Sarah Ludlow.

Jenny Kristal.

I felt tempted to do what I usually did on computers when I was about to get booted. I felt the pull like a drug. Like my mom must've felt every time she got bored going straight.

You're not a kid anymore. You'd go to jail for this.

Yeah, I wasn't a kid anymore. I'd already done enough jail time at juvie hall, thank you very much.

Sorry, Mom. Time to break with the family tradition. No more other childhoods for me. No more impersonating other girls. Alert the media.

Or don't.

I thought about Ben. About what he'd done. About what they'd done for him. Was he a monster? Were they? Ben had been a kid in true peril, who'd felt entirely alone. I could relate. They'd been out-of-their-mind parents faced with a monstrous choice.

Lose one child. Or both.

Okay. Sure.

Speaking of threats. Of going to jail.

I thought I should probably hold on to Ben's file. Why not? As collateral. Just in case.

I'd create that hole-in-the-wall like Tabs had told me to.

Bury it right here. In the lake-house computer. Close to where something else was buried. If I ever needed it, I'd know where to find it. In a new file, deep in some random program directory. With its very own password protection. Something simple I wouldn't forget.

Let's see . . . how about J-E-N-N-Y P-E-N-N-Y?

Sure.

The computer wouldn't let me.

Ever play hide-and-seek and stumble across another kid in the very hiding spot you were going to use, telling you to get lost? Sorry, no room.

There was already a hole-in-the-wall in the computer.

That password was already being used.

J-E-N-N-Y P-E-N-N-Y.

Okay. I went where it led me. *This* way. When I clicked on that file—her picture appeared. Jenny's. The one from the poster they'd nailed to the telephone pole in front of that pizza place—her first-grade school photo.

Why would Jake bury it? I was assuming it was Jake—Jenny Penny had been *his* nickname for her.

Because he couldn't bear to look at it. That's why.

Because even after all this time, it hurt too much.

The photo album Laurie pulled out that night had been covered in dust. Maybe Jake climbed the stairs to the loft sometimes so he could stare at her picture by himself. Allow himself to cry over his dead daughter. Alone. Without Laurie seeing.

I hoped it was like that. It made me like him a little more. Made the times he called me Jenny Penny seem less like playacting and more like wishing.

I clicked on the picture to enlarge it.

Other pictures suddenly popped up.

Hundreds.

Even as I tried to stop the vomit hurtling up my throat, even then, I remembered Tabs saying you could hide stuff in pictures too.

The door opened.

"Two more things to do," Jake said. "Then we'll get going."

I nodded—it taking every ounce of my remaining strength to get my head to move because I was using almost all of it to stop myself from screaming.

"You on the computer?" Jake asked.

I nodded.

The desk faced the door, so the computer faced away from it. Away from Jake. He hesitated. Like he wanted to walk around the desk and see what I was looking at. Like he thought he really should do that.

"Just checking out Twitter," I said.

He stayed there in the doorway.

"Okay. Another hour maybe, that's all."

I waited till I heard him walk down the stairs and into the back of the house.

I threw up. Over the computer. Onto the rug.

I lurched back off the chair.

I went out the door he'd just left through.

Down the stairs.

Seeing the pictures.

Those pictures.

Jake's.

I went out the front door and ran into the woods.

The vomit-covered computer. I hadn't bothered turning it off.

FIFTY-ONE

Ben

He wasn't aware of actually driving.

He glimpsed pieces of road, the bleached-white sound walls that lined the New York State Thruway, a toll booth or two.

He was seeing something else.

A couple of times he almost turned on the windshield wipers to clear away the raindrops. It wasn't raining.

Doing some chores up at the lake, Mom had texted. See you tonight.

When he'd jumped in the car, he hadn't known that's where he was going. He was running away from the house. That's all. It took him a while to realize he was headed to another house.

There was this show he'd seen on Netflix where everyone had to wear blindfolds so you wouldn't see the monster and end up killing yourself. Just the sight of the monster was enough to push you to do it.

This was Ben. He was trying to not see the monster. He was trying to not kill himself.

A couple of times he'd thought of steering the car right into the sound wall.

Two seconds and it'd all be over.

He stuck to the road. Tried to concentrate on passing signs.

ALBANY—112 MILES.

OVERLOOK MOTEL—6 MILES.

ROCKING HORSE RANCH—NEXT TURN.

Goldy was eating a blue carrot in the picture on Jenny's door. She'd spelled Goldy's name with a backward G.

He passed a state police car squatting on the highway shoulder like a spider waiting for passing flies. Stock-still until it was ready to pounce.

Hey, Officers, might I have a word with you?

Jenny was talking to her imaginary friend again.

Through the bedroom door.

Do I look pretty? Do I really?

He thought of the broken highway lines as a fence—his job was to stay behind it. On one side was him. On the other, the sound wall. Which would make the sound of Ben's head-on crash disappear maybe. The police looking through their windshield and seeing a silent thunderbolt of flame.

The smoke was still there in his lungs. In his eyes. The fire was in him now.

Count the miles. Something to do. The odometer moving in tiny, painstaking increments.

Fifty-two and one-tenth miles . . . and two-tenths . . . and three . . .

Miles to go before I sleep. A poem they read in English class. He had miles and miles to go before he'd be able to shut his eyes. So he could finally stop seeing. Please.

He shoved her door open.

NO, BEN!

He shoved her door open and there was Jenny.

PLEASE, Ben! NO!

He shoved her door open and there were Jenny and Dad.

GET OUT!

Jenny and Dad.

On the bed. With no clothes on.

Dad was hurting her. Hurting Jenny. Trying to stop Jenny from screaming now. His arm around her mouth. Around her neck. Squeezing.

NO, DADDY . . . PLEASE . . .

He raised his arm—the one with the cast. To block out the sight forever. To stop him from hurting her.

The world went black.

Black as sleep. Black as nothingness. Black as death.

Over and out.

FIFTY-TWO

I didn't know where I was running.

It didn't matter.

Through the woods. Fast as I could.

Branches whipped at my face. Thorns ripped my pants. I tripped over a tree root and went down.

I was multitasking. Running and thinking. Thinking and running.

When he'd looked at me on the couch that night. That gagging nausea that overtook me like a bolt from the blue.

It was Father's look.

Those times they'd get out the video camera and pose me. *Open your legs a little bit more . . . good girl . . . that's right . . .*

Jake had been trying to watch the Knicks that night. When I opened my legs, he'd watched me. That same sick, sweaty stare— why I'd almost thrown up.

Those same sick pictures. And I had thrown up.

I found myself in the clearing of yellow grass. Stumbling past the gray stone.

I whispered a prayer. "Sorry, Jenny . . . sorry . . . God bless . . ."

I was in mourning.

For her. For me. There wasn't a difference now.

I kept running.

Lurching into the thick trees. My heart hammering.

It started around four. Her problems. One day she was a perfectly normal little girl. Then one day she wasn't. She just changed.

Four years old. When something else changed. When Jake must've stopped reading Jenny bedtime stories and begun making up his own. When he began paying her early-morning visits, with Laurie and Ben still safely asleep.

He'd paid her a visit that last morning—after she'd dutifully locked her brother in the downstairs closet during a game of hide-and-seek.

He's locked in, she'd whispered to her imaginary friend that morning. *Be right up . . .*

Then she'd tried to set Ben on fire.

She looked like she wanted to kill me, Ben said, the morning he'd woken up with a pillow over his face.

I understand, Jenny. I do. I do.

Ben wasn't the one being sexually abused every night.

He was magically exempt.

Those friends of hers—them, too. Toni and Jaycee. Able to go to sleep at night without having to wonder if they'd be getting a visit from the tooth fairy.

Jenny couldn't lash out at her tormentor. At Jake. It's not allowed—the fucked-up heart won't allow it. The rest of the world would have to do. Anyone within arm's length.

What had Toni said? *You were violent. As in physically the fuck harmful to me and Jaycee.*

The trees were thicker here. Crowded together at jagged cross angles. I felt a sharp stitch in my side. Stitch one, slip two . . .

Snakes.

The one part of Ben's dream Krakow hadn't bothered explaining. Maybe the symbolism was lost on a priest—at least, a priest who wasn't ass-fucking altar boys.

Snakes equal *dicks*. Dreams 101.

I wasn't aware till this second that I was crying. This whole time tearing ass through the woods. Sobbing. Snot and tears and scratches making a mess of me.

Then I heard it.

I was making the tangled twigs and roots snap, crackle, and pop. So was someone else.

First my racket, then seconds later another one. Like an echo.

We weren't in Tom Sawyer's cave.

He was coming after me.

I went down again. Twisted an ankle. When I sprang back up, pain shot straight through my leg like an electric current.

I needed to move faster. Faster and faster and faster. I was slowing down.

I saw a patch of light through the trees.

I went for it.

When I stumbled out the other side, gasping for air, holding my side, I was staring straight into the sky. As if I'd been running toward heaven.

I was.

I was standing on a cliff. Eagle Cliff.

Jake had burst out of the brush and was standing there blocking the only way back.

You sick motherfucker."

This time I understood I'd stated it straight out loud. Screamed it.

"Daughter fucker. Jenny fucker."

It tumbled out of me—an incoherent torrent of rage. I knew I wasn't just shrieking at him. At Jake. Father and Mother were here. *See* them? I was letting them know what they'd done. To that little girl they'd bought for a bag of crystal meth. The girl in the closet. The girl with the Raggedy Ann mouth. The girl they'd strapped to a bed. The girl who'd grown up and wanted to be anyone on earth but Jobeth.

"You had no right . . . you destroyed her . . . you killed her . . . you *did* . . ."

"I didn't mean it. It was an accident," Jake stated calmly.

Huh? *What?*

Jake had killed her? Jake . . . not *Ben?*

I'd been raging at him about murdering the child inside. Her tiny innocent soul.

He'd murdered the child.

Jake had.

"You told Laurie it was Ben. All these years. Blamed it on him."

Jake didn't bother answering. His eyes were scanning the surroundings—the thick trees . . . the flat area of cliff . . . the steep drop.

And now, what should have been obvious the moment I'd turned around and seen my only way out was blocked suddenly became ice clear. My anger morphed into something else. Fear. Searing heat into sudden bone-cold chill.

"Too bad . . . ," Jake said.

How far was I from the edge of the cliff? Five steps, maybe less.

"You getting on that computer. You seeing. I loved her, you know. She loved me. We had a special relationship."

I almost gagged.

"Is that what you call it?"

"You wouldn't understand."

"I understand fine. I had a special relationship too. My parents were real fuckers. I was the fucked."

"Jenny loved me."

"She didn't have a choice. She was six. You did."

Jake shook his head.

"Shit. I really wish you hadn't gone on that computer. Fuck . . . fuck . . . fuck . . ." Like he was wrestling with what I was forcing him to do. One thing to *have* an accident. Another to make someone *else* have one.

Eagle Cliff is like a hundred million feet high . . .

"I'll keep my mouth shut. Just like you said."

Jake snorted. "Sure you will."

"It's mutually beneficial. You're right. I don't want to go to jail." A strange thing to beg for your life. I'd begged for plenty of other things—food, money, a place to sleep, not to have to walk into a pitch-black closet or get strapped to a bed or let a stranger in a tracksuit come into my room. This time was for keeps.

"Sorry. Neither do I." His face was flushed. Not just from running after me through heavy brush. From what he was about to do.

"Please . . ."

"Shhh . . ." He was walking toward me. Face flushed, eyes narrowed, arms out as if he were zeroing in for a hug.

When I first went to my new house, I would try to dodge them, dart past their outstretched arms and down into the basement, where I'd hide, shivering and terrified. I made it a few times. Mostly they'd manage to snag me—by my neck, my nightgown collar— then I'd be dragged back to bed. Tied down. Raped.

It felt like death. Every single time. It was death now. For real.

I almost got by him.

Almost.

He hooked me by my belt—the one Laurie bought me that day at the Roosevelt Field Mall. Jammed his fingers in there good and tight and yanked me back hard. The back of my head hit the hard stone. I felt the jolt of pain all the way down my spine. He began dragging me to the edge of the cliff.

I fought back.

Hard as I could.

Just like I'd done at the edge of the sink that morning when they'd forced my chin up so they could sew my mouth together. Just like those times in the basement, when they'd yank me out from behind those mildewed cardboard boxes stacked with old Superman comics—I wasn't Super Invisible Girl—and I'd imagine Superman flying right out of those comic books to save me like the girl in the burning house.

He didn't ever.

Not once.

Eighteen years old and way past believing in comic book heroes and my last thought on earth was that: Superman coming in to cradle me in his two superstrong arms as I went flying out into space.

Because I could swear—really swear—he was there flying toward me—as I tumbled, tumbled, to my death.

AFTER

Thelma and Louise.

I kept bringing it up on the endless drive to Minnesota.

"Which one am *I*?" Tabs said. "And didn't they end up going over a cliff?"

"Bingo."

We were about halfway through Ohio. There was some question as to whether Tabs's weathered blue Mustang would make it all the way to Duluth. I put it at fifty-fifty. The car had a persistent cough and a serious case of the shakes, debatably making it in only slightly better condition than me.

The final toll: Four broken ribs. One fractured clavicle—collarbone for the anatomically ignorant. A few other grotesquely misaligned bones here and there. I had four pins in me—I'd have to inform airport security about that from now on—or risk being strip-searched by some latex-gloved TSA agent. Not that I'd be getting on a plane anytime soon.

"Hey, Thelma," I said, seeing myself more as the spunky Louise. "Thanks again."

I was thanking Tabs for the road trip. I'd already thanked her plenty for taking me in and helping nurse me back to a reasonable facsimile of a functioning human being. Her parents too. I think my notoriety made me something of a novelty—even for two soulless dullards—though to be honest, they seemed pretty okay to me. I guess if you're trying to keep up with the Joneses, this was something the Joneses couldn't possibly match. Her dad even made the evening news: "Jobeth is doing fine but would rather not speak to reporters right now."

He could've added: *Or ever. Way too much to explain.*

I'd already been forced to sit down with Hesse and Kline, this time to spill the beans on the *real* Father and Mother—but I made sure to mix in enough half lies to send them in the wrong direction.

"No problem, Louise," Tabs said, squinting through the windshield, bathed by a blinding late-afternoon sun.

"Fuck it . . . stick with Jo," I said.

Now that I was out of my adopt-a-family phase, I enjoyed hearing my actual name said out loud. I'd spent my life doing everything I could to *not* be Jobeth—but I'd made a kind of peace with her. Not an easy one. Eternally wary of each other but willing to give it a shot to prevent further bloodshed.

There'd been enough.

I would've been added to the list if it wasn't for the root of a dead tree. Maybe the very same tree whose branch Ben grasped thirteen years ago to keep himself from going over Eagle Cliff. Call it the Kristal Family Tree—where even fake members get to claim a piece of it.

I'd grabbed on for maybe all of ten seconds—just enough for

it to halt my free fall and deposit me on this sort of ledge. When I looked at the photos later—news photos splashed across the internet—it looked more like a dent. Maybe it was the perspective— the ledge was at least twenty feet down from that gnarled hanging root. Which explains why I have four pins in me and needed Tabs to help me to the toilet for three straight weeks.

What happened on that cliff was pieced together by those news articles, by Tabs, and by yours truly, once they took the methadone drip out of my arm, which I screamed for them to do as soon as I understood it was in me, screamed at them to replace it with some- thing else—anything else, something without the word *meth* in it, thank you. You understand.

Jake had thrown me off Eagle Cliff.

Jobeth—yours truly—discovered 384 pictures of Jake Kristal raping his daughter. Jobeth (alias Jenny, but that's another story) ran out of the house. Jake followed her. Cornered her. Tossed her.

Then Jake jumped off Eagle Cliff.

Killed himself.

Unable to live with what he'd done. To his daughter, Jenny. To the girl *pretending* to be Jenny. Blah, blah, blah . . .

That flying figure I'd seen hurtling toward me—remember? It wasn't Superman. It was Jake. On his way to the bottom.

And that was that.

Except.

It wasn't true.

The Jake-killing-himself part.

Okay. This is between you and me. Deal? You, me, and Ben.

Once I could move around without saying ouch, Tabs drove me to the house to get my stuff. Laurie had let her know that all those clothes she'd bought me were still mine. I could have them. Tabs had been sharing her own stuff with me, but I'd gotten tired of Alice Cooper T-shirts, Metallica tank tops, and bell-bottoms with yellow plastic daisies on them.

I stayed in the car waiting for Tabs to reappear—milking my convalescence for all it was worth. Plus, I didn't want to go in. Someone else appeared. Ben stepped out on the porch, staring at me through the car window. For almost the first time I could remember, his expression was devoid of any *fuck you*.

I say almost.

Because the only other time I'd seen his face like that was on Eagle Cliff.

Sure, it was upside down, so maybe I got it wrong, but just as I was going over the ledge, I could swear I saw Ben standing right there behind his father, staring at me with a look that seemed, well, almost empathetic.

This was seconds before Jake came tumbling down after me.

Ben had that same look now.

Like, *I get it*. Like, *I understand*.

So I returned it in kind.

I get it, Ben. I know. I understand.

I do.

It's 1,197.6 miles from Long Island to Minnesota. According to Google Maps. Eighteen and a half hours, if you don't break it up.

I didn't want to. Because I was afraid if you gave me half a chance, I'd turn back. Exhaustion won out—we stopped at a Motel 6, where we watched *Thelma and Louise* on Netflix while munching on popcorn we procured from an outdoor vending machine.

When they sailed over the cliff at the end, I cried.

Hard as nails, meet soft as sugar.

Somewhere during the drive, Tabs had asked me what I wanted to be when I grow up.

We both knew I already had. In a real hurry. Anyway, I'd been giving it some thought—amazing what things you can think about when you're not spending every second thinking about just making it to the next day. You can start to see the next year. And the year after that. And you can maybe see yourself doing something worthwhile with it—this thing called the rest of your life.

"I don't know . . . maybe something with drawing . . . art therapy or something like that. For kids who've been through trauma."

"That'd be pretty cool, Jo," Tabs said. "*Really.*"

Yeah, I thought. It would.

But first this.

When we got within a mile or so of her house, I said, "I want to turn around, Tabs."

"But we're here," she said.

"Yeah. That's the point. We're here and I don't think I can do it."

"Sure you can."

I'd called J. Pennebaker.

Rang him up after everything went down—my rescue from the ledge after Laurie wandered out looking for Jake, the police and ambulance showing up, the fifteen minutes of lurid news stories that followed—and told him he'd been right. Half-right, anyway. Jenny hadn't been kidnapped on her way to Toni Kelly's house that morning. She'd been murdered. But Ben wasn't the murderer.

He'd been wrong about that.

And I told him something else.

"You were my Facebook friend. Lorem."

"Guilty as charged."

"Why?"

"Why? You want the short answer or the long one?"

"I'm covered in casts. I've got time."

"Okay. Let's just say I was close to figuring it out—until you showed up, of course. So I called off the dogs. Called you, I believe—think you were the one who answered the phone—and I said to please tell them I'm sorry, I won't be calling again. But then I got to thinking. Occupational hazard. How it seemed just a little too perfect. For them, I mean. The timing and all. So I started looking at you. It wasn't that hard. Discovering you probably weren't who you were saying you were."

"So why didn't you say something?"

"I said probably. Wasn't one hundred percent sure. Besides, you made the cover of *People*. I'm a retired detective about to start cashing social security. When I called off the dogs, there was just one dog—a pretty toothless one these days. I thought I'd make sure you stayed safe instead. At least warn you. Try to. That you weren't the only one in that house who was lying. Someone else was—even if I wasn't exactly sure who. Guess I did a fairly shitty job on the keeping-you-safe part."

"I was a fucking imposter."

"Life is relative, sweetheart. If you learn one thing as a policeman, you learn that. You were an imposter—fine, and by the way, I think we can probably find it in our hearts to excuse you just a little bit for that, no? They were worse. *He* was, anyway. As it turned out, a whole lot worse."

Imagine that. A Facebook friend who really was one.

"Anyway, thanks for calling and letting me know," Pennebaker said. "I spent a lot of time looking for you. Well . . . not you. Your namesake, I guess we'll call it. You mend up . . . okay?"

But before I said good-bye, I asked him for a favor.

It was the actual reason I'd called.

"You probably can track down just about anyone, can't you? Being such a hot-shit detective, I mean."

He laughed. "Maybe so. Who you talking about?"

I gave him a name.

It didn't take him very long. Less than a week.

Then two weeks more as I went back and forth deciding if I was really going to contact her.

Yes. No. Yes.

When I got a response back, I didn't open it for a day and a half. I just stared at it like it was maybe a bad test result from a doctor. Like if I actually opened it, I'd be finished.

I clicked on it.

Is this really YOU? she'd written. I've been looking for you. For YEARS.

I burst into tears—right there in front of the computer. Shook and sobbed and bawled like a baby.

I answered her. Tentatively.

She answered me in a New York City minute.

We kept it up.

A conversation that turned into a dialogue that turned into a plan.

She'd been straight for almost six years. Stone-cold no-relapse swear-on-Scout's-honor straight. She had a job counseling other addicts. A nice place to live. Even a nice man to live with, who sounded like someone I might even like to know.

The one thing she didn't have was peace.

With the unforgivable thing she'd done so long ago by a short-rate motel.

But maybe that's exactly what I needed to do now.

Forgive.

When Hesse and Kline came calling again, I knew if I'd told

them the whole truth about Father and Mother, it would've eventually led them to *her*.

I didn't want that now.

Because that's where I was going.

"There it is," Tabs said. "Ninety-five Weatherly, right?" She stopped the car across the street from a gray clapboard house that had rosebushes lining the walk all the way up to the front door. From here, you couldn't see a single thorn on them—just a solid bloom of bright, welcoming pink.

I waited.

"So. You gonna do this?"

I nodded.

"Want me to come?" She was unclasping her seat belt.

"No. Don't think I need help walking anymore."

I got out of the car, crossed the street. Limped past the roses up to the front door, swallowed hard.

Ding-dong.

A woman I barely recognized opened the door. Her eyes were wet and welcoming. Her arms were already reaching out to grab hold of me. Her daughter.

Safe at home.

Safe at last.

Acknowledgments

I would like to thank my brilliant editor, Lindsey Rose, and my wise and indefatigable agent, Richard Pine, without whom this book would not have been possible.

About the Author

S. K. Barnett is a pseudonym for a *New York Times* bestselling author whose previous book was turned into a major motion picture.